Up in her room with trembling hands Miss Lavinia was opening her letter. It was only a few lines, but such amazing words were in them! Miss Lavinia could scarcely believe her senses. She had to get up and hunt a clean handkerchief to wipe her glasses before she read the words again. Out of the stilted maze of legal phrases she gathered at last that a miracle had come to pass!

Some money had been left to her!

Tyndale House books by Grace Livingston Hill.
Check with your area bookstore for these best-sellers.

MISS LAVINIA'S CALL
(and other stories)

LIVING BOOKS ®
Tyndale House Publishers, Inc.
Wheaton, Illinois

This Tyndale House book
by Grace Livingston Hill
contains the complete text
of the original hard cover edition.
NOT ONE WORD
HAS BEEN OMITTED.

Printing History
Harper & Row edition published 1949
Tyndale House edition/1991

Living Books is a registered trademark of Tyndale
House Publishers, Inc.

Library of Congress Catalog Card Number 90-71920
ISBN 0-8423-4360-1

97 96 95 94 93 92 91
8   7   6   5   4   3   2   1

CONTENTS

Miss Lavinia's Call

MISS LAVINIA was in her sister-in-law's kitchen, washing dishes, when the letter came.

For the last twenty-five years she had been most of her time in that same kitchen washing dishes; and it seemed to her that she would probably be there—washing dishes—when her call came to leave this earth. She sometimes wondered vaguely whether there would be a call for her; or whether, perchance, she might not be forgotten and go on washing dishes throughout eternity. Forgotten! That was what she felt herself to be.

Not that she had grown sour and hard over it; she was anything but that. There was always a gentle word upon her lips, always a patient, ready acquiescence in any of the family plans that involved, as the family plans of the Wests always did, a shouldering of the heaviest part of the burden by Aunt Lavinia.

When times grew hard and her brother George decided to take his small capital and start in business for himself, it was his sister Lavinia who herself suggested that the kitchen-maid be dismissed and that she could take the

Reprinted by permission of *The Christian Endeavor World*.

extra care upon herself, while the children were little and demanded their mother's attention; then George could get on his feet and not be hampered by heavy household expenses. She had been sure that she could bring expenses down. And so effectually had she done it that there had never been a time in all those twenty-five years, with the children growing up and the expenses growing with them, when the family had felt they could afford to make a change in their domestic arrangements.

To be sure, she was entirely dependent upon her brother for support. That made some difference. She would think it over sometimes and remind herself that she ought to be most grateful that a home and work were provided for her. This was a new age in which women did strange things, and she was little fitted to cope with the business world in any way that could have supplied her living. She ought to be exceedingly glad that she had her work, work that she could do, and could feel that she was making return for the respectable, comfortable home which she occupied.

She never murmured as the two girls grew up and found life too full for the help they had by tradition been expected to render when they were old enough. Harriet and Mabel were pretty and popular and bright. Of course she wanted them to go through high school, and was proud when their father decided to send them to college. Without a thought she kept on washing dishes that they might have good outfits for their four years' course of butterflying through an education, and accepted without a murmur the cast-off gowns which they said weren't good enough to wear at college, but would be plenty good enough for "Aunt Viny" to wear afternoons at home. As if Aunt Viny ever had time to dress up "afternoons at home"! Miss Lavinia turned up the hems—she was smaller than either of the girls, and pieced down the sleeves—she couldn't bring herself to wear them elbow-length; it hadn't been seemly in her young girlhood, except for evening wear. She accepted gratefully the botched-up bonnets which her sister-in-law pieced for her out of the girls' cast-off finery. She wore Alice blue, grass-green, gaudy tan and purple, large black-and-white check, uncomplainingly, and dyed the cerise poplin brown, meekly answering not a word when they jeered her for the streaks it had acquired in the dyeing.

Without a murmur she took the much-darned stockings of the family, and "adapted" them for her use, setting in new feet, though the seams always hurt her tender flesh. She wore shoes that were too tight for her and gloves that were too large, and scarcely ever had a new thing out of the store in all those twenty-five years.

When George Junior came into the kitchen while she was frying doughnuts, she always gave him as many as he wanted, and wiped up the mud-tracks on her neat oilcloth pleasantly. She picked up after him, and took his outrageous impudence patiently, acquiring a sweet air of protest like a frightened dove in his presence; yet she would have given her life at any moment to save his.

Maria, her sister-in-law, dealt in sarcasm; and it was to Miss Lavinia's gentle nature like vitriol in a cut. It grew to be the habit always to think that anything that went wrong in the family was Aunt Viny's fault; and she was perpetually anticipating blame, and trying to prevent it by little nervous actions that only precipitated trouble.

Five years ago there had been a time when Miss Lavinia fully expected her brother to hire a servant and make things a little easier for her. Indeed, he spoke about it once or twice, for he was getting on well with his business; then another brother out West died, and his orphaned boy Donald came to live with them, making what George Senior called "added heavy expenses"; and so Lavinia stayed in the kitchen, and washed dishes.

Those five years had not made things any easier for Aunt Lavinia. The coming of Donald had not brought harmony. George Junior bullied him, and there was constant friction between them. When Donald had finished two years of high school, George Senior told him it was time for a boy in his position to go to work. He got him a clerkship in a freight office, and Donald swallowed his desire to be a boy a little longer and finish high school. He went to work, while George Junior loafed through three more years of high school and barely got through without honor. Aunt Lavinia sighed a great deal in those days. She loved Donald. He had great frank brown eyes like her younger brother who was his father, and he always brought her a chair when she came in after the supper dishes were washed and she was free to sit down and read the morning paper a few minutes before going to bed. Sometimes when she crept into her narrow bed in the third-story back, the room that would naturally have been given to the servant, she lay a long time staring up at the dark ceiling and thinking how beautiful it would be if she could do something for Donald. But then of course she never could. She was nothing but a dependent. Donald was a dependent too. It was hard to be dependent. She almost wished at such times that she might go out into alien kitchens and earn a wage, that she might save it up and do what she would with it, rather than be a dependent and have others order her life, no matter how kindly the ordering. But then of course that would hurt the family pride, and she mustn't think of it.

Thinking her meek, sad thoughts, and sighing her deep, hopeless sighs, she gradually grew to have an expression of hopeless submission, eyebrows up high in the middle, down at the outside corners; mouth drooping; gentleness written over her whole face. The family thought she was happy. They blamed her, and berated her, and depended on her, and loved her in their way; but they never dreamed of her rebelling. She was theirs, and this was her life, what she was born for. Why should she not like it?

And then the letter came like a meteor dropped into the midst of the household!

Aunt Lavinia hadn't had any letters in years. The old schoolmate, a quiet girl who had married a missionary and gone to India, and who used to write to her once a year, was gone to her reward. Nobody ever thought to write to her any more. And when Harriet went to the door at the postman's ring, and found that long, thick envelope addressed to "Miss Lavinia West," she stared at it in wonder, and was about to open it as she sometimes did her mother's letters, thinking it an advertisement of some patent medicine, when her sister exclaimed: "Why, Harriet West! that letter belongs to Aunt Viny! Who on earth do you suppose she is getting a letter from? Aunt Viny, O Aunt Viny! You've got a letter!"

"Nothing but an 'ad,' of course," said Harriet disdainfully. "I'll put it on the mantel till you get done your dishes, Aunt Viny."

And Miss Lavinia meekly washed her dishes, pared the potatoes for dinner, and made a pudding before she washed her hands carefully at the sink, and went to get her letter. Of course it couldn't be anything but an advertisement, as Harriet had said; but even that was something. There was a bright pink spot on each cheek. Did some fine instinct tell her that a crisis had arrived in her monotonous life?

"I'm going up to make the beds now," she explained to the curious girls, who by this time had discovered that the envelope bore the name of a famous firm of lawyers in the city. "I'll be down in time to put on the potatoes." And Miss Lavinia fled to her room.

"Isn't Aunt Viny queer?" said Harriet impatiently. "Just see how she acts about that letter, carrying it off by herself as if it were some great thing. I believe she's getting childish."

"I shouldn't wonder," assented Mabel, looking up from her perusal of the new fashion magazine, which had just arrived in the mail. "Look how unreasonable she was about going to that funeral the other day, when we were going to have the Five Hundred Club here, and cake to bake, and sweeping to do, and all. Why, I believe she would have gone in spite of everything if I hadn't hid my old black coat, and it was the only decent thing in the house she could have worn to a funeral. Queer what a whim she took, and he was only an old schoolmate. You don't suppose she ever had a case on him, do you?"

"Not that I ever heard of," said Harriet. "Fancy anybody having a case on Aunt Viny!"

Up in her room with trembling hands Miss Lavinia was opening her letter.

It was only a few lines, but such amazing words were in them! Miss Lavinia could scarcely believe her senses. She had to get up and hunt for a clean handkerchief to wipe her glasses before she read them over again. Out of the stilted maze of legal phrases she gathered at last that a miracle had come to pass! Some money had been left to her! How much, or for what purpose, or from what source she did not stop to question. It might have dropped from heaven for aught she knew. With a strange elated impression that the occasion demanded her utmost she dropped upon her knees beside the neat bed which she had conscientiously "spread up" before opening her letter. No word came to her agitated mind or her trembling lips; but, when she arose, there was a radiance upon her as if she had received a benediction; and, when she went down-stairs to put on the potatoes, there was a gentle dignity about her that kept the girls from questioning. Not for worlds would she speak of the matter until she was sure it was true. It seemed to her yet that there must be some mistake.

The letter had spoken of Mr. Stanley K. Washburn. Miss Lavinia's heart beat quicker and the pink grew softly in her cheeks as she thought about it. Why should Stanley Washburn leave her money? He had given her a rose once, standing by her father's gate in the dim twilight years ago, the night before he went back to college for his last semester before graduation. She had kept the rose carefully for years in her handkerchief-box, until Mabel rummaging one day came upon it and crushed the withered leaves to powder, scattering the precious dust in the drawer. It had been so with most of the precious things in Miss Lavinia's life. She had only their memories in her heart.

Stanley Washburn had come back from his college commencement on a stretcher, the result of a railroad accident on his homeward trip. The years following had been filled with pain and a useless round of going from one physician to another in his own and foreign lands, until he had finally given up hope and settled down bedridden in the old home with his invalid sister, two invalids, the last of the family.

Meantime, Lavinia's father and mother had died, and she had gone to a distant part of the city to live with her married brother. The years had passed, and the two whose lives had almost touched went far apart with nothing but a crumbling rose to bind them. Lavinia had visited her old friends occasionally through the years; a gentle, formal call with sadness in their eyes and a show of cheerfulness on their faces; but gradually, as the cast-off garments that fell to her lot were less and less to her liking, she ceased to go; and at last his sister died. That had been three years ago. She had been only once since. Something Maria said once about her "traipsing off to see a *man*" had made her cheeks burn, and kept her away. It hadn't even been possible for her to go to his funeral when he died. She had shed bitter tears about that in the secret of her chamber in the night. It had been like all the other things in her life, something that had had to be given up.

But now he had left her some money, a sort of good-by present, she supposed, if indeed it was really true, and the lawyers hadn't made any mistake about it. It was beautiful in him. The tears filled her eyes at the thought. She held her head with more of an uplift than usual, and she managed to stay in the kitchen doing little things most of the time during the noonday mean. She wasn't hungry, and dreaded lest the girls should speak again about her letter. Somehow she wanted to be by herself, it was so wonderful that some one had thought of her and left her a remembrance.

At half past two Mabel and Harriet went off in their prettiest garments to the house of a friend where they were going to "pour" at a reception.

At half past three Miss Lavinia, having prepared the vegetables for the evening meal, made a lemon-meringue pie, and washed up the lunch dishes, went quietly up to her room, and prepared to go out.

She sighed as she put on the old brown poplin, and wished she had something a little more respectable in which to go to see the lawyers. It was due to her old friend that she look as well as she could. But she found Mabel's black cloak, which covered a multitude of discrepancies, mended a pair of black silk gloves, straightened out the bows on her rusty black hat, and then, dressed as neatly as her wardrobe allowed, she slipped down the stairs to the sitting-room door.

"I'm just going out for a little while, Maria," she said quietly, as if it were a common occurrence, and closed the door before Maria had a chance to take in what she was saying and object. She felt like a truant from school as she hastily shut the front door and hurried down the street to the corner, glancing furtively back, half expecting that Maria would recall and cross-question her.

Fortune favored her with a car almost immediately; and she climbed in excitedly, scarcely able to believe that it was really herself who was going secretly on this daring expedition. She paid her fare out of a worn old pocketbook whose gaunt sides touched over a solitary dime, and whose antiquated clasps were brassy with disuse.

The dime was all the money she had in the world. Her

father had given it to her forty years before, when at the age of five she had repeated for him perfectly the twenty-third Psalm. She had hoarded it carefully all these years, and had hoped to keep it all her life. She sighed as she laid it venturesomely in the conductor's hand. It seemed a sacrilege, but there had been nothing else to do. She could not ask any member of her family for car-fare without explaining her errand, and that she would not do until she was sure there was no mistake. How they would jeer at her! Her cheeks grew crimson at the very thought. If there was nothing to it, her family need never know. Perhaps this was the time of need for which she had been keeping it. At least, there was no other way. It was too far to walk.

When she got her breath, she took out the letter and looked at it again to make sure of the street and number, and to wonder again over its stately phrasing. It came to her to wonder for the first time how much the legacy might be. Probably five or ten dollars. That would be a great deal for her to have of her own after these years of absolute poverty.

But what if it should be as much as fifty dollars? Incredible thought! It almost took her breath away. She could buy Donald a brand-new suit of clothes, so that he wouldn't have to wear George Junior's old ones that didn't fit him. She knew those baggy clothes were a great trial to Donald. Perhaps she could even pay for a term at night-school for him. Donald had ambitions to be an electrical engineer some day, but the prospect looked rather dim. Night-school would help him a great deal. Then, if there was enough left, she would buy a pair of nice new gray kid gloves for herself. It would not be selfish for her to do that much. Her old friend would be pleased if she did.

Then suddenly she reproached herself for such wild fancies, and her eyes filled with tears over the thought that any one had cared enough for her to remember her in his will.

Tremulously at last she entered the lawyer's office, murmured her meek name, and handed out the official-looking letter as her excuse for being there. But, behold a miracle!

A gray-haired man of fine presence came forward deferentially, just as if she had been a queen, and conducted her to an inner office, where he placed her in a great leather chair. He could not have given her more honor and consideration if she had been the dead man's wife. The poor little woman was overwhelmed.

It appeared that the lawyer had been the lifelong friend and confidant of Mr. Washburn. The will, which left everything to Miss West, save a few small bequests to faithful servants, had been made some years ago; in fact, as soon as the sick man was told by his physicians that his case was hopeless and he might pass away at any time. The lawyer added that the making of the will had been a great pleasure to his friend, and that he had written a letter which was to be given to her after his death.

Miss Lavinia listened as in a dream to the wonderful story. She was endowed with what seemed to her a vast fortune. "Comfortably off" the lawyer expressed it. The property was well invested and bringing in an annual income of at least thirty-five hundred dollars in addition to the old Washburn homestead, which could be rented or sold as she chose. There was besides about two thousand dollars of ready money in the bank subject to her check. They gave her a bank-book and a check-book, explaining their mysteries carefully, and even handed her a roll of bills, fifty dollars in all!

Dear little Miss Lavinia in her dyed garments and her darned gloves grew white and pink as she looked at the lawyer and tried to understand. It was too marvellous, too wonderful, too incredible to happen to her. She looked at the money, and she looked at the lawyer. All that money in her hands at once! It simply could not be!

But, when they put his letter in her trembling hand, and she saw the old familiar quirk to the L in Lavinia, the same he had written on the commencement-invitation envelope, a great light broke over her face. It was as if she had heard his voice speaking her name. A something seemed to rise within her, something that had long been crushed and forgotten. Was it her sweet self, rising in wonder to a new life wherein some one really cared for her aside from what she might do for him?

She was overwhelmed no longer. She had his letter in her hand, and the mere touch of it enabled her to rise to the occasion. So quietly, so gently, with such well-bred dignity of thankfulness, she received the news that the old lawyer thought within himself, as he escorted her to the elevator a few minutes later, what a pity she could not have been permitted to cheer the last lonely days of her friend! Surely here was a woman who would have been unselfish enough to give a few years of her life to an invalid.

In a kind of sweet daze Miss Lavinia climbed into the homeward trolley, and paid her fare out of a crisp new bill. At least, she could now keep the other half of her precious dime as a reminder of her dear father. Her heart thrilled anew with gratitude to her old friend as she paid her fare and felt independent for the first time in her life.

It was not of the money she thought most as she rode home, but of the letter, the wonderful letter held close in her little darned glove. How wonderful after all these years to have a letter from Stanley Washburn! The years were bridged, and she stood once more beside the gate in the dusk, with a rose in the breast of her white gown.

When she reached home, she slipped quietly up to her room and changed her dress, buttoning the letter safely inside her blouse. Then she tucked her fat pocketbook away under a pile of clothes in her bureau drawer, giving it a loving pat, and went hurriedly down to the kitchen, for she could hear Maria rattling the range with indignant vigor.

"Well!" said Maria, straightening up from her self-imposed task. "So you've come back! Where in the world have you been? If I'd known you were going out, I wouldn't have begun to cut out Harriet's shirt-waists. One can't do everything at once. Look at the time of day! George will be here in half an hour, and this is his Building-Society night, you know. He can't be late with supper."

"I guess I sha'n't be late," said Miss Lavinia serenely, glancing at the clock to make sure Maria had as usual exaggerated the time. Then she lifted the range-lid capably, gave a glance at the fire, and pushed forward the kettle of hot water. In this brief time the kitchen seemed to have assumed its normal complacency after the hurried on-slaught of Maria.

"Go back to your shirt-waists, Maria; I'll manage alone," Lavinia said gently, and there was that in her tone that made Maria turn and stare curiously at her sister-in-law. There had been times during the years when this sister showed a calm superiority that made Maria uncomfortable; but never before had she seen quite the look that Lavinia's face wore now, filled with a sort of soft glory that radiated from her eyes and seemed to set a halo above her prematurely silvering hair. It was almost as though she glimpsed for an instant the gentlewoman in this humble dependent of the family, their heretofore meek burden-bearer. It was like a rebuke, as if Lavinia had been a great lady in disguise all these years. And yet she did not seem to have taken on any airs. Maria gave her a second puzzled glance, and hurried out of the room. There had always been something about Lavinia she could not understand.

The dinner was only five minutes late, after all, and Miss Lavinia did not hear the family jokes at her expense as she brought in the steaming dishes. She was thinking that it was only a little time now until she would be free to read her letter. She gave Donald a bewildering smile as she turned back to the kitchen, and he answered it with a grateful one. Donald was tired and discouraged that night. George Junior had been particularly trying with his lordly airs.

After dinner Donald slipped out to the kitchen, and wiped the dishes for Aunt Lavinia. He often did it. It was their only chance to talk together alone, and it did the boy good to hear her kindly sympathy and brighten her monotony with tales of the office. Tonight, however, he was unusually silent. It seemed a long way ahead before he could hope to get where he could do anything worth while. Perhaps he would never get there.

Suddenly, however, his aunt looked up.

"Donald, I want you to write and find out what it costs to go to that college you were talking about the other day."

"What's the use?" said Donald dejectedly. "I couldn't ever go to college, no matter what it costs."

"Yes, you could!" said Miss Lavinia decidedly. "There's going to be a way. I see a way now, and I want you to write the letter this very night and find out all about it."

"Aunt Lavinia!" Donald never called her "Aunt Viny," as the others did. It was one of the things about him that made him different from the rest. "What do you mean? You can't mean anything, of course. And, besides, I couldn't go to college; I've never finished high school."

"There are preparatory schools, aren't there? I want you to write and ask them what preparatory school they want you to go to."

"Aunt Lavinia!" Donald almost dropped the big yellow mixing-bowl he was wiping.

"Never mind, child. You do as I tell you," said Aunt Lavinia alertly. "I'll tell you all about it to-morrow. Don't say anything," she added under her breath as George Junior banged into the kitchen, loudly demanding the hatchet.

It was late when Miss Lavinia finished and got up to her room at last. With trembling fingers she opened her letter, touching the page gently as if it were human and sensitive.

My dear Lavinia, [it read.]

When we stood in the dusk by your father's gate that night so many years ago, I was happy in the thought that I would soon be in a position to ask you to be my wife. When I gave you a rose, I hoped you would understand that I loved you. How beautiful you looked to me with that rose tucked in your little white dress!

You know what happened, and will understand that the time never came when I, a hopeless invalid, could honorably ask you to share my broken life. But I have loved you all these years.

I am not, however, going to burden you with the tale of my love and disappointment; for the years have gone by, and I no longer know whether my love would interest you; but it has been a great pleasure to me to think that I might at least when I was gone have the privilege of leaving to you my possessions, and so providing for you as I would have loved to do if you had been my wife.

I have thought sometimes that I saw in your eyes an answer to my feeling for you, but then I have reproached myself, for how could any woman care for a broken man upon his bed?

And so, my good friend, if nothing more, as my friend I am leaving you all that I have in this world. Yet if, in the providence of God, you ever cared for me, then know that all man's soul may give to woman my soul gave to yours, and, whatever place in your heart and thoughts you choose to give me, I am content. It is enough for me now to think that I may leave you independent for the rest of your life.

I would suggest that you leave the money invested as it is. It has been my study and pleasure to place it safely where it will bring you a steady continual income, and I commend to you my old lawyer friend, who will advise you wisely in all business matters. You will hardly care to live in this old house. The neighborhood has changed since the days when we all lived about here, but I should be glad if you can find time to look after and dispose of the things in the house, my sister's and my own. We were the last of the family. I have full confidence in your sweet judgment; and I leave you unhampered, and rejoice that I may have so much part in your dear life.

I bid you farewell.

Your friend or lover as you choose,

STANLEY K. WASHBURN.

She crept into her bed at last, and lay there staring into the darkness of the room as if it were filled with glory-light. No thought of death or darkness or separation came to blight that first joy of her knowledge that she was beloved. It was enough that he loved her, had loved her through the years. She could live her days out joyfully now. She would make his money bring joy to others. She was happier than she had ever dreamed of being on this earth.

Once a great pang shot through her to think of his long years of suffering and wanting her, and she not knowing it, or being able to minister to him. Then it came to her like a revelation that through it his greatness of soul had been born, and so she was content.

She told them the next morning at the breakfast-table, quietly as if it were quite a common occurrence.

"George," she said, as she passed her brother his second cup of coffee, "I want to tell you that I've had a little money left me by an old friend, and I sha'n't be a burden on you any longer." As if she had ever been a burden in that house!

"Money!" screamed George Junior jubilantly. "Then you'll buy me that motor-cycle I've wanted so long, won't you, Aunt Viny?"

"Money?" said George Senior, putting another lump of sugar into his coffee. "That sounds good. Money's always welcome when it's coming our way. How much is it?"

He spoke as if it were coming to the common coffer.

"It's enough to keep me quite comfortably," said Miss Lavinia in the self-effacing tone she had used during the years to put herself into the background.

Her brother laughed.

"I guess you don't have much idea how much it does cost to keep you, Viny, do you? You never had much to do with money matters. You've always been well taken care of and not had to bother where your daily bread came from."

"Yes," sniffed Maria, "I guess you don't have much idea about what things cost, Viny." There was righteous implication in her tone that intended to convey the high cost of Miss Lavinia's living all these years.

Miss Lavinia's soft brown eyes told no tale of how distasteful this conversation was to her nerves long accustomed to such as this. She only answered with dignity,

"I shall have an income of about thirty-five hundred a year."

"Great Scott!"

George dropped his teaspoon into his cup with a clatter. "Thirty-five hundred a year! Why, Viny, you're crazy. You don't know what you're talking about. You mean thirty-five hundred in all, don't you? Even that's a great deal for *you* to have left you."

"Aunt Viny doesn't realize what a big capital an income of thirty-five hundred a year would mean," said Harriet patronizingly. Harriet had been a stenographer in a business office for six months after she left college, and thought she knew a great deal about business matters.

"Well, I should like to know who on earth would leave Aunt Viny money, anyway," said Mabel saucily. "I guess you'll likely find there's some mistake, Aunt Viny. People don't leave big sums to strangers that way."

"Be still, Mabel," said her father sharply. "Let your aunt talk. Viny, who'd you say left this thirty-five hundred to you?"

Donald's face was red with indignation, and his fists were clenched under the table-cloth; but Miss Lavinia answered with a sweet lifting of her radiant eyes and a gentle dignity that was both convincing and awe-inspiring:

"It was my old friend, Stanley Washburn, George, who used to live near us on Chester Avenue when we were young. There's no mistake about it, for I went to see the lawyer yesterday. I shall have an income of at least thirty-five hundred a year."

"You don't say!" said Mr. West, sitting up excitedly. "Stan Washburn! that poor fellow that got knocked up on the railroad? So he's dead at last! Well, I must say it was decent of him to leave you his money."

"Well, he's better off," sighed Maria piously. "I'm sure I shouldn't want to live a long life of suffering. I should think you'd be glad now, Viny, that you took my advice and didn't keep running out there. It can't be said of you that you were after his money."

"Is that the man whose funeral Aunt Viny was so crazy to go to?" broke in Mabel. "*Now* we see what *you* were up to, Aunt Viny."

But Miss Lavinia had fled to the kitchen, and no one but Donald had seen the tears in her eyes as she reached for the empty coffee-pot.

"It's a pity this couldn't have come three years ago, when you were building the new store," suggested Maria in a low tone to her husband. "You could have managed the double building then and enlarged the business."

"Yes, it might have come in handy," said George reflectively, folding up his napkin and putting it into the ring. "Strange! Stan Washburn! I never knew he was stuck on Viny. Viny!" he called to his sister. "You say you went to see the lawyer yesterday. Well, you'll be wanting to get the business part settled up right away. It's always better. I'll arrange to get away from the store this afternoon and go down with you. I think I can fix it up to invest your money in the business."

But Miss Lavinia was standing in the kitchen door, her soft eyes bright with the recent tears, her cheeks red, and her soft lips set firmly.

"Thank you, George," she said gently. "But I shall not need you. Everything is all arranged. The money is well invested, and Mr. Washburn wished to have it remain where it is. I shall not need any help."

Then she turned, and shut the kitchen door quietly after her.

"Well, upon my word! Such airs!" said Harriet. "Mother, how are you going to get along with an heiress in the kitchen? I'm sure I didn't suppose Aunt Viny would get her head turned like that by a little money. She seems to have forgotten all we've done for her."

"Done for *her!* What have you ever done for her?" muttered Donald under his breath. "What has *she* done for *you,* you better say!" and Donald marched off into the kitchen, followed by George's sneering, "Well, there's a pair of you, I should say!"

Further conversation, however, was interrupted by the reappearance of Miss Lavinia.

"I've been thinking," she said; and the family, looking up, perceived about her a new air of confidence that commanded their attention, "I shall have a great deal to attend to the next few days, and shall scarcely have time for my usual work. Mr. Washburn has asked me to look after some of his sister's and his things, and this must be attended to at once. If you're willing, Maria, I'll run over to Chloe Whitely's, and get her to come for a week or two till you can look around and see whom you want to get permanently."

"Certainly, if you have the money to pay her," said Maria contemptuously. "Of course I suppose you'll run the house, now that you have a little money."

"O, why, Maria, I don't want to do anything you don't like, of course," said Lavinia, conscience-stricken, "but I'll be very glad to pay for some good help, anybody you'll select to take my place. I thought you'd like Chloe because she's washed for us so long, and knows all our ways, and how we cook. You see I shall have to be away for several days; it may be longer. I can't tell how long it will take me, nor what plans I shall make."

"O, of course," said Maria, still offended. "I should have supposed you'd want some of your family to advise you, but you seem sufficient to yourself. Perhaps you'd like one of the girls to go with you."

"Thank you," said Lavinia dubiously; "but I think perhaps I ought to go alone; at first, anyway."

During the next few days the West family suffered a physical and mental disturbance somewhat similar to a volcanic eruption; and when it was over, they found a decided change in the face of their landscape. Through it all Miss Lavinia went her serene ways untroubled and untrammelled. For in truth she was a new being. The sharp words, and broad hints, and covert sneers that would have crushed her meek soul to earth in former days went unnoticed in the high altitude to which she had attained.

She went shopping for three whole days.

Donald appeared in a new suit at dinner the second night, to the discomfiture of his cousin, George Junior, who expected to shed his own suit before it was half worn out, on the pretext that Donald needed it. However, he forgot his grievance the next morning in the arrival of a shining new motor-cycle.

All that day packages began to arrive, and were stacked up on the hall hat-rack until they overflowed its ample limits.

"Gee!" said George Junior, coming home to lunch black and blue from his first ride. "But she can spend the money. Guess I better strike her for some more things before she gets away with it all."

"Yes," said his mother anxiously, "she needs a guardian. She'll just spend it all, and be back on our hands to support again. I declare, George," turning to her husband, "some one ought to stop her."

"Guess no one can stop her. The money's her own," said George Senior, drumming reflectively on the window-seat.

But the third evening Miss Lavinia brought down a lot of those packages. There was a rich wonderful satiny silk of purple, with deep black and rich green shadows in it, such as Maria had coveted for many a day. There were two charming gold wrist-watches for Harriet and Mabel, besides a lot of pretty things in jewelry and lingerie that the watchful aunt had long wished to buy for them all. Also before she went up to her room she handed her brother a check for five hundred dollars, which she said she hoped would pay for some one to take her place for a while and also get him the big leather chair and desk he had coveted for his library.

Somehow the atmosphere of the family changed a good deal that evening. They weren't exactly overwhelmed by their gifts, munificent as they were; but they were mollified. After all, you wouldn't have expected them to bow down to her, meek, quiet little woman that she was, still in her handed-down and dyed and made-over garments, her hair combed in the same plain way they had known it for years, her feet incased in an old pair of Harriet's shoes with the heels worn down at the side.

But the great surprise came the next morning.

It was strange enough not to have Aunt Viny down in the kitchen before any one else was up; but to have her actually late to breakfast was a thing the family quite resented, even in spite of the gifts of the night before.

"Well, really! So you've come down at last!" said Maria in her sharp tone, forgetful for the moment of the luscious purple silk. And then the family dropped their knives and forks, and sat back, and stared.

For there on the threshold stood not Aunt Viny in her faded poplin, rusty bonnet, darned gloves, and shabby shoes, but a lady! A stranger she seemed to be at first. She was attired in a simple, exquisitely tailored fine gray suit, a coat and a skirt with a glimpse of a soft gray silk blouse beneath and a fine white lace collar. On her head was the sweetest little gray hat of fine straw, with gray and white wings that seemed to nestle like a dove about the fluffy silver hair that waved over her calm forehead. Her hands were incased in soft gray suède gloves; her shoes were trim, well fitting, and new; over her arm was thrown a long soft camel's hair coat of gray; and she carried a small hand-bag of gray leather, and a larger travelling-bag of black.

After observing these details their eyes travelled back to her face. A beautiful one, sweet and gentle, with soft brown eyes that had in them something familiar. What was this beautiful stranger doing in their dining-room? A feeling that the indignity was somehow due to Aunt Viny arose in their breasts; and then the lady spoke, and the voice was the voice of Aunt Viny!

"I'm sorry to be late," she said; "but I thought I'd better be all ready before I came down. Mr. Benson, the lawyer, is coming pretty soon to take me to the house; and it won't do for me to keep him waiting."

The family caught its breath as one man and one woman in a sudden relief and indignation. Aunt Viny had no right to startle them all that way. But astonishing thought! *This* was Aunt Viny, and she was *beautiful!* How had she managed it just with clothes? Who knew she could look like that? The girls turned sick with envy and mortification. They hadn't taken in yet what she said; they had only taken in that it was Aunt Viny.

Calmly, as if her new belongings had been with her all her life, Miss Lavinia walked over to the dining-room couch, and deposited her cloak and bags, and drew off her gloves, apologetically saying, "I put these on to be sure they would go on quickly the second time." Then she took her seat at the table.

Mechanically and in silence they handed her a plate. Maria, disturbed as by the presence of a guest at table, rang for hot coffee, and said she hoped the rolls were not cold. When had she ever taken so much solicitude for Lavinia before? But a lady clothed in tailor-made trimness was somehow different from Viny in her kitchen gingham.

"I thought I better tell you all that I don't suppose I'll be coming back to stay; so you can fix up my room as you like," said Miss Lavinia. "I know the girls have been wanting a bay window in their room, and I left something up on their pincushion that will help build it. I shall be back and forth, of course, but not probably to stay overnight. I'm going to take Donald with me; so you can have his room for the extra guestroom we've needed so long. I can't tell just how long it will take me to get the house ready to sell; but I may be there a month yet, anyway. Donald has to give his month's notice before leaving the office. Then we are going to hunt around and find a nice little home near the college he wants to go to and settle down for the next five or six years. We haven't got our plans made yet, but we hope you'll all come and see us often."

Had a bomb been thrown into the room and exploded, it could not have more completely knocked the senses out of the family. They simply sat and gasped, as the erstwhile meek burden-bearer brought out one after another her calm, astonishing facts.

And then, before a single one could summon a word the door-bell rang, and the lawyer arrived.

It was quite obvious that nothing suitable to the occasion could be said with only a pair of thin portières separating the imposing stranger from their voices. And in five minutes more Miss Lavinia was seated in the lawyer's great shining car, waving her pretty gray glove to them happily, with Donald in the front seat beside Mr. Benson.

The family stood on the front porch and watched them go, still speechless from astonishment.

"Who ever knew she was *beautiful?*" exclaimed Harriet as the car turned the corner and was lost to view.

"Any one can look that way if they can buy such clothes," said Maria with a toss of her head.

"Wasn't that hand-bag a peach?" said Mabel. "It was lined with moire silk, pale rose color, and mounted in gold."

"I mean to ask her to buy me a car next Christmas," said George Junior, mindful of his cousin Donald on that front seat.

"That's the way mother used to look when I was a little kid," said George Senior. "Mother was beautiful like that. And she always wore soft gray things." Then with a sort of wistful sigh he turned back to his house that seemed suddenly desolate. Was it possible that Aunt Viny had made so much difference?

Something Quite Forgotten

BETTY ANDERSON carefully folded her wisp of a black velvet dinner dress, and laid it without a wrinkle, tissue paper between each fold, into the cardboard box that exactly fitted into her suitcase.

There was a pleased eagerness in her face as she smoothed the velvet across the shoulders, just above the tiny triangle of great-grandmother's bit of old English Honiton lace in the neck.

There was absolutely nothing the matter with that dress. It was really distinguished in style, cut, and elegant simplicity.

Betty had always wanted a black velvet dress, but she hadn't thought she could possible afford it until she found that wonderful remnant of transparent velvet on the bargain counter, a short-length marked absurdly low. And because she herself was a short-length she had been able to get that darling little dinner gown out of the remnant. There had even been enough by careful piecing to make the dear little puffed sleeves that were so short they could hardly be called sleeves at all. But Betty liked a bit of sleeve. She was not the kind of girl who took to low backs and slender straps.

She glanced toward the bed, where was assembled the rest of her meagre wardrobe, at least all that was respectable to take to the wonderful Christmas house-party. Fortunately the party was to be held in a great log cottage up on a mountain, and it was to be supposed that the dressing would not be elaborate in such surroundings, but one could never tell.

"Bring sports things and two or three of your prettiest evening frocks," the hostess had said in her casual invitation. So Betty's glance was anxious as she reviewed the collection.

There was a little pool of pink lingerie and the right kind of stockings, quite beyond criticism; black satin slippers with bright buckles, a smart little pair of sports shoes that she had bought for a song because they were too tight for a classmate. Nothing the matter with any of those. It was the dresses that worried her. Had she enough?

There were two hand-knitted dresses which she had made herself in odd hours between studies, and when she had to look after the office, for she was working her way through college and but little of her time was her own. One was brown with vivid orange in the border, the other a lovely Lincoln green with a creamy white blouse with lacy crocheted revers. They were both stylish and distinctive. And of course the black velvet was perfect; but besides it she had only two others: a little scarlet silk that she had made and dyed herself from an old white china silk of ancient pattern, but it was berry red, Christmasy and becoming. The other was a white satin she had fashioned from her mother's precious wedding dress, highwaisted and quaintly eloquent of days long gone by.

Well, it was too late to question now. The train left in a little over an hour. She had had to work up to the last minute putting rooms in order before she was free to leave.

It was the first Christmas in three years that Betty had

spent away from college. Three years since the terrible accident that had swept away Father and Mother and home and fortune in one stroke. It had been a long, hard time, and this was the first bit of change that had come to her. She must not be too particular about whether she had everything that other girls had.

She packed rapidly and gave a quick glance around the room to see if she had left out anything. Ah! There was her Bible. That must go along of course. She put it in and snapped her suitcase shut. Then swiftly donned her little close green felt hat and lovely new green cloth coat with its beautiful beaver collar and cuffs, rejoicing that some extra coaching she had done in French had made it possible for her to purchase these. Her old hat and coat had been so shabby.

She barely caught the train to the city where she was to meet the party of young people who were to be her fellow guests. Her heart was in a tumult of excitement as she made her way out of the train into the station. But almost at once her ardor was somewhat dampened, for it was a chauffeur in livery who met her at the train gate instead of the bevy of friendly college girls and boys she had pictured.

When she shyly took her place in the middle seat of the third car which the chauffeur assigned her, the young people who already had possession were anything but friendly. A cool stare, an indifferent "Oh, hello!" was the utmost greeting they gave her.

There was a lovely drive of several hours through the woods ahead of them, but she had not gone many miles before she most earnestly wished she had never come.

"What's the matter, Baby? Doesn't your mother know you're out?" cried out a girl with the reddest lips, entitled "Zaza." For Betty had refused both cigarettes and liquor.

Betty's cheeks flamed crimson and she wanted to cry but she knew she mustn't. They were climbing a hill now, far from any railroad station. It was too late to go back. She must brave it out, and she mustn't let them think her a baby either. She suddenly remembered that she was a witness for the Lord Jesus. She must think of her testimony. A sentence from a book she had read a few days ago came back to her:

"The world can only see the Lord Jesus today through men and women who know Him and are willing to slay self and let Him live in them."

Well, she had tried to do that. She had prayed that Christ might be in her all through this Christmas time even though she might be in a world that did not know Him. But she had not dreamed it would be like this. She would not have chosen to come if she had. Ah! perhaps she had been wrong to be so eager to come—to have just the right clothes and everything. Perhaps she had thought more about those things than a child of God should. Well, it was plain now anyway that she must somehow bear a clear testimony among these people while she had to be in their company.

So she endured her discomfort in silence, even taking it sweetly when Rilla Munson, a girl with gorgeous red hair and a sharp tongue, carelessly upset her glass on Betty's beautiful new coat sleeve.

That ride was as utterly unlike what she had anticipated as possible. Betty tried to enjoy the woods, the tall forest trees, the plumy pines; tried to forget the noisy company about her. Once she even tried to be friendly again, calling attention to a frisky chipmunk in the branches, but Rilla set up a yell to one of the boys:

"Oh, Bartley, shoot him for me, that's a darling! and I'll have him stuffed for a souvenir!"

And the young man actually got out a flashy little revolver and shot several times at the gay little atom of life in the branches. Betty was glad that the yells and screams of the party warned the tiny creature in time and he whisked into a protected hole in a tree trunk, scolding away and looking almost as if he were laughing at them.

After that Betty kept her words to herself.

It was early dusk when they arrived at the great palace of logs in the wilderness. It was a wonderful place, with wide rustic galleries, and an immense fireplace filled with burning logs. There were thick rugs and deep soft skins of wild animals on the floors, and great easychairs and bookcases everywhere, not to mention a grand piano and a number of beautiful works of art not usually found in a wilderness. Betty gazed about in wonder and only wished the company were different. What a wonderful time she could have if they were all nice people!

The hostess was very gracious. She kissed Betty on her cheek, and told the others that Betty's mother had been her school-mate and she hoped they would show Betty a nice time. But the young people scarcely noticed her and went on about their own concerns.

Betty was given a tiny room at the far end of the upper gallery, only a cot, a dresser, and chair in it. The hostess apologized, "You won't mind, will you dear? I had to give you this small room because Ted, my son, is bringing home a man he met in Europe and he insists he must have a room to himself."

No, Betty didn't mind. She was only too glad that she did not have to room with some of those other girls. Having a room to herself, even the tiniest one, might make it possible to endure a good many unpleasant things. She could always get away by herself when things got too hard.

The evening meal was an elaborate and hilarious one. There were twenty young people besides herself, and Betty found it easy to keep in the background. A few smiles seemed all that was expected of her.

A great deal of the table talk was about the stranger, Graham Grantland, who was to arrive on the morrow, presumably with Ted, the son of the house. Mrs.

Whittington told how brilliant he was and how much Ted adored him, and the girls each began clamoring to have him placed beside her at the table. But Zaza declared that he was hers. And then they all began to plan how they would drive down the mountain to meet him on the morrow. Betty took no part in this talk, quietly resolving that she would not be one of those to meet the wonderful expected arrival.

To that end next morning she asked her hostess if there was anything she could do to help.

"Oh, my dear, *would* you?" exclaimed the lady sweetly. "I do want to go down the mountain on an errand, but there hasn't been a thing done about decorations. I wonder if you would look after that for me? You look so sweet yourself I just know you are artistic. The servants will be here to help of course, and Decker will do all the heavy work. There are plenty of hemlock branches, and holly and mistletoe. Decker will put up the tree. I've told him about that. You'll find the tree ornaments in the attic, and lots of tinsel and tissue paper and silver stars and things. Do you think you could do something to make it look sort of Christmasy here, my dear?"

"Why, I'd love to!" said Betty with her eyes sparkling. "Have you any special plan or directions?"

"Oh, no, dear! Just fix it as you like, make it gay and pretty, that's all. Use anything you find in the house."

With a sigh of relief Betty turned from watching the noisy guests troop off to the cars and drive away. Then with a zest she went to work.

The three servants took hold with a will. The tree was up in no time, and blossoming out with balls and luscious, expensive ornaments. They talked like four happy children as they worked. Betty sometimes burst into a Christmas carol and they all joined in timidly, until Betty began to wish it were the servants she was visiting instead of the aristocracy.

All around the second story of the great living room ran a rustic gallery from which opened the guest rooms, and this gallery they interlaced with hemlock boughs. Laurel ropes were festooned from the peak of the lofty roof to the gallery rails till it looked like a tented forest. Holly and mistletoe bloomed out behind antlers on the wall and over doorways. It really was wonderfully pretty. And the great tree towered and glittered at the upper end of the long room opposite the fireplace.

Everything was done at last but the mantelpiece. Betty looked at it with a catch in her breath. It was a wonderful place to work out an idea. Dared she?

Up in the attic she had found a great electric star among the tree trimmings, and a good many rolls of different-colored crepe paper; also a lot of children's toys, among them several large boxes of stone blocks and a whole Noah's ark and zoological garden of animals. These had given her the idea.

She called Decker to help her, and with her heart beating a little wildly she set to work.

She made Decker hang up several lengths of deep blue crepe paper reaching from the mantel to the ceiling and these she peppered over with different sizes of little silver stars which she found in small boxes among the wrappings that had been provided for Christmas gifts.

She feared it was a little temeritous to dare to take down the great deer's head, crowned with wonderful branching antlers, which had occupied the place over the mantel, but she hung it on the gallery just over the main front door and gave it a lovely collar of holly about its neck. And then she had the electric star hung in the place over the mantel where the deer had been, and framed the whole space in hemlock like a bit of starry sky among the branches.

The servants with growing admiration watched her place a row of little boxes of different heights across the back of the mantel shelf and then cover them with crumpled green tissue paper. Then suddenly they saw it was not boxes and green paper at all, it was a row of green hills against a midnight sky. Betty was setting little toy woolly lambs on the hill to the left, with a toy Noah in a brown crepe paper tunic as a shepherd to watch them.

They stood in wonder and watched her deft fingers as she began to build little flat-roofed stone houses from the blocks, with miniature outside staircases on the different heights of the hills to the right. A twig of spruce or hemlock stood here and there for trees. Then all at once there was a little hilly village, and the cook, who had come in to take a look, exclaimed in wonder: "Sure, that'll be Bethlehem! An' will ye be makin' the stable an' a manger?"

So Betty made the khan with little stone arches for entrances, and found three camels with riders for the wise men. It was really a lovely picture when it was finished, and it would look quite real when darkness came and all the other lights but the electric star would be turned out.

After a delicious little luncheon by herself, she put on some old togs she found in a closet and went out with a pair of skiis to find out if she had lost her old skill acquired several years ago when as a little girl she spent a winter among the mountains.

She was enjoying herself so much that she scarcely noticed how far she had gone until she suddenly began to realize that she was very tired and ought to go back to the house.

But just then she swept around a clump of trees straight into a half broken trail, and there before her not a stone's throw away stood a horse and wagon, the horse with his head bent wearily down snuffing the snow, and behind him on the wagon seat two rough-looking men, one drinking from a black bottle, the other reaching to get it for himself.

They both turned as Betty swept into view, a maudlin

evil light leering into their eyes, and the younger of the two sprang unsteadily down and started toward her.

Betty was too frightened to know just what to do, but she gave a quick turn to the right and plunged out through the snow blindly, not noticing until she was actually upon it that there was a great chasm just ahead across her path that separated her from another rise of the mountain. She caught her breath an instant. She had taken greater leaps than this when a child, but could she do it now? But there was no time to think.

"Oh, God, help me!" she cried, and leaped forward skimming like a bird over the great crack, and sailing on down the mountain. When she dared to look back her pursuers were mere specks in the distance.

But now, what should she do? She dared not retrace her steps to find her footprints back to the house and she was completely turned around. She had no idea which direction she ought to take.

After a time she came into a quiet place on a higher level and paused to get her bearings. Was she surely safe from those awful men? But how was she to get back and be sure not to meet them again? How foolish she had been to come so far. No one would know where to look for her. Somehow she had the impression that the house-party wouldn't even notice her absence when they returned, wouldn't bother to hunt for her. Still of course some one would eventually make a search. But she mustn't be the cause of all that fuss. She would so much rather get back quietly by herself.

Wait! There was a sound! Were those men still on her track? Perhaps they had skiis or snow-shoes in their wagon. Ah! Was that a shout?

The sound drew nearer and she stood listening, alert, but somehow unable to decide which way to move. And then to her great joy the sound grew into words and a voice of gorgeous fulness. It swept throbbingly among the silence of the trees and snow, like some great organ voice of praise:

> *"Joy to the world! the Lord is come;*
> *Let earth receive her King;*
> *Let every heart prepare Him room,*
> *And heaven and nature sing!"*

Then her heart leaped with great relief. Whoever that was, he was singing about her Lord and Savior, and she had nothing to fear. The voice was coming closer now, ringing out gloriously in the vast mountain silence with thrilling sweetness and power. It almost seemed as if it must be some great Christmas angel come down from the realms above in answer to her need. Her throat throbbed with longing to join in the song, but she stood waiting, silent, breathless.

Suddenly the singer swept around the mountain and came face to face with her! A tall splendid-looking man striding along on skiis!

He came to a sudden halt, lifting his hat.

"I beg your pardon," he said. "I supposed I had the mountain to myself. I hope I haven't startled you."

"Oh, I'm so glad you were singing!" cried Betty with a tremble of tears in her voice. "I've been so frightened by two drunken men that tried to chase me, and when I heard you singing a hymn I knew I need not be afraid."

His face softened and a light came into his eyes.

"You know the Lord, too?" he asked, and his voice was almost as if he were claiming kinship.

"Oh, yes!" she breathed shyly.

"That is good. Then we are not strangers. Is there anything that I can do for you?"

"Why, if you could direct me to Storm Castle Mountain, where the Whittingtons live, I shall be grateful. Somehow I'm all turned around."

"Why that's just where I'm going," said the young man. "Do you happen to be one of the other guests?"

"Oh, yes!" said Betty with relief. "Isn't it a coincidence that I should find you?"

"Well, my name is Graham Grantland. May I know yours?"

"I'm Betty Anderson," she said, giving him a troubled look. "But if you're Mr. Grantland, how is it that they missed you? They all went down to the station this morning to meet your train. They'll be terribly disappointed."

"They did!" said the stranger with a grin. "Well I'm sorry to have made them all that trouble, but I particularly told Ted not to expect me till I got there. I've been visiting friends on a neighboring mountain. I took a fancy to come on foot and so sent my baggage over by express. However, there's no great harm done, I guess, and I certainly am glad I got here in time to find you, since you were lost."

"I'm afraid," said Betty gravely, "that they're going to be terribly cross at me for having met you first."

"Indeed!" said the young man, studying her keenly. "Well, let them try it!" And suddenly Betty felt deeply thankful that he was here, and that she had come to the party.

"How does it happen that you didn't go down with the rest to meet me?" he asked, a gleam of a smile on his pleasant lips.

"Why,—I—" hesitated Betty a bit embarrassed, "I stayed behind to help with the decorations."

"I see," he commented, watching the lovely flushed face and glowing eyes, and reading between her words. "And now, tell me about yourself, please."

As they climbed together to the house on the mountain, the miles flew by on wings. Betty forgot that she had been tired. It seemed as if they had known one another a long time.

And even though they loitered they reached the house before the others had returned; for, failing to find Grantland on the noon train, they had waited for the late afternoon train to come in. Betty was glad that she did not have to make a spectacular appearance with the lion of the hour. She could imagine just what black looks she would get from the other girls under such circumstances.

But they came a few minutes later, tired and cross and much upset to find that Grantland had arrived during their absence.

Decker with rare good sense had turned on only the lights over the front door, and in the galleries, so that the full beauty of the decorations did not burst upon the guests until after dinner, for everyone hurried to dress and came rushing down to the dining room.

And so it was that Betty escaped much notice from anyone. She sat at the other end of the table from the guest of honor, beside a disgruntled youth who had been displaced from Zaza's side for Grantland's sake. But occasionally Grantland's understanding glance sought her eyes and she felt somehow that he knew just how out of place she was in this gathering.

Finally, in a pause when everybody had been saying how dreadful it was for him to have to walk up the mountainside in all that snow, and how sorry they were that they had not been there to make the afternoon pleasant for him, he raised his voice just the least bit and smiled openly down Betty's way.

"Thank you, that's very kind of you all," he said, "but you needn't apologize. I assure you I had a wonderful time with Miss Anderson. We were out on skiis together for a while. She is a charming substitute hostess, Mrs. Whittington."

"Indeed?" said Mrs. Whittington, turning a cold eye on Betty. "I'm very glad, I'm sure," and a chilling silence fell upon the crowd.

But Grantland still had the ear of the table.

"I don't suppose you knew that our families were old friends," he said, looking at his hostess with a disarming smile. "You see, Miss Anderson's father and my father were close friends and classmates in college, and I was named after Mr. Anderson. Graham Anderson Grantland is my full name. So I am doubly thankful to you for inviting me here, you see."

Betty looked up, a warm thrill running around her heart. So that was why he had asked those questions about her dear father: what college he attended and what his exact name was. And then at once the atmosphere about her grew just a trifle warmer. Mrs. Whittington smiled at her and asked her if she had been lonely while they were gone, also remarking that she had noticed there were greens on the galleries and thanked her for attending to the decorations. She hadn't had time to look at them yet, but she was sure they would be very pretty. Even the young man on her left, who hadn't even looked at her before, suddenly grew interested and asked the name of the college she was attending.

With the dessert came a new order of things. The hostess decreed that everyone at the table must tell a story or sing a song or perform some sort of stunt.

The hostess picked at random the performers until all had taken part except Betty and Grantland. They were evidently used to such demands. They had ready the latest joke, the last jazzy song, and several risque acts that brought forth wild merriment from the company.

Betty sat with troubled gaze, wondering if she would be called upon, sending up an unspoken prayer for help. Then her eyes sought Grantland's. What did he think of this? What would he do when they called upon him? The two were the only witnesses for Christ—The Christ who had been forgotten and left out of this Christmas—and what could they do? What would she do if she was called? She couldn't decline, it would not be good sportsmanship or good testimony either.

And even while she was thinking this her hostess called her.

"Betty dear, I'm sure you have some cunning stunt. Give it to us now, please."

Betty's frightened eyes glanced down the table catching Grantland's strong, steady gaze. It seemed to put strength into her, and give her courage to follow the idea that had flashed into her mind.

Steadily she arose in her place with a little smile about on the hostile, astonished company and spoke in a cool clear voice:

"Would you mind going into the other room for mine? I think everybody has finished dinner, and I need the decorations for a setting. Decker, will you please turn on the lights—*all* the lights please?"

"Oh, but my dear!" protested the hostess, "everyone hasn't performed. Mr. Grantland hasn't had his turn yet, and I imagine his will be the best of all."

"If you don't mind, Mrs. Whittington, I think I too could do better with the setting of the other room," said Grantland courteously, and rose as he spoke.

"Oh, very well," laughed the hostess indulgently, rising and signalling to her guests.

So Betty passed behind their chairs and preceded them into the other room. When the whole company arrived she was standing in her bright little scarlet dress beside the fireplace, with the fire light shining on her dark curls. Her eyes were bright with excitement and her face was flushed. As she lifted her eyes and glanced up toward the Bethlehem city she had built, Grantland watched her and thought how lovely she was, and how she might almost have passed for one of the maidens out of the Old Testament, Ruth or Esther or some Israelitish queen in her oriental loveliness. Then, just at that moment, the great star flashed on, for Decker had left it till last, and the whole little company saw the Bethlehem hills for the first time and a hush fell upon the room, followed by a soft murmur of astonishment and delight.

Then Betty's voice rose, clear, with arresting attention:

"This is Christmas Eve," she said, as if she were calling attention to something they had quite forgotten. "May I recite the words that belong with this picture on the mantel?" And then without more preamble she repeated from memory, slowly and distinctly the majestic words of the Christmas Gospel.

As she finished the last words amid a strange awed silence Betty suddenly felt frightened at what she had done and shrank back into the shadow.

Then softly into the hush came a tender chord, and another voice, fitting right into the picture as if it had been rehearsed. Grantland had seated himself at the piano and was singing:

> *"O little town of Bethlehem,*
> *How still we see thee lie:*
> *Above thy deep and dreamless sleep*
> *The silent stars go by:*
> *Yet in thy dark streets shineth*
> *The everlasting Light;*
> *The hopes and fears of all the years*
> *Are met in thee tonight."*

The room was very still as the glorious voice rolled on making the words of the old hymn live anew, and forcing their meaning into the hearts of the listeners.

Betty from her shadowed corner looked out in wonder over the hushed company. Over on the stairs young Ted Whittington stood, his eyes glowing, watching his friend and drinking in every word. Just below him Dick Atkinson sat on a step with his elbows on his knees, his head in his hands. Everyone in the room looked serious. Even Zaza had shaded her eyes with her hand, and Rilla was openly wiping her eyes with her handkerchief. Back in the open dining room door the servants stood in the shadow with bowed heads. Suddenly the tears rushed into Betty's eyes and she had to put her own head down and struggle to keep them back. Ah, the Christ had come back even to this Christmas! And all those careless young people were listening to His story.

On swept the wonderful resonant voice, making a prayer out of the last verse:

> "O holy Child of Bethlehem,
>   Descend to us, we pray;
> Cast out our sin, and enter in,
>   Be born in us today.
> We hear the Christmas angels
>   The great glad tidings tell;
> O come to us, abide with us,
>   Our Lord Immanuel."

There was somehow a holy spell over the rest of that evening. The hilarious mood that had ruled at the table did not return. The singer was applauded again and again, and responded with a few more Christmas carols, in some of which they all joined in. Then there was a distribution of the gifts, a rich heap of costly little packages in elaborate wrappings; but even when they laughed over some particularly appropriate gift, or a bit of a joke in an expensive trifle, there was a subdued undertone in it all.

Zaza did attempt to turn on the victrola and suggest some dancing, but Rilla shook her head.

"Don't!" she said sharply. "Not tonight! It doesn't belong!"

When at last the company broke up to go to their rest, Grantland sought out Betty in her shadowed corner.

"How about an hour on the skiis in the early morning," he whispered, "before the others are up?"

"Oh, that would be wonderful!" she answered, her eyes like two bright stars.

"All right, then, I'll wait for you here, at five o'clock?" She gave eager assent.

"Then good night, little new friend, and thank you for the wonderful Christmas story. It was a brave thing to do."

"Oh, but it would have fallen flat if it hadn't been for your singing!" said Betty earnestly.

"Oh no!" he said quickly, "God's Word never falls flat. Don't you know He has said, 'My Word shall not return unto me void, but shall accomplish that whereunto I have sent it'? But I thank God I was here and was allowed to help in the wonderful message your Bethlehem and your story started. Good night, dear new friend! I know I'm going to be thankful always that God brought us together." He pressed her hand quickly, smiled and was gone.

Betty, full of new joy and wonder, hurried to her little room, to thank her Heavenly Father for the way He ruled over the evening.

But she had scarcely closed her door before there came a tap, and opening it she found to her dismay the girl Rilla.

"I want to ask you what it is that makes you different from the rest of us," she said when Betty had offered her the only chair and sat down herself upon the cot. "How do you get this way?"

"Why, what way?" asked Betty puzzled.

"So kind of happy and satisfied-looking," responded Rilla. "You don't seem to have so much to be happy over. Mrs. Whittington says your people are dead and you've lost your money. I don't see how you can look the way you do. Now I've got money to burn, and I've tried every thrill in the universe, but I'm just as miserable as I can be. What is it that makes you different? Can you show me how to find it?"

"Oh, yes," said Betty, a great light dawning in her eyes. "It is Jesus Christ! Certainly I can show you how to find Him."

And there in the little back room, Betty led the way to the manger again, and to the cross, and pointed out the dying Savior. And presently, with the lights turned out, the two girls knelt beside the wide window where the Christmas stars looked down, and Rilla prayed for the first time in her life, accepting the great Christmas gift of a Savior.

It was long past midnight when Betty at last crept into her cot, a great joy in her heart. Oh, it was wonderful to have had the privilege of leading a soul to Christ!

And in the morning she was to meet her new friend, and she would tell him all about it and he would be glad. Oh, life was wonderful witnessing for the Lord Jesus! And God had been good to send her a friend like Grantland. A real friend! Oh, this was a glad Christmas Day, indeed!

And she fell asleep thinking of Grantland's good night, hugging the words to her heart: "Good night, dear new friend, I'm going to be thankful always that God brought us together."

A Government Position

LUCY JANE WATSON and her mother were sorting out the mail and putting it into the glass-faced compartments which separated their living-room from the space set apart for the village people when they came for their mail.

Lucy Jane and her mother had had the Dewville post-office ever since Captain Watson died. People felt sorry for them, and no one tried to get it away. Everybody liked Mrs. Watson, and naturally she and Lucy Jane took a great interest in the village mail, and tried to do their duty by it.

"Another one come back?" whispered Mrs. Watson, peering over the shoulder of her daughter, who by virtue of her better eyesight usually distributed the letters.

Lucy Jane nodded sadly, as she held up a large manila envelope to scrutinize it more closely.

"Yes, and it's from the same folks. I'd think she'd get discouraged. I should s'pose her family pride would keep her from tryin' the same ones over again. But then, poor thing! I s'pose there ain't only jes' so many publishers, an' she's got to begin all over when she's been around once." This in a low, sad whisper that could not be heard by the

Reprinted by permission of *The Christian Endeavor World*.

sharp ears of even little Lizzie Prye, who stood waiting outside the window for the paper which was reposing in the box, and at which she had squinted several times, flattening her nose against the glass to read, "Joseph W. Prye, Dewville."

Mrs. Watson sighed heavily, and held out her hand for the envelope. "Let me see it," she said.

They studied it again with their heads together, while the doctor's boy who had been sent for the mail whistled impatiently, and rapped on box forty-six with his dirty knuckles.

"Well, don't put it in the box just yet," said Mrs. Watson, handing it back reluctantly. "Poor thing! Give her one more mail for thinking they've took it."

"No, mother!" said Lucy Jane in so vehement a whisper that her mother rustled some old newspapers in a panic lest the waiting populace should hear. "The last time I kep' one out for twelve hours I couldn't sleep at night, thinkin' maybe the poor thing would get her hopes high from its not comin' direc'ly back, an' it would only be harder to bear. I'll put it in the box, whatever happens. She may not send for the mail before night, anyway."

Then she walked with decision to the lower end of the rows of boxes, and put the envelope in the first of a row of six which were deeper than the others, and had locks and keys and little glass windows set in brass.

Lizzie Prye applied her eye to this window, and read, "Mrs. Robert C. Lyman." She wondered what nice package had come to Mrs. Lyman, and fell to dreaming of what it might contain.

The rest of the mail was distributed at last, and Lizzie Prye and the doctor's boy, with others who had dropped in, were sent on their way. There was not much time for the mother and daughter to talk, and would not be for another hour; for people would be coming "right along" for their mail, Mrs. Watson said; but she kept her anxious eye looking out of the door for the owner of the yellow envelope.

It was near five o'clock; and, as the work was all done, and there would not be any rush with getting the evening mailbag ready for almost an hour yet, Lucy Jane went to the front door to rest and watch the street. She had not sat there long before she came flying back into the little dining-room beyond the post-office, where her mother sat reading Deacon Bassett's paper. As it was Wednesday, the night for the evening prayer meeting, Mrs. Watson knew the Deacon would not drive into town for his mail till near meeting-time; so she had plenty of leisure to read the news and get the paper back innocently into its wrapper without fear of being flurried.

"For goodness' sake, Lucy Jane, how you scairt me!" exclaimed her mother, quickly folding up the paper and looking around for the wrapper. "What's the matter? You're gettin' too excitable."

"She's comin', mother! I see the phayton an' pony down the street. Theodory's drivin'. Oh, dear! I wisht I had done as you said, an' not put it in the box yet. It seems too bad to spoil their nice afternoon. They look so comfortable an' expectin'. I'm jes' sure I shall shake all over. You go in, ma, for she most always forgets her key. I believe I'd take it out of the box yet; only that hateful Lizzie Prye saw me put it in, an' it might come out somehow."

Mrs. Watson, forgetful of Deacon Bassett's paper, hastened into the post-office long before Lucy Jane was through talking.

"Sh!" she said, holding up a warning finger as the girl peered in at the doorway. "She's comin', poor thing!"

A sorrel pony stopped before the door, and a girl with merry eyes and curly brown hair got out and ran in, leaving the reins in the hands of a slender, pale woman dressed in black.

"Good afternoon, Miss Theodory," said Mrs. Watson, to conceal her agitation. "Mail? No, there wasn't anything of any 'count, I guess, jest a cirk'lar"; and she shoved the large manila envelope through the little window, while Lucy Jane in the background hovered near a crack in the boards, and held her breath in pity.

"Oh, dear! nothing but that!" exclaimed the girl as she looked at the envelope and frowned.

Mrs. Watson looked at her daughter, her eyes filling with helpless tears.

"It's too bad the little one has to see her disappointment. It must make it that much harder for her ma," whispered Mrs. Watson, as she and Lucy Jane both hastened to the window to watch the lady in the carriage.

They saw the lady draw her brows down and bite her lips as she examined the envelope. Mrs. Watson fancied she grew pale. There was some low talk between the two in the carriage, but the watchers at the window could not hear, though the window and slats were open wide. The lady in the carriage looked at her watch, and the little girl looked disappointed, and seemed to coax; but the mother shook her head, and the little girl turned the pony's head around.

"They're a-goin' back home. She feels too bad to go a-ridin'," said Mrs. Watson.

"No, ma, she's a-goin' to try to get it ready to send off to another publisher 'fore the next mail goes. Didn't you see her look at the time? Poor thing! It's too bad. If she'd only quit tryin', and go to dressmakin' or somethin' sensible, she'd do a great sight better."

They both went to the door, and watched the pony till it was out of sight. They stood there talking till it was time to get ready the mail-bag for old Joe Jeffries, when he would come to hang it on the long arm for the evening express to pick off and carry with it as it went by.

Mrs. Watson grew flustered when she saw how late it was, and almost put some eastern mail in the western bag; but they had it ready at last, all but fastening the bag, and old Joe stood lazily on the front steps, waiting.

"Ma, can't you wait another minute," said Lucy Jane, "while I go see if Theodory ain't comin'? They'll be dreadful disappointed if they don't get that manuscrip' in this mail after all their hurry, an' givin' up their ride, an' all."

"It ain't much use, Lucy Jane! That manuscrip' jest come back again, poor things!" said Mrs. Watson; but she looked at the the clock and held the mail-bag open.

"She's a-comin'!" said Lucy Jane, hurrying behind the glass-fronted pigeonholes. "The carriage is past Mis' Riddle's, an' she'll be here in a minute. I told Joe you was most ready."

Then the phaeton drove up, and the little girl came flying through the door, another large envelope in her hand.

"Is this too late for the evening mail, Mrs. Watson?" she questioned sharply.

"Jest in time," answered Lucy Jane, snatching it in so businesslike a way and slipping it into the bag that you never would have guessed she had all but made the mail too late to wait for it.

After old Joe had gone, and the mother and daughter were free to prepare their supper, Lucy Jane hurried in to her mother, who was cutting bread in the kitchen, and said excitedly,

"Ma, did you see the address on that envelope?"

"Why, no," said her mother, pausing interestedly. "Did you? Was it to any folks you know?"

"Yes, I did," answered Lucy Jane tragically, lowering her voice to a whisper. "Ma, it was sent back to the identical same folks it come from. You know they had their names printed up to the left corner of the envelope, and I remembered it was the same."

"Lucy Jane!" ejaculated Mrs. Watson in a calamitous tone. There was silence in the room while the two pondered what this might mean.

"Mebbe they've writ her to send 'em another try," said the mother meditatively with a gleam of hope.

"No," said Lucy Jane decidedly. "She couldn't have writ it so quick. There was too thick a bundle for that. An' she wouldn't have dared send some old thing that had been sent back from somewhere else. She's had too many discouragements fer that. I'll tell you what 'tis. She's jest got to the end of her rope, an' she's a-sendin' it back, and beggin' 'em to take it, please, an' jest pay her a little fer a start. I expect she went home, and fixed it up a little, and changed somethin' to try 'em once more. It's jest too bad. Now, ma, it that comes back, *somthin'* ought to be done!"

"I know it," said Mrs. Watson deliberately; "I've knowed it fer some time back, but what could it be? We couldn't do a blessed thing at helpin' her through anybody else without lettin' on how we know, an' she's that proud it don't seem right for folks to know how hard she's tried and failed. Poor thing, why didn't she see how full the world was of wimmin writers, an' none of 'em gettin' their bread, to say nothin' of their butter? Maybe we ought to have gone an' warned her about Drusilly, an' how she failed with her poetry books, when we first found out she was sendin' a manuscript and gettin' it back week after week. But somehow I couldn't bring myself to expose my own sister's shame; for Drusilly did set such store by her poetry, and it was jest as good as any I read in the Deacon's paper."

"Ma, I've been a-thinkin'. We've got to help her our own selves some way," said Lucy Jane impressively.

"Well, Lucy Jane, I don't know but you're 'bout right, as you mostly are. It does seem too bad to see a young thing left like that, an' her not knowin' how to lift her hand to do a thing, an' we with a good bit in the bank laid by. An' she's proud, an' wouldn't take help. It would have to be givin' her honest labor to do. She'd never take money out 'n' out. My, I can see her now when she was a little thing, a-ridin' by with her curls a-flyin', an' her nurse tryin' to keep her little white sunbonnet on. I never thought to see her come to this. Not as I knew her folks so amazin' well, Lucy Jane; but I always did admire her afar off, as it were. Yes, somethin' must be done."

Nothing more was said about the matter for two days, though Mrs. Watson waited breathlessly for another manila envelope every time she opened the mail-bag, and Lucy Jane hovered nervously by the door watching for the pony phaeton whenever she had nothing else to do. She felt a morbid interest in watching little Theodora as she flitted by on errands and ran in to see whether there was any mail.

At last, one rainy afternoon, as Lucy Jane and her mother sat listening for the whistle to sound which would tell them that the afternoon mail had arrived, and lifting uninterested eyes from the stockings they were darning to the window to watch for old Joe's coming, Lucy Jane broke the silence.

"Ma, I've thought what we must do!"

Then she got up, and closed and locked the door which led into the little outer office, and knelt down beside her mother, and whispered low. The mother listened thoughtfully, a shadow coming over her face the while; but she nodded assent as one to whom the proposition was not new.

"Yes, Lucy Jane, I've been a-thinkin' just that. It would be hard—but land! Think of the poor thing havin' to bear what she's done, a-seein' the work of her hand and heart— yes, an' you might say of her mind, too, for it must take a good bit of mind for story-writin'—a-flyin' back in her very face. It's like havin' one's very own children turn against one. What she needs is heartenin' up. An' my belief is that a little payin' work would do that more'n anythin' else."

The front door opened, and old Joe thumped the mail-bags down, and grumbled as he rattled the fastened latch. Behind him they could hear the feet of the villagers eager for their mail. Some of them were women who never got a letter a year, and yet were always hovering about the delightful possibility.

Lucy Jane's fingers trembled as she unfastened the bag and took out the letters. She had calculated that, if that manila envelope was to come back as usual, it would be likely to be in this mail. She worked with nervous energy. The mother halted with her papers to look over her daughter's shoulder. One comprehensive glance told them both that their fears were realized. It was there. Mrs. Watson's heart sank, and her face took on a gray look. Lucy Jane lifted her head in one sublime act of sacrifice. The worst had come, and they must offer the remedy.

Without the usual interest they distributed and dealt out the mail. Then silently they went about getting their tea, though neither felt that she could eat. They forced down a few mouthfuls and drank a little tea for form's sake, and no word was said about the subject uppermost in their minds until Lucy Jane had risen to clear away the cups and plates and put the bread away in the box.

Mrs. Watson drew a long sigh, and murmured, "Poor thing!"

After Lucy Jane had come back from putting the milk and butter in the cellar she asked,

"Are you going to tell her to-night?"

"Certainly," said the mother with unusual decision. "She mustn't be kep' in anxiety any longer. Get your hat, and bring my bonnet. We won't need to dress up. It's dark in the streets by this time, an' it's likely she's been cryin', an' 'll be settin' without a light."

"Mamma," said Theodora, coming into her mother's library, where she was hard at work beside her desk, "Mrs. Watson and her daughter are in the parlor and want to see you, and they say you need not light the gas. I guess they feel bad about something."

Mrs. Lyman went at once to the room across the hall, where the soft light of an open fire played with the shadows around the room; and from their deepest recesses arose two dark, embarrassed figures.

"We hope you'll pardon our comin'," began Mrs. Watson, getting out her handkerchief to wipe her eyes, "but we felt so sorry for you, havin' known you, that is, watched you, ever sence you was the size of your own little girl and younger, an' I couldn't forbear——" Here a tear rolled down her cheek, and she stopped to wipe it away. She would not have the lady suspect how great was the sacrifice she was about to make.

"You are certainly very kind," said the little woman in black. "I am very lonely since my husband's death, and it does me good to know I have the sympathy of my old friends, who would not be to blame had they almost forgotten me, I have been away from Dewville so long."

Lucy Jane felt they were not comprehended, and put in a word.

"You see, we couldn't help knowin' all about it; for the very first one the little girl brought she wanted weighed, and said it was a manuscrip'; an' we watched every day, hopin' it wouldn't come back. We always take great interest in our customers. An' ma, havin' experience with Aunt Drusilla, we couldn't help understandin' it all."

"Yes?" the lady said, puzzled and awaiting an explanation. "I don't think I remember your Aunt Drusilla."

"Drusilly was my sister," spoke up Mrs. Watson, having gained control of her emotions. "You wouldn't remember her much. She was Drusilly Garnet. She married Mark Keeler, an' he went off an' got killed on the railroad; an' she had to support herself, an' she took to poetry. She wrote faithful every day, so many lines, an' got whiter an' whiter; an' every time she sent any off it come back reg'lar. We got a hold of a book by a big writer once that told how he had suffered of hunger an' all sort of want a-tryin' to get famous, an' how he never did till it was too late. I made Drusilly read it, an' I think if I had 'a' got it sooner it might have cured her in time; but it was too late. She'd jest put her heart in them rhymes, an' she couldn't give it up; an' she wrote an' wrote, an' at last she had 'em printed herself, two hundred copies as a start, an' there never was but five of 'em sold. One her doctor bought after she died; one was sold to me, and one to Deacon Bassett, one to her Uncle Garnet, and one to the hired girl who took care of her in her last sickness. All the rest are packed away in my attic now. I brought along a copy to give to you, so you might see how good they was; and yet they never brought her nothin'."

Mrs. Watson paused for breath, and her hostess murmured how sad it must have been for the poet, and wondered what errand had brought these strange callers. Lucy Jane saw her opportunity, and burst in.

"An' soon's we saw your manuscrip' come back, we understood, an' felt so sorry for you; an' we thought we'd come an' tell you, an' we didn't want you to have any trouble—an'—"

"I beg your pardon, do you mean there was not postage enough on the last manuscript my daughter mailed?" said the lady, interrupting Lucy Jane's illucid remarks.

"Lucy Jane, you keep still; I can tell this," said her mother severely, and Lucy Jane subsided into the shadow.

"No, my dear, there was nothin' wrong with the postage. They always have enough. Once I suspicioned it was half a stamp too much, but I weighed it, an' found it was just right; an' that was one reason why I always felt so bad, you payin' out stamps an' never gettin' anythin' back. So, when we found this last come back again to-night, we just made up our minds to come an' offer you the post-office. We've got money put by in the bank, and we can get along without workin' any more, I guess; an' the post-office is real nice work, not hard a bit. It would be a sight easier'n dressmakin', bein' as you wasn't raised to any of them things. Then 'twould be lots of company for you, too. Lucy Jane an' I would help you when you didn't understand, an' I guess there wouldn't be any trouble gettin' you sworn in till you got your appointment reg'lar. The folks would all sign for you if we told 'em to, an' fix it up permanent for you."

She halted trembling at the magnitude of her sacrifice. The hostess sat bewildered.

"My dear woman, what do you mean, and what is this about my manuscript? I do not understand."

It was some time before the mother and daughter could make the story intelligible; but at last it dawned upon Mrs. Lyman, the kindly pity and the willing sacrifice. She broke down, and laughed and cried at once, while the two sat bewildered, and looked guiltily at one another.

But the lady recovered herself, and said: "Mrs. Watson, my dear, kind friend, I do not know how to thank you for your interest and your offer. I appreciate it fully, but I am thankful for your sakes that I do not need it. Come into the other room, and let me show you something."

And then she led those two astonished women into her library, and showed them the corrected proof she had just finished and placed in another manila envelope addressed to her publishers. And she showed them magazine after magazine with her own name printed at the head of articles, and gave them copies of her books to take home, that they might read and understand how successful a writer she was, and how unnecessary was their pity.

"Lucy Jane," said Mrs. Watson when they had reached home and lighted the kerosene lamp, "cut us each a slice of that fruit-cake, an' set the teapot on. I'm hungry. Doesn't the post-office look good? I never loved it so

much as when I thought I was goin' to have to give it up.
I'm a-goin' to read this book a while."

Said Lucy Jane as she handed her mother a plate which
contained a huge slice of black fruit-cake,

"It isn't safe to judge from appearances ever; is it, ma?"

Star of Wonder

THE invitation came a week before Christmas and plunged the Whitman household into a whirl of bewilderment. Beverly read it aloud at the breakfast table without realizing what it would contain. (The boys had gone early to school and only her father and mother were there.)

> Dear Beverly;
>
> I'm stranded in a New York hotel over Christmas so I'm having a house party. Won't that be great? Besides you I'm asking Floss Everill, Vic Saunders, the Sheldon twins and Violet Fletcher, all our end of college hall.
>
> Of course it's only a hotel, but we have connecting suites and all New York for a playground. Cousin Lew is bringing some of his men friends down from Hartford and there's one particularly stunning young architect I want you to meet.
>
> Now wire me at once what train you'll take and I'll meet you at the Pennsylvania Station. Come not later than Monday afternoon, the 24th, and Saturday

if you can make it. I'm dying to see you again. Don't bother about clothes. Anything will do. You always look nice. And anyway there are the darlingest shops right in the hotel if you should need anything.

Yours for the time of our lives,
Carolyn Kramer.

Beverly read more and more slowly, a troubled look coming in her eyes, and there was a dead silence in the room when she finished. Finally her father spoke, a kind of hesitancy in his voice.

"Well, that's certainly kind of her! That will cost them quite a good deal —in a hotel!"

Then the mother spoke in a noncommittal tone.

"She was your roommate at college, wasn't she?" Beverly could see they were both trying to be very polite about it and not intrude in her decision. She experienced a sudden relief that her brothers had left before the mail arrived.

"Yes," she said, glad to be able to answer a commonplace question. "She's a grand girl and very generous. Of course they have loads of money. But she's a dear. These girls she's invited made up our clan. It would be wonderful to see them all," she added wistfully, "it seems like six years instead of six months since we parted at commencement."

There was another silence and then her mother said hesitantly: "You would like to go?"

Beverly cast a quick look at her mother, but she was carefully pouring another cup of coffee for Father and kept her eye on the cup. Her father was thoughtfully crumbling a bit of bread in his fingers. He did not look up.

"Why, I scarcely know," said Beverly in a troubled tone. "It's such a surprise! Of course it would be nice but I hate to be away from you all at Christmas."

"You mustn't think of us," said her father with forced

cheerfulness. "This is an opportunity of course. You haven't had many. It's always an education to go to New York."

"I'm not out for more education at present," laughed Beverly, "I'm not half using what I've got you know."

"Well, settle it for yourself, child," said her father rising, "I've got to get out and finish that chicken house before we have a snowstorm on our hands."

Father went out and Beverly and her mother began to clear off the breakfast table.

"I'd have to have some new clothes," said Beverly speculatively as she gathered up the silver.

"Not so much," said her mother thoughtfully. "She said not to worry about clothes."

"Yes, but you ought to see her clothes, Mother. She buys a hand-knit dress or two at seventy-five or a hundred dollars apiece and thinks nothing of it."

"Well, you can't compete with that of course," said her mother with a sigh. "Still, since you're working in the bank, making your own money you ought to be able to afford one or two good things. And perhaps your father would feel he could help a little."

"I wouldn't let him!" said Beverly quickly. "Father's got enough financial load with Aunt Lucile in the hospital, and all his money tied up in a closed bank. If I go I'll get what I need myself, but—I had Christmas plans!"

"You mustn't let Christmas plans interfere," said her mother firmly. "You mustn't think of us. We want you to have every advantage. It's a great grief to Father and me that we can't do more for our children."

There was something wistful in her mother's tone that brought the tears to Beverly's eyes.

"Don't, Mother, please!" she said earnestly flinging her arms about her mother's neck. "We have everything we want. I've had a grand life, Mother, and a wonderful family! I wouldn't have a thing different!"

"You're a good girl," said her mother, brushing a bright

tear away and managing a little trembly smile. "We thank God for our children every day. That's why we want you to accept this invitation—if—you really *want* to!"

Beverly gave her mother another quick look. "Why, of course it would be wonderful but—I'm not sure I ought to. Christmas has always been such a very special time with us."

"Well," said her mother with forced cheerfulness, "it's for you to decide, and you mustn't let any thought of us stand in your way. It would be foolish!"

Beverly went slowly, thoughtfully upstairs after the dishes were done, to examine her wardrobe. She would need a new evening dress, and she really ought to have a new winter coat. The old one was terribly shabby. And then—a wool dress of some kind.

Of course she could easily afford to get them if she hadn't ordered those expensive extra Christmas presents for them all, her lovely surprise! They ought to be here today or tomorrow! The new hockey skates and shoes for Stan, the set of books that Graham so longed for, the lovely fur neckpiece for Mother, and the new overcoat for Father. He hadn't had a new one for ten years and wouldn't get one himself. He said he didn't need it yet. But she knew his old one was worn thin and thread-bare.

Of course she had other gifts for them, little things that she had made, hemstitched handkerchiefs, neckties, and picture puzzles she had bought some time ago. But these things were special since she got her job. They wouldn't be expected so they could all be returned and nobody the wiser. She could get them again later in the season when she had earned more money, and they would likely be cheaper then. But it wouldn't be like giving them for Christmas!

She turned from the window where she had been staring out at the drab-brown hills set off by the darker green of pines on the distant mountains. The sky was leaden gray and her heart was heavy. She couldn't quite make up her mind whether she wanted to go to New York or not.

Her father came in to lunch and said there was a storm brewing. He warmed his hands at the fire that snapped cheerfully on the hearth. Oh, home was a pleasant place! Mother was making mincemeat for the Christmas pies, and if she went to New York she wouldn't be here to eat them nor have a part in the thrill of Christmas morning and the cosy happy time opening the presents. A pang struck to her heart, but she told herself crossly that one couldn't be a child always.

Father went out to his work again, but came back to get his old sheepskin jacket. He said it was turning bitter cold and went to his bones, and Beverly thought of the new overcoat with another qualm.

She was upstairs looking over her wardrobe again when the boys came home from school.

"Gee, it's cold," she heard young Stanley say. "There'll be skating sure for Christmas, but my skates are too small. Boy, I wish I thought I might get new ones for Christmas. You don't spose there's any chance, do you Mother?" he asked wistfully.

"I'm not sure, dear," she heard her mother's troubled voice. "Your sister has had an invitation to spend Christmas—" and her voice dropped so that Beverly could not hear the rest. But she heard Stanley's dismayed answer.

"Spend *Christmas!*" he fairly shouted. "You don't mean Beverly would go away from us for *Christmas* do you Mother? When Graham's going ta make that star and all, and she not here?"

"Hush dear, don't make her feel bad. We mustn't let her know we mind her being away. She doesn't get many chances for a good time."

"Aw, good night! She has as many chances as the rest of

us! *I* wouldn't *want* good times if she wasn't in 'em. Not at Christmas anyhow." There were almost tears in the indignant young voice.

"Aw, Gee," he went on plaintively, "and we had some surprises for her, too. I've run errands for the grocery every noon for weeks ta get money ta get 'em, and now there won't be any Christmas at all!"

Suddenly Graham's voice broke in upon the dismal wail.

"Who says no Christmas? Sure we're having Christmas! Aren't you and Beverly and I going to surprise—"

Then her mother's voice broke in with a hush. She was telling Graham about the invitation.

"But you don't mean that she's *going!*" broke in the older brother incredulously.

"Why, yes, I think perhaps she should," said her mother sadly.

There was a dead silence below stairs for a minute, then Graham spoke indignantly: "I didn't think Beverly would do a thing like that!" he said furiously, "I thought she— *loved* us!"

"But Graham—" her mother's voice protested, and then the dining-room door was shut and Beverly heard no more. But she did not need to.

She turned back into her room, closed the door, and sat down in dismay. She hadn't realized how they all would feel. She had been thinking only about herself. And now suddenly she realized that she didn't really want to go at all. She didn't want to be away from the dear fun and frolic of home. She wanted to see her mother's face when she wrapped the fur piece about her neck, to watch the boys when they found their gifts, to hear Stanley say, "Oh, boy! Hockey skates!" and see Graham's eyes light up when he discovered the whole set of books for which he had longed, hidden in different parts of the house as she had planned. She wanted to sing the carols and sit around the fire while Father read the Christmas story from the Bible and prayed. She wanted to help hang up the stockings and trim the tree, and then steal down when the others weren't looking and hide the presents where they wouldn't be seen till morning. There wouldn't be anything like this in New York. There wouldn't be any atmosphere of holiness, no thought of Bethlehem among her gay friends. Christmas was only a holiday to them, a time of giving expensive gifts and having a good time. And all at once she knew that if her father and mother knew all about it they wouldn't think it was such a wonderful opportunity for her either. They were all modern girls, nice, and good fun, but none of them Christians. She would be losing Christmas and all that it had always meant to her, losing it utterly, right out of her year! All at once Beverly knew that she could not go. That she did not want to go!

She got up quickly and went to her desk to write her telegram.

> Sorry but impossible to come. Have made other plans.
> Many thanks. Love to all. Am writing. Beverly.

Then she put on her old brown beret with the tiny red feather, her old brown coat and warm gloves and went downstairs.

"I have to go to the village to mail some letters and send a telegram," she called out, opening the dining-room door on the dismayed faces, "who wants to go with me?"

"Why, Beverly, ought you to take time for that? The telegram can be sent over the telephone, and Stanley will take the letters if they must go tonight."

"Time?" said Beverly gaily. "I have plenty of time before I help get supper, unless you need me for something. I thought I'd like a little exercise, and if I telephone my telegram Tilly Watrous will be sure to listen in and broadcast it all over the neighborhood. Besides, the boys and I have some Christmas secrets to talk over and we don't want you spying on us, Mother dear. Graham, how about you taking this telegram over to the office while Stan and I go to the five-and-ten?"

She threw her telegram down on the table. The boys huddled gloomily together and read it without seeming to do so. Her mother gave her a puzzled glance. Then Stanley suddenly cried out with a shout: "She isn't going, Mother! I told ya she wouldn't!"

"Of course she wouldn't!" growled Graham, a great relief in his voice as he pulled on his gloves. "Come on, Kid, I'm with ya!"

The mother glanced at the telegram and then back to her daughter. "Why, Beverly," she said with almost a tremble of joy in her voice, "are you *sure* you want to send that telegram?"

"Yes, I'm *sure!*" said Beverly throwing her arms about her mother's neck and giving her a resounding kiss.

The father came in just then. "It's very cold!" he said with a shiver. He looked blue around his lips. "I think we're going to have a real old-fashioned winter. I hope it won't storm while you're on your way to New York, child!"

"She's not going!" shouted the boys in chorus.

"Now, boys, you haven't been whining around and coaxing her to stay have you?"

"No, Father," said Beverly winding her warm young arms about his neck and kissing him on his cold cold nose. "I wouldn't go for anything, not at Christmas time. I wouldn't want to miss Christmas with you all for anybody."

Then they went out for their two-mile walk to the village, gay and full of Christmas plans, and when they came back they had many mysterious packages, and among them were wire and electric sockets and tiny electric bulbs, and strings of lights and silver rain for the tree. They entered their home fairly sparkling with joyous plans,

Beverly just as happy as the rest. The spirit of Christmas seemed to have come in with them, and peace and harmony and joy to abide.

All that week they went about with their happy secrets and there seemed to be among them a sweet intangible something that thrilled the whole family. Even a long protesting, pleading telegram from Carolyn and finally a lengthy long-distance conversation on the telephone failed to disturb the joy, since Beverly was not going away.

Saturday morning the boys got the tree, a beauty, from their own woods up on the hill a mile away, and set it up in the corner of the big living room.

"It's beginning to snow," said Father as he came in Saturday night from feeding the chickens. "Just lazy flakes but I think it means business."

"Oh, good!" cried Stanley, "a real Christmas!"

It snowed a little at intervals all day Sunday, and when the family drove home from church Sunday night it was three inches deep on the running board and coming down in little fine grains.

"She's off for an old-time blizzard!" said Graham jubilantly. "I thought she was fooling, but I guess she means it!"

Monday morning it was still snowing harder than ever, but the flakes were broad and heavy, big white feathers, piled firmly on top of the hard grainy foundation. Then the wind arrived and hurled the falling snow into fantastic drifts, heaping it higher and higher every hour, till the drifts were getting so deep they had to make tunnels to the chicken houses and bring some of the chickens into the barn for safety.

"Isn't it lovely!" cried Beverly, pausing in her busy preparations to look out the window. "Look what I would have missed if I had gone away! What fun would there be in a hotel in such weather? They don't have such lovely snow in New York City I know."

"You dear girl!" said her mother smiling happily.

"There's a drift ten feet high between here and Harrises," announced Graham coming in from taking a basket of good things to a less fortunate neighbor. "Tom Harris had to go around by Bogg's Corners to get to the village."

"Yes, it's a real blizzard all right," said Father, piling another log on the fire. "I'm glad you're at home, little girl."

"So am I," said Beverly smiling happily. "Graham, don't you think it would be good to hang that star about an inch lower so it can be seen at night through the arch of the front window?"

"Who's going to see it?" laughed Graham. "There won't be a soul abroad for many a night."

"Somebody might be lost and it would guide them," said Beverly thoughtfully.

Gideon Ware climbed stiffly from his car and for the thousandth time that day wiped the heavy coating of snow from his windshield. It lay in great flakes overlapping one another on the glass like frosting on a cake. His windshield wiper was utterly useless. His common sense had told him to get a defroster before he left his home city, but he had started late and was in a hurry at the last to get away from the city, free from business and everything, and he had taken a chance trusting to his well-proven ability to fight through difficult situations.

Gideon Ware was a big strong good-looking young fellow with an attractive manner, a rising business, and just now a lonely bitterness in his heart that made him restless. He hadn't wanted to go to this Christmas affair at the big country estate. He had told the girl who asked him that he would come if he could, but he hadn't meant to go. Yet at the last minute he couldn't stand the thought of Christmas alone in the city, so he had hurriedly purchased a few costly trifles to serve for Christmas gifts if they were in order, and had started, rather craving the long drive through the storm. The journey would have taken him only about five hours in ordinary weather, but he had already been twice that number and he was not by any means at the end yet if he could judge by the map. He had a horrible fact to face, and that was that he could not now find himself on the map at all. Again and again he had got out and cleaned off a sign board only to read, "Drive slow, School ahead!" or, "New York 90 miles." That didn't help much because he was no longer sure which direction he was coming from. The detours had been most bewildering to his tired brain.

The dark had come down since he had stopped at the last filling station and the old man who served him had been vague in his directions.

There had been occasional windswept glares of ice where he skidded around wildly, even with chains. Then he would turn and forge ahead again, wallowing into a dip in the road where the snow lay deceptively deep. He could not follow the line of the fence in the darkness and suddenly the car lurched into a ditch by the roadside. It was more than two hours before he finally got it back again into the road. His feet were wet, his wrists were wet, there was snow down his neck and up his sleeves. He was nearly frozen. Why had he started on this fool journey? Just because he was tired of plugging away at business with nothing else in life! He didn't especially care for the girl who had invited him. She was pretty and heartless, out to have a good time at any price, like all other girls he knew, but there wasn't anything else to do, so he was on his way, plodding through snowdrifts, not even knowing if he was going in the right direction. Nothing was visible even with his powerful headlights, save this thick blanket of snow through which he was moving. Why hadn't he turned around long ago when there was a place to turn? He could have stayed in his apartment, slept through the day and moped alone. What was a party anyway, and what was

Christmas but bunk? An illusion gone that used to make rosy his childhood, when there was a mother and father and home and cheer. He would never see anything like that again.

He was deadly cold and tired. He wished he could drop his head down on the wheel and sleep. His hands and arms were numb. He could scarcely move them they were so cold. People froze to death this way growing numb, not knowing they were freezing. Well, if he froze to death there was nobody to care!

Was that a light off there to the left or only a mirage, a winter will-o'-the-wisp? It certainly was a blurred brightness, or else he was dying of cold and couldn't discern that it was the light of another world.

And then, as if the car were alive and had seen the light too, it stopped dead in its tracks, stalled, *thump,* with a great white wall looming up ahead, higher than the car, deeper and higher and wider than the universe! The car had buried its nose in the drift and stopped.

He tried to go backward, but the engine just churned away for a minute and stalled again, as if it had given its last breath to save him. He lifted his tired hands that were so heavy and numb and tried to open the door. His feet were aching with cold. The heater had gone dead miles ago and the car had been growing colder ever since.

He managed to get the door open with his numb fingers at last. The world outside seemed terribly still and shut in by that soft white deadly blanket of snow everywhere. What was the use of getting out? It was only colder. There wasn't anywhere to go and if there was, he couldn't get there. That wasn't a light over there, it was a mirage, and he wasn't Gideon Ware going to a Christmas party, he was just one man freezing to death and it didn't matter. Oh, he was so deadly sleepy. And cold! He would close the door, crawl into the back seat and go to sleep. No one would ever know or care.

It was at that moment that the star blazed out clear and steady. Such a bright star, penetrating that white blanket, able to shine through the window because the house on that side was sheltered from the wind and the snow was driving from the other direction.

A star! And then a sound! Music! Was he dreaming? Could that be angels? Perhaps there was a heaven after all. He didn't belong there of course. But his mother must be there. She had taught him to pray. Perhaps in passing he might get a chance to speak with her before they sent him away. Hark!

It was only a soft humming at first, several voices tuning in on the melody, just a low humming like wings far away yet somehow strangely familiar. Then they burst out clearly in the white stillness:

> "Oh,—*star of wonder, star of night;*
> *Star with royal beauty bright;*
> *Westward leading, still proceeding,*
> *Guide us to Thy perfect light."*

"I'm coming!" called Gideon Ware in an unsteady voice half to himself. "I'm coming! Don't leave me!"

He stepped down into the snow and fell to his knees, his stiff cold knees, but he struggled up again and the motion woke him to reality. He was waist deep in the snow, wallowing!

Ah! There was a shallower place! He could feel flagging under his foot. He wasn't frozen yet. He would hold out to get to the star! Or was it a house? Maybe it was like travelling after a rainbow, never reaching the pot of gold. But there might be warmth in that star, even if it were but a star, if he could only get there.

With a last struggle he arrived at the door and fumbling found the knocker, though it fell from his numb fingers and stopped the music inside, the heavenly music!

"What's that?" said Graham suddenly rising from the floor where he had been sitting with his back against the wall. "No, Dad, you sit still. I'll go!"

But they crowded behind him as he flung open the door.

Gideon Ware stood there like a snow man, covered with white from his head to his feet and struggling for words as his mind slowly came back from a white dead world where he had almost slipped away.

"Would you mind—" he said slowly, blinking his snowy lashes, "if I came in for a minute—and got warm—by that star? I think I've been—freezing—to death!"

Strong young arms drew him inside and laid him on the couch. Stanley ran out for a pan of snow to rub his hands and face, Father put more wood on the fire, Mother went for blankets and towels, and Beverly made some coffee. In a few minutes they had brought him back, all the way back to the room, with the star shining full upon him.

An hour later, warmed and fed and beginning to feel like himself again Gideon looked about him with his own pleasant grin.

"I must have been pretty far gone, when I saw that star," he said. "I thought this was heaven. And I guess at that I wasn't so far wrong."

"We are certainly thankful God sent you to us before it was too late," said Father heartily. "And now what more can we do for you? Would you like to telephone your friends that you are safe and they needn't worry about you?"

"There isn't a soul in this world worrying about me," said Gideon with another grin. "I was only on my way to a foolish Christmas party that I didn't want to attend. I would have turned back long ago if there had been a place to turn."

"Well, telephone your Christmas party then that you are going to attend another one instead," said Father. "The roads are practically impassable."

"They are," said Gideon. "I found that out. But I don't need to stay around in your way. Can't I get a mechanic at some garage to tow my car? I can surely make it to a hotel near by."

"There isn't such a thing near by," said Graham, "and I can tow your car when it's time for you to go. You can't go till the storm's over, that's a cinch. And as for a mechanic, you couldn't bribe one out here tonight, even if he could get here!"

"You are very welcome here," said Mr. Whitman heartily, "isn't he, Mother?"

"Of course," said Mrs. Whitman with smiling eyes. "We'll be delighted to have a Christmas guest. It will just put the crowning touch to our festivities. Beverly, go make up the guest room bed."

Gideon saw the welcome in the girl's eyes as she hurried off upstairs and felt more than ever that he had reached at least the vestibule of heaven.

"Now, boys, let's get out and look after that car so nobody else will run into it in the night," said Mr. Whitman bringing out his old sheepskin coat and cap and mittens.

"Indeed, you will not," said Gideon springing up, "I'm entirely able to do anything that has to be done."

"Now, Son, lie still," said Father putting a firm hand on his arm. "You would catch your death of cold after the steaming we've given you. The boys will count it a privilege, a joke!"

Gideon finally succumbed to the Whitman determination, and felt like a big child, sitting wrapped in blankets, in the armchair beside the fire.

Outside the boys were working with snow shovels and whistling Christmas carols. Beverly's voice from above sounded softly in tune with them, humming as she worked. It seemed a blessed place into which his lines had fallen. And presently he heard the chug-chug of a flivver backing out of the old barn and coming to rescue its aristocratic brother from the drift. A strange sweet lassitude of blessed comfort and rest settled down over the guest.

"Now," said Father a little later, as they came stamping in shaking the snow from their garments, "we must get this man to bed at once!"

"We must hang up our stockings first!" cried Stanley. "Can't I get one of Father's socks for Mr. Ware, Mother?"

"Of course," said Mother smiling. "Here, I'll get one."

"Oh, please don't bother about me," begged Gideon, "I haven't hung up a stocking since I was a kid."

"All the more reason why you should now," said Father. "There are plenty of apples and nuts and maple-sugar hearts to put in it," he laughed.

"You are very kind," said Gideon deeply touched.

When the stockings were hung they all settled down quietly as Father took up the Bible and read the Christmas story of the star of long ago. Beverly was seated on a low stool by the fire and Gideon watched the firelight playing over her sweet face and wondered at himself that he should be there. Then the father prayed, not forgetting "the stranger within our gates," that he might have great blessing, and thanking the Lord "for saving him from the deadly peril of the storm." That prayer somehow made Gideon ashamed of his indifference and unbelief, and hardness of heart and gloom. If there were people like these in the world, a home like this, and a girl like that one over by the fire, life must be somehow worthwhile after all.

Up in the quiet of the guest room he searched his suitcase for the Christmas packages he had bought so indifferently for those other strangers. He swept aside the gold cigarette cases and jeweled vanity cases and bridge sets, but there was a pin he had liked, a delicate thing of amethysts and pearls that would do for the sweet mother, and there was a bracelet, a slender hoop of platinum set with emeralds and tiny diamonds. Would the girl like that?

There was a handsome silk muffler for the father, and a pair of cuff links and fur-lined gloves that would do for the boys. He got into the big lavender-scented bed well satisfied, and fell asleep at once.

There were buckwheat cakes and homemade sausage for breakfast. Gideon thought he had never tasted anything so good. There was a brief happy worship again at the table, and then they all adjourned to the living room around the fire to open the presents.

Gideon was taken right into the circle as if he belonged, and he entered into the spirit of the day as if he had always been having such Christmases.

His stocking was bulging, and there was a bag of butternuts and another of apples, down on the hearth underneath it. There was a pair of fine woolen socks that Mother had knit, a handsome compass from Graham that he had won as a prize in a school contest and treasured greatly, a trick flashlight that Stanley had saved pennies for months to buy for himself, and down in the toe of the stocking a small exquisitely bound Testament in dark blue leather and gold, one of Beverly's recently acquired treasures. She had written in it, "Christmas Greetings to Mr. Ware from Beverly Whitman," and been a little troubled lest he should be offended at such a gift, as if she thought he had no Bible. Yet she had nothing else suitable to give.

But the look he flashed across the room to her when he opened it, and the smile that went with the look, showed that he liked it.

Gideon entered into everything all day as if he were one of the family. He watched the stuffing of the turkey, and even helped Beverly to set the table; and later in that wonderful day when the big brown turkey had been eaten, with all its accompanying vegetables and cranberries and mince pie and the like, and more carols had been sung, the sun shot out for a while. They they all issued forth into the white wonderful world and shovelled paths and made snowballs, and a marvellous snow man.

When the dusk came down and they came in, there was the firelight and the star gleaming. Gideon and Beverly stood together by the big arched window and looked at the star for a moment silently. They were alone for the rest of the family were busy about some household matters.

"I shall always be grateful to that star," said Gideon in a low voice, his face lifted thoughtfully to its soft shining. "It not only saved my life," he suddenly looked down into the girl's sweet eyes, "but—it—led me—*to you!*"

He hesitated just an instant, and added in a solemn tone as if he meant it with all his heart: "And I think it has started me—on the way back to God!"

He put out his hand and laid it over the girl's, and Beverly, not drawing hers away, looked up with a joyous light in her eyes.

"Oh, I'm glad!" she breathed softly. "Then, you didn't mind my giving you the Testament?"

"I loved it!" he said solemnly.

After a moment, his hand still over hers, he spoke again. "I have never seen a girl like you, Beverly. May I come soon again to see you?"

The look she gave him as she said quietly, "I wish you would," bespoke a royal welcome for him when he came.

Late that night, up in her own room alone, she said as she knelt down to thank God for the blessings of the day, "And oh, suppose I had gone to New York instead of staying at home. I'm so glad God showed me in time before I went off on my own selfish way."

The Ransomers

MOTHER peered anxiously under the old green shade, and watched Old Gray come plodding slowly up the road. She strained her eyes, and tried to make out from Father's bent attitude whether he was bringing good news or bad, but could not be sure. Then Old Gray passed behind the thick growth of lilac-bushes in the front yard, out of sight; and she turned from the window with a sigh.

The simple dinner was all ready but she had not the heart to take it up till she knew. She opened the door and looked out.

Old Gray, according to habit, stopped in the green drive in front of the stone flaggings, and Father looked up; but he did not smile. The look in his eyes was weary, as if something hurt him.

"Well?" said Mother.

"Nothing from Theodore yet," evaded Father with an attempt at lightness in his voice.

"Didn't the notice come yet?" Mother's voice had a quick catch in it, half impatient at Father's feeble efforts to save her from the truth.

Reprinted by permission of *The Christian Endeavor World*.

"Yes, it came." Father's voice took on a hopeless note.

"Nothing else in it? You know it's several days late. I didn't know but it might be put off, 'r the date changed, 'r something."

"Nothing else, Mother; jest the us'al notice that the int'rest is due the fifteenth o' this month. It's dated jest as us'al. They don't change dates on things like that, Mother."

Father's tone was gentle, patient, indulgent, as one would explain to a little child.

"Let me see it." Mother put out her hand, and took the envelope eagerly, almost fiercely, as if somehow she might still be able to extract hope from the single sheet of paper folded within.

Father handed it to her with a sigh, and took up the reins.

"Git up!" he said. Old Gray walked staidly, obediently into the barn, and drew a sigh of anxiety. He was very susceptible to voices, and he knew something was wrong with the family. Mother usually had a kind word for him, even if there were no apple-core or lump of sugar. He loved to nuzzle with his old pink nose in her worn hand. The old horse took to his small portion of corn, and ate daintily, reflectively, making it last as long as possible to seem like a big meal; but it did not taste so good as usual. Something was the matter with Mother. And Father! Come to think of it, Father hadn't talked to him nearly so much as usual on the way home from the post-office. Something *was* the matter! He took a long breath, and wafted a stray bit of last week's chaff from a corner of the manger, gathered it up carefully with his pink velvet lips, and wished he knew.

Father and Mother ate their meal in silence. There wasn't even any chance to comment on the cooking; for there were only warmed-ups, and Mother didn't say a word about Father's not bringing home the things she had told him to get from the store. He had forgotten those, of course; but they could get along without them. With that twenty-five dollars interest money looming ahead, how could they buy such things as sugar and coffee and butter?

It was while Mother was washing the dinner dishes that Father, standing by the window, looking down the road, asked quaveringly, "You don't s'pose Theodore could 'a' forgot the day the int'rest falls due?"

"No, Father; he said it over and over. He said: 'Now, Mother, don't you worry. I'll be sure and have that money here in plenty of time. The fifteenth of September is a long way off, and I'll have the money here by that time!' He marked it down, too."

She wiped her hands on her apron, and went over to the old almanac hanging over the desk in the corner. Adjusting her spectacles, she found the place where a pencil-mark testified to Theodore's knowledge of the date.

"Theodore never would let it run this close to the time unless something had happened to him," said Mother, brushing the back of her hand hastily across her eyes.

"O, nonsense!" said Father feebly. "Nothing has happened to Theodore, Mother; don't you worry 'bout that. Most likely his letter hes miscarried, er else he ain't been able to git the money together's soon es he 'xpected. There couldn't nothing happen to Theodore up there in those big woods in the lumber-camp. It ain't like he was in a big city with autymobles flying round thick."

"A tree could fall on him," said Mother with a catch in her breath as if she had spoken now the awful dread of her heart, and almost feared it would bring the calamity.

"Now, Mother, you've jest got to trust in the Lord, and not think o' things like that. You know you promised you would when Theodore hed that fine offer and went up there. Moreover, this ain't a time to be thinking of trees falling. We've got that mortgage to pay, an' how we going to do it? That's the question."

They settled down to the inevitable talk which both had known was coming all the week, and both had tried to put off, hoping something would happen to make it unnecessary.

"You don't think 'twould do to tell the man—jest go, explain how 'tis—that Theodore is going to send the money in a few days?"

It was the temptation that had been hovering on the edge of Mother's mind all day; she knew it in the secret of her soul for the weakness that it was, but somehow it had to come out for Father's condemnation before she could quite get rid of it.

"No, Mother," said Father decidedly, as if he too had thought of that and dismissed it forever. "That wouldn't be businesslike, and 'twouldn't be egzactly honest. What 'd we do ef Theodore didn't get the money? We hev to think of some other way."

"Yes, I s'pose so," sighed Mother, relinquishing the weak way reluctantly. "Well, what you going to do? Ef Aunt Jane had only left me those spoons instead of leaving 'em to Sar' Ann, who didn't need 'em, having plenty of her own, we could mebbe have sold them. They ought to have brought that much; there was two dozen, big and little, and not bent a bit."

"Well, we ain't got the spoons; so we won't consider 'em," said Father impatiently, after the manner of men with the impractical "if onlies" of their women folks.

"Well, you're going to do something, I suppose. Or are you just going to let it alone, and have him *foreclose?*" She brought the word out impetuously, that awful word that was like a blow on both their hearts, the fear of which had hung over them for days, ever since they had begun to watch for word from their absent son, and it had not come.

The old man turned his hurt, sorry eyes toward her; and a hard, set look came about his mouth.

"You ain't supposing I've quite took leave of my senses," he said; and then, because she had stung him with the word, he was nerved to say the thing that had been in both their minds for a week. "I don't see nothing for it but to sell the old horse, Mother."

The word was spoken, and they both sat dumb, quivering at the thought. Mother was glad she had not been the one to voice it. She would have had to if Father hadn't done it first; now she felt a strange resentment at him rising up in her, that he could bear to say it. Old Gray was so like one of themselves. Sell Old Gray!

The tears coursed down her cheeks silently, and her hands dropped helplessly in her lap. The awful thought was out at last. It could be no more hidden in the recesses of their spirits and bidden take leave. It was with them to stay.

The old man cleared his throat several times.

"I know, Mother, I know." He got up nervously, and walked over to the window. "I know, it's hard; but I don't see no other way. We've got to be honest, an' we can't let the house go. It's all the place we've got to live in while we stay."

There was silence in the room, save for the soft little sobbing sound of Mother's breath. The old cat realized that something was the matter, and got up from the mat by the stove, going over to Father and winding herself lovingly about his feet. She purred loud comfort as well as she knew how, but there were tears on Father's face and in his eyes. He could not see out the window. The lilac-bushes were blurred upon the pane, and he could not see the cat when he tried to look down.

Supper that night was a mere ceremony which each got through somehow for the sake of the other; and bedtime, though welcome, did not bring relief. Neither slept at all; and about four o'clock in the morning Mother said quaveringly, out of the flatness of her damp pillow.

"We'd have to be sure he had a good home."

"Of course," said Father briefly, and silence reigned again till five o'clock, when Father got up and hurried out to the barn. He had purposely fed Old Gray after dark the night before. He couldn't bear to look the kind old horse in the face. Both he and his wife had been conscious all night of the animal's presence out there, as if he were another human being lying awake and wondering why they acted so strangely toward him, he who had been a faithful part of the family for so many years.

There was very little corn left in the bin; but Father gave Old Gray an extra helping that morning, and patted him on the nose as if ashamed. Then he bolted from the barn.

When he came into the house, Mother looked up anxiously from the mush she was frying, as if to ask whether Father had told Old Gray, and how he took it; but Father only blew his nose hard, and went and looked out the window.

Three days they stood the agony, going through the forms of eating and sleeping without the spirit, and both were overborne with sorrow. Twice each day Old Gray plodded to the post-office two miles away, and Mother went along. She felt as if she couldn't bear to lose a single ride now with the old horse, there were so few left; and with a pang she watched his bony body plod along ahead.

Each time the post-office came in sight new hope sprang up in their hearts, only to die away in utter sadness when Father came out empty-handed.

The road lay along the old canal, and usually Mother loved the view, the bright still water with its green banks, and purpling hills in the distance. She usually looked back at the turn of the road to get another glimpse of the white church-spire back in the village. But that day the tears hid the water, hills, green banks alike, in one misty blur.

At a little roadside store on the outskirts of the village Father drew up and began to speak to the man who reclined on a barrel-head in front of the door.

"Say, Dave, d'yeh know any one wants to buy a horse?"

Mother quivered at the words, and neither of them dared look at Old Gray, who turned an inquiring eye around at the words, and drew a long sigh of astonishment. So it had come to that!

Dave Hardy shifted his position against the barrel-head, crossing the other foot over; took in the outfit with a final, lingering, comprehensive glance at Old Gray; and replied at leisure: "Wall, I dunno. Yeh might try Lym Rutherford. He's gen'ally ready fer a good bargain in horse-flesh. That the horse? He's gettin' on in years, ain't he?"

"He's not so old," said Father with asperity. "He's got a good deal of spirit left in him yet. I was thinking of Rutherford. Git up, Gray!" and Old Gray, always ready to play up to the part assigned, threw up his ragged tail, and pranced off at quite a lively pace considering his heaviness of heart. But Mother leaned back toward the man on the barrel, and called anxiously: "Is he kind, Mr. Hardy? Is Mr. Rutherford kind to his horses?"

"Wall, neow," laughed Dave Hardy, "I never considered that he made a speciality o' kindness t' anythin' but himself, but I guess he's es kind 's the gen'ral run of 'em." And Mother had to be content with that.

They drove straight to Lyman Rutherford's farm, a mile and a half from their own home.

"Guess we better get it over with, hadn't we, Mother?" asked Father as they turned into the road that led to the Rutherford farm.

Mother wiped her eyes, and nodded. She had no more words left.

Lyman Rutherford was standing in the open barn door with two other men, a neighbor and a hired man, when they drove into the lane by the house.

Father got out, and left Old Gray standing by the house, with Mother sitting under her umbrella in the buckboard, her heart beating like a triphammer. Father walked slowly, determinedly down to the barn. He wanted to get the preliminaries over out of Mother's hearing. It was hard for Mother. Men had to bear such things, but women somehow couldn't.

Mother sat holding on to her umbrella and trying to keep from trembling. She was afraid Mrs. Rutherford might be at home and come out to talk to her; but no one came, and the minutes passed. A great Newfoundland dog lay on the porch as if he were set to guard the house, and the hens clucked about in the lane noisily. Mother found herself wondering how they could bear to make such ugly, contented sounds. She watched the four men in the distance, and wondered just what Father was saying, half hoping that Mr. Rutherford would say, "No" at once, and end the agony. Then a panic seized her lest he would, for how could they pay the interest if they did not sell Old Gray?

As if to give Father an opportunity to talk with Lyman Rutherford, the hired man and the neighbor sauntered leisurely up the lane to Old Gray, and began to examine him critically, taking no further notice of Mother than to pull their old hats half off and jam them on again. They became at once absorbed in the horse.

They pointed out the lame spot on his leg where an old swelling sometimes showed itself and gave a limping gait to the beast. They slapped his sides in what seemed a most unnecessarily cruel manner, making the dignified old horse start and quiver as if the contact hurt his spirit rather than his body. Then the neighbor seized his kind pink nose roughly, and, holding him uncomfortably by the under lip, forced his mouth open to examine his teeth. It appeared that they were telling his age in some mysterious way by this indignity; and Mother sat as quietly as she could, trying to control her wrath and her anguish, her mild eyes snapping with indignation.

It seemed ages to Mother that the men poked and

mauled and slapped the beloved Old Gray, muttering half-laughing jokes about his ribs and his years; but at last they turned and went back to the barn, and a conference was held by the three men. Father came hurriedly, and stood beside Old Gray, touching him gently here and there, as if to find out whether he had been hurt, and to try to explain or make up to him for the insults he had suffered.

There followed a period of silence and waiting. Mother didn't dare say a word, and Father didn't dare look at her. It seemed like the awful silence that precedes a funeral service.

Then Mr. Rutherford came forward, the other two men following slowly.

"Wall, I'm willin' to give twenty-five dollars, no more, fer the hawse, an' I'll add five more fer the waggin ef you want to sell it. It ain't wuth much to me. In fact, I don't need any more *ve*hikels 'bout the place, but to 'commodate you I'll give you five dollars fer it."

Father looked helplessly at Mother, whom tears and anger were beginning to threaten; but, when they turned to each other for support in resisting this old skinflint, lo! there rose up between them the stern wall of necessity, and each saw in the eyes of the other the fatal words: "We must! It is probably the best we can do!"

"Wall, I'll take it," at last said Father, his voice choking miserably as he turned away to hide his emotion.

"You'll find you've got a good market price," said the bargain-maker, stooping to look at Old Gray's lame foot.

Father did not reply.

"You'll want to take your wife home, I s'pose," said Lyman Rutherford, looking up in the uncomfortable silence.

But Mother arose in her might, and began climbing down to the ground.

"No, I'll walk," she said decidedly. "We'll have it over with. I couldn't stand it to take him home again, Father."

Father wheeled sympathically.

"Ain't you 'fraid it'll be too much fer you, Mother? It's a good mile and a quarter from here."

"No, I got to get used to walking. I might's well begin," Mother said decidedly. Father knew it was of no use to argue when Mother spoke like that.

Mother walked straight up to Old Gray, and put her hand on his kind old face. He leaned his head down to her affectionately; and she laid her cheek against his nose for a minute, and closed her eyes. Then she turned with a quick catch of her breath like a sob, and started off down the lane. Mr. Rutherford looked after her a moment furtively, and began fumbling in his pocket. He took out a roll of ragged bills, and counted out thirty dollars, handing them over to Father, who took them without a word, and hurried after Mother as if ashamed. He felt as if he had sold one of the family. He did not turn to look at the horse, whose kind eyes watched him down the lane forgivingly as if he understood the necessity.

When they were out of hearing, Lyman Rutherford chuckled amiably. "Beats all what fools women is with animals and childern," he remarked, and then turned toward the horse with a strange feeling that he had been overheard by one of the family.

"Guess I was a fool fer buyin' 'im," he said reflectively, kicking at Old Gray's fore hoof. "But mebbe I kin fatten 'im up an' sell 'im over in the next county fer a lady's drivin'-hawse. Ladies don't know much 'bout age.

Father and Mother walked silently down the lane and into the road. Mother was crying, and Father was not far from it. They said not a word to each other, but plodded on in the hot sunshine. When they had gone about two-thirds of the way, Mother was almost exhausted.

"Sit down and rest a few minutes, Mother. Here's a nice place on the bank all shaded by that haystack. You're all beat out."

Father helped her, and she sank down on the bank exhausted, and sobbed a minute or two.

"Seems like I just couldn't bear it!" she said, trying to hold the tears back again, for she saw how hard it was for Father. "I got to thinking while you was bargaining how Old Gray stopped stock-still and looked round at our little Betty that time she was riding him bareback, an' fell off. That was two years 'fore she died. He was young and coltish then, an' he might 'a' killed her; but he didn't! An' now we've gone an' sold him fer twenty-five dollars to pay off a miserable little interest on a mortgage. Seems turrible. I don't know what Theodore 'll say when he comes home. He meant to send that money. We might 'a' waited another day. P'raps his letter 'll come by morning with a check."

"I know, Mother; but that int'rest had to be paid, an' there's only one more day. We couldn't wait. It's hard, but there wasn't nothing else to do."

"It seems awful, jest fer that little money, an' he having our Old Gray. You could see he wasn't caring a bit about him. He jest cared how much he'd be worth to him. And our comfortable buckboard going for five dollars! It's dreadful. How can we go to church?"

"Never mind, Mother, bear up! Bear up! I know it's hard; but mebbe Theodore 'll make money up there in the lumbercamp, an' come home an' buy you a new one some day."

"I don't want a new one. I want the old one we saved and scrimped to buy. It suited me better 'n any autymoble could. And I want our old horse!"

"Yes, yes, Mother. Bear up! Mebbe Theodore 'll be able to buy Old Gray back."

"He may be dead by that time," sobbed Mother, utterly giving way now. "He can't stand hard treatment and hard work. He's old. They said it, and he is. He'll die of a broken heart."

"Now, now, Mother," comforted Father; but his own heart was almost broken.

Now on the off side of that haystack, well sheltered from observation, sat three boys, practising the manly art of smoking, as their fathers had done before them.

It added zest to the entertainment that they were sitting in the shelter of a haystack that was of all things most inflammable, and that the owner of the haystack had threatened dire vengeance if he ever caught them there again smoking.

Unable to make their escape, the three were obliged to listen; and perhaps there could not have been found three more uncomfortable boys in the county than they were as they endured Mother's sobs and Father's feeble attempts to comfort her. Down the sensitive spine and into the alert young mind of each boy gradually the whole story crept, and stirred his emotions as he never would have allowed them to be stirred if he could have helped it. It was worse than being flogged by the farmer who owned the haystack. Yet they could not get away.

Three warm, dusty, red-faced boys crept out at last from under the straw, and looked furtively down the road after Father and Mother.

"Gee! Ain't that fierce?" said "Spud" Smith as he mopped his warm brow with his shirt-sleeve.

"Good night! Fellers! That gets my goat! D' ye know who they are?" asked James Leander Richardson, otherwise known as "Leany Rich."

"Who are they?" said "Beany" Johnson, leaning around the haystack to see better.

"Why, they're Ted Brown's folks!"

"That's right! So they are! Ain't that fierce?"

There was silence for half a minute.

"Who'd they say bought that horse? Rutherford? Jest like him. He's an old skin. Say, let's go up an' have a look at the horse."

They scrambled down the bank and were off silently, hands in their pockets, kicking the dust viciously now and then by way of easing their emotions. Scarcely anything was said on the way.

They skirted the surrounding fields until they reached the old pasture. Yes, there he was, Old Gray, standing alone in the pasture, looking reflectively over the bars at the cows in the next meadow. Old Gray was not enjoying his chance to eat the plenty of grass that was about him. He was looking off into space, meditating on the sad ways of life. He was trying to understand. His thin face, visible ribs, and lean haunches all showed that his had not been a life of luxury. His kind eye told that he was ready for whatever sacrifice might be demanded of him.

The boys mounted the fence, took out their knives, and began to hack at the top rail, watching the old horse silently. At last Spud spoke.

"Say, fellers, let's can that deal. Ted would feel something awful. 'Member the flies he used to knock out to us down on the old ball-field? He sure was the best coach we ever had."

"No chance!" said Beany decidedly. "We'd just get canned ourselves fer swipin' him. What good 'ud that do Brownie?"

"Aw, what 'r yeh givin' us? I don't mean swipe him, you boob. Course we'd get pinched if we did that. I mean *buy* him, out 'n' out, like anybody."

"*Buy* him!" screamed Leany. "Own him an' ride him! Gee! Wouldn't that be some class? We could keep him out in our old machine-shop."

"Not buy him fer ourselves, y' poor dunce, yeh!" Spud's indignation fairly exploded, and he punctuated his words with a thrust in Leany's ribs. "Can't yeh ever see anything but yerself? What 'ud Brownie think o' you, my son, if he was to come back an' find you ridin' round on his dad's horse? No, sir! We're going to buy him an' send him back to 'em safe an' sound."

"Where 'll yeh get the money?" damanded Beany. "I ain't got but a nickel, an' I owe that to Jonesey."

"Easy 'nough," said Spud with assurance. "I know where we can get a job right off, an' we'll buy the horse on th' 'nstalment plan, a few dollars at a time. We'll likely have to raise a little on the price, 'r he won't sell. Come on; we've got to hustle 'r he'll sell him to some one else mebbe, an' anyhow we want to get it back to 'em 'fore Brownie gets home again."

The boys obediently descended from the fence, and followed their leader through the pasture, down the road, and into the village at a lively pace, he dilating as he went on the possibilities of labor and wages for the three.

To his own back yard he led them, where was a great pile of old iron, wire, nails, and tin roofing.

"There!" said Spud, waving his arm dramatically over the field of action. "There's yer work. Dad said last week if I'd have that sorted an' take it down to the foundry before next week, he'd give me three dollars. We c'n get it all done 'fore dark if we work hard. We gotta rake up the yard, too. Then we'll take that money up to Rutherford's t'night if it ain't too late, an' pay the first 'nstalment. Come, get to work!"

"Good night! All that? We can't ever get that done!" groaned Leany, bracing himself against the weathered fence, and looking discouraged.

"Mebbe you don't want to be in this combination?" threatened the demagogue darkly. "'Cause, if you don't, there's plenty o' friends of Brownie's we c'n get dead easy. Can't we, Beany? Say the word. D' you want to, 'r don't yeh?"

If Spud had held a revolver in his face, Leany could not have straightened up quicker.

"Sure! I'll do it," he said in quite an altered tone.

"Well, get to work then; we ain't got any time to lose. You take wire. It's easiest." There was a covert sneer in his tone which completely finished poor lazy Leany. "Beany c'n take nails an' iron, an' I'll take tin; there's more o' that 'n' anything else. Put 'em in piles. Beany, put the nails on the porch. Leany, you stack the wire by the fence here, an' I'll pile the tin down by the gate. I'll take the first wheelbarrowful to the foundry an' 'xplain, an' you hev a lot gethered up time I get back. Hustle now. See which c'n get his heap biggest." With the skill of a born contractor he marshalled his forces, and soon the back yard began to look like a junk-shop. But load by load it was hurried away to the foundry in the wheelbarrow by three excited boys, urged on by a furious driver who had no mercy.

As they returned from their last trip, dirty, weary, and hungry, triumph in their eyes and a thought of supper in their minds, helped on by the savory odors that were floating on the village air, Spud halted in front of a house where a generous sprinkling of new bright shingles on the roof showed that repairs had just been finished.

"Here's where we get out next job," said Spud with satisfaction in his voice. "Come on in. We better see about it now." He swung the gate open.

"No chance!" declined Leany. "I'm tired; and, besides, we ain't got that doggone yard raked up yet. Come on; I gotta get home. It's supper-time."

Spud stood grimly in front of him, a smouch of iron rust across his fierce young face.

"Are you goin' to turn yellah? 'Cause, ef you are, now's the time. There comes Pete, an' Jonesey lives just up the street. They're pretty good frien's of Brownie's."

Leany turned without a word. He was weary, but he was not "yellah." Spud was in earnest, and Pete was an old enemy of whom Leany was deeply jealous. He stood without further protest while Spud made the contract for cleaning up Miss Lamson's yard.

"We'll make it fine es silk fer a dollar and a half," said the young contractor, mentally estimating how long it would take and how many shingles there were to be picked up.

"Pile the shingles neatly by the kitchen door?" asked Miss Lamson doubtfully.

"Sure," said Spud.

"Could you possibly get it done by to-morrow noon? I'm going to have the Aid Society here in the afternoon, and I'd like it to look nice."

Spud shook his head doubtfully, then brightened into a winning smile as if a happy thought had struck him.

"You couldn't make it two dollars?" he said insinuatingly. "'Cause then I could get another feller to help, an' we'd get it done sure."

"Why, yes, I'd pay two dollars if it was all done by one o'clock," she said.

"Then we'll be here at seven o'clock in the morning," said the contractor, and marched out, followed by his meek supporters.

"For the love o' Mike, Spud, seven 's awful early. Can't yeh make it eight?" protested Beany when they were out in the street.

But Leany was looking across the street at Pete and wondering who that "other feller" was likely to be.

"Say, Spud, I guess we could get along, us three alone, ef we began that early," he said.

"Sure!" said Spud easily, looking his satisfaction furtively at Leany. "I meant to all th' time, Leany; only I wanted more money. No, Beany; we gotta get another job fer afternoon; so we gotta get this one done."

"O, say, now, Spud, this is vacation," growled Beany, but was stopped by the sudden appearance of Spud's father, from whom the young contractor demanded his pay.

They followed Mr. Jones back to the yard, finished raking it, and received three crisp new dollars, after which neither Leany nor Beany made further protests, but gathered up their stiff limbs and hurried home for supper, agreeing to meet Spud and go out to Rutherford's to see about the horse.

Scrubbed and shining they appeared at the farmer's back door an hour and a half later, and made their astonishing proposition to buy Old Gray, harness and outfit, for thirty-five dollars, on the instalment plan, producing their three new dollars to bind the bargain.

Lyman Rutherford had heard of several young horses which were for sale cheap over in the next county, and was already sorry for his purchase of the afternoon. He was too shrewd a man not to see an advantage in the boys' proposition. At least, he would lose nothing by it. If the boys were foolish enough to want the horse, it was nothing to him. He agreed that, when they had paid ten dollars, they might take the horse away, bringing at least a dollar a week thereafter, and promptly, until the amount was all paid.

"We gotta get more fellers into this, I guess," said Spud doubtfully as they stood outside under the stars once more. "We gotta make this thing go now, and we must have that ten dollars by Saturday. Brownie might come back most any time now."

"Jes wait awhile, an' see what we c'n do," said Leany eagerly. "An', anyhow, let's not have Pete 'r Jonesey. They always want to run things."

"We'll see," said the boss briefly. "Come on now; we'll go an' have a look at *our horse.*"

Silently they stole around the house, across the barnyard to the pasture fence, and down through the pasture to where Old Gray was spending his first night for years under the stars without care or keeping, the dews of heaven upon his patient gray head.

It is curious what a feeling of proprietorship will do.

Old Gray had suddenly become to the eyes of those boys the most beautiful horse that ever cropped pasture, and they stood around him, admiringly telling over his good points in a low tone, and touching him almost reverently. Who shall say that those rough, kindly young hands did not comfort the spirit of the lonely old horse on the hillside that first night of his exile?

The days passed, and vacation was slipping away unnoticed. The boys were having the time of their lives, working with mysterious zeal. The other boys of the village couldn't understand it, and weren't allowed in the combination despite their most wily attempts; for Leany was "making good," and Spud meant to let him have his way as long as he acted "fair."

"I'm sure John's up to some mischief or other, Papa," said Spud's mother anxiously. "He comes home terribly dirty every night, and goes to bed without my saying a word. I haven't had to call him to breakfast once this week. Maybe you better speak to him. I'm real worried about him."

"Let him alone," said Spud's father. "He's only got something on his mind. Pity he wouldn't keep it there and help him get up mornings."

The jobs hadn't all been so plentiful or so remunerative as on the first two days, and the boys had to work hard, and pick up little errands here and there. Fifty cents, a dime, a nickel—they all counted. No more tobacco or soda; they couldn't spare the money, and even gum was tabooed. They worked night and day whenever they could find anything that paid. They had hoped to be able to pay the ten dollars by Saturday night and take their horse away; but there were no more three-dollar jobs, or even two-dollar ones, and the yards and gardens seemed to be singularly well cared for around their neighborhood. However, they did not lose heart, and Saturday night, counting up, they found they lacked only seventy-five cents of completing the first ten-dollar payment.

"My grandmother promised me a dollar once if I would learn the books of the Bible. I know 'em all but the minor prophets," confessed Leany reluctantly.

"You're the stuff, Leany!" cried Spud, slapping him on the shoulder. "Learn 'em, old boy! The rest of us 'll get a quarter apiece at least somehow, and we'll get some corn to put in the wagon. We'll go get the corn now out o' this money, an' then you go home an' learn them prophets. We'll pay fer the horse t'night, an' in the morning we'll take a little joy-ride out toward the crossroads. Then in the afternoon we'll put the corn in the wagon and take him home. School begins Monday, but we sure can earn that dollar a week fer a while. I bet I c'n make two dollars a week easy."

They carried out their plan, but not the least hard of all the tasks of the week was that of James Leander Richardson, sitting heavy-eyed and stolid beside his astonished grandmother, learning the names of the minor prophets!

Sunday morning dawned bright and clear, and the boys were astir early. Spud did not wait for breakfast, but took a "piece" and slid out. Eagerly the three took their way to the Rutherford farm, and presented themselves to receive their property, assuring Lyman Rutherford that the weekly instalments would be paid regularly. Gravely they took the harness and climbed the pasture fence. Old Gray received them almost effusively. He had been lonely that long week, and sad thoughts had dwelt with him. He bowed his neck to the bit, and walked majestically behind the boys to the barn where the buckboard stood. Almost reverently the boys lifted the shafts, and buckled him in. Their own horse, bought and partly paid for by the honest sweat of their brows! It was almost too much to believe!

They climbed into the buckboard, and picked up the reins. Spud of course was to drive first.

Old Gray seemed to realize, and, lifting up his fine gray

head, lit out over that country road as if it had been a racecourse and he a blooded courser.

Perhaps the week in the fresh air had done him good, or the break in the monotony had lifted his hope and given him new strength. However it was, he certainly did take a tremendous pace that Sabbath morning for a staid old horse whose Sabbath days' journeys had always been to church and back again. He may have lost count of the days there alone in the pasture, or perhaps his grateful heart thought he was rendering service in taking the boys over the hills and valleys that beautiful September morning; but he seemed to enjoy it as much as the boys, whose eyes sparkled and whose shouts rang out on the air gayly. For that one morning Old Gray was their own horse, and rightfully. It was all they were asking for their hard task; but it was enough, and they meant to enjoy it to the full.

It was the first time in fifteen years that Father and Mother Brown had stayed away from church, and the day went hard with them, hardest of all the hard week. Yet Mother could not walk so far, and Father would not leave her alone, not this first Sunday, anyway.

After dinner, when the dishes were washed up and everything quiet and Sundayfied, Mother put on a clean white apron and sat down in the big rocker by the desk. Father took the old coarse print Bible, drew up the rush-bottomed chair with the patch-work cushion, and adjusted his spectacles for the afternoon chapter.

In the desk behind Mother was the receipt for the interest on the mortgage, and the house was safe; but the old horse was gone from the barn; and every one of them, even the cat, was conscious of the sadness that brooded over the whole place.

Father opened his Bible and read while Mother closed her eyes, trying to listen and not think of the empty barn and the dear boy far away who had not written when he said he would.

Old Gray approached his home from the upper road, and could not be seen from the window that looked down the road to the village, even if Father and Mother had been looking. They boys tied the horse to the fence a little way up the road, and stole softly up to the house to reconnoitre. They crept behind the lilac-bushes around the house, and Spud shinnied up a tree a little back from the window till his eyes were on a level with Father's grave head and he could see Mother sitting with her eyes closed. Father's quavering voice was reading the sacred words. The sight of it all was service enough that day for Spud, and he slid softly down the tree with a mist upon his eyes. Not even the cat, dozing in her ample furs by the stove and pretending to listen, had caught a glimpse of him. The look on his face when he came down to the ground and muttered, "They're there all right!" made the other two boys curious, yet almost afraid to look; and each came down with that same awe over him.

They led Old Gray slowly, softly into the green drive. It was like a triumphal pageant. The basket of corn was in plain sight on the seat, a whole bushel, besides some oats in a box and a little hay under the seat.

Around Old Gray's neck hung like a gigantic locket an old pasteboard box cover on which was painfully inscribed,

I have bought myself back, and have come home to stay.

By the stone flagging at the side door, where Mother always got in, the old horse stopped of his own accord. Then Spud, because of his leadership, gave three loud knocks on the door, and the boys fled around the corner of the house, and lay flat behind some alderbushes.

What they saw and heard that day as they lay behind the alders peering out, the three boys will never tell. They never spoke of it to one another. They crept away when all was safe and quiet and Father had ceased to look for any one who might have brought the horse back. The look on each boy's face was as if he had gazed into the depth of two human hearts and learned a great deal of life.

Six weeks later Theodore came home in a panic from the lumber-camp to see what was the matter with Father and Mother. His letter and check had been returned to him from the Dead-Letter Office. His writing was blind sometimes, that's a fact; and he could pitch a ball better than address an envelope.

All that Lyman Rutherford had told Father was that a couple of boys had bought the horse on the instalment plan, and he didn't know them nor know as he'd recognize them if he saw them again. It was nothing to him so he got his money.

But, when Ted Brown got home, things began to be found out; and it wasn't long before Ted had the three culprits, as sheepish for all the world as if they had stolen Old Gray, and was telling them what he thought of them.

"Great work, old man, great work!" said the former coach, gripping Spud's grimy hand. "You're right there with the goods and no mistake about it. You're great, all great, every one of you, and I sha'n't forget it of you. You've made a home run, and I'm proud of you!"

He gave them their money back, and associated with them freely before the jealous eyes of the other boys; and when he left them, Leany looked down at the roll of bills in his hand exultingly.

"Gee!" he said reflectively. "Say, we was workin' fer ourselves, after all, wasn't we? Ain't that great?"

Sometimes in his stall when he is wakeful Old Gray remembers his exile in the pasture, and the three silent visitors under the starlight, who stroked his old lonely coat, and made him feel better. He sighs contentedly, for he feels that his time of sacrifice is over, and home is good at last.

The Esselstynes*; Or,
Alphonso and Marguerite

*A Story written on purpose for "Mother's Boys and Girls,"
by one of the Girls, who is just 12 years old, and
whose name is Grace L——.*

CHAPTER 1
AT THE BREAKFAST TABLE

"FRANK," said Mrs. Esselstyne, "I do wish there were some children in this house."

"So do I, Laura; suppose we adopt one or two; eh; how will that do?"

Oh; do you really mean it! That will be perfectly *splendid.*"

Yes, Laura, I really mean it; would not you like to begin this morning? I mean to hunt up some child, and——"

But no knowing what was going to be said, for the servant, who had just stepped out, returned, and having overheard the previous talk, and being very fond of children, thought this would be a good chance for getting some. She

*The author's first book. Published when she was twelve by her "Auntie Belle" Alden, as a surprise.

told her mistress that there were two of the prettiest little darlings out in the kitchen that she ever in all her life saw.

Mrs. Esselstyne gave a look at her husband that said as plainly as words could say:

"I think God has sent them here, don't you?"

Her husband nodded assent, and they both got up to go and look at the children.

"Jane," said Mrs. Esselstyne, "take these children to the bathroom, and give them good baths, and dress them, and bring them to my room."

"Yes 'm; but what shall I put on them?"

"Why, sure enough! Well, wrap them in blankets, and bring them down to me."

"Yes 'm," said Jane, and she went off delighted.

CHAPTER 2
THE QUESTION DECIDED

"WHERE do you live, children?" asked Mrs. Esselstyne, when Jane had brought them to her room.

"Nowhere."

"Where are your father and mother?"

"We haven't got any."

"What are your names?"

"We haven't got any names either, unless 'Ragbags' is a name; that is what the boys on the street call us."

"But what do you call each other?"

"We are brother and sister."

"Is that all the name you have for each other?"

"Yes 'm."

"That is strange! Well, would you like to come and live with us, and be our children? (Mr. Esselstyne had come in the room while they were talking.)

"Oh, yes, ma'am, so, *so so* much! *Can* we?"

"Why, I think so, if you are good children."

"Oh, goody! goody!" and the poor things clapped their hands, and jumped up and down.

"Jane," said Mrs. Esselstyne, take the poor darlings out, and give them some breakfast; they look very hungry, and I will see at once to getting them some clothes."

CHAPTER 3
GETTING DRESSED

"Oh! here are my darlings!" said Mrs. Esselstyne, as she came into the nursery. "Now, my little girl, I am going to give you a name; you shall be my Marguerite. And my boy, your name is Alphonso; you may call me mamma, and the gentleman whom you saw down stairs, you will call papa.

"Now, I am all ready to have you dressed. Alphonso, we will dress you first."

Now I will tell you how he was dressed; first his hair was combed and curled, then his dainty under-clothes were put on; the way his hair was combed was this, it was parted at the side, and rolled over in a lovely roll on top of his head, and the ends behind were arranged in wavy curls, (I forgot to tell you that his hair was quite long); then his pretty little brown pants and coat were put on, of course he had on a pretty little shirt, and last of all, a white rolling collar, and a lovely blue necktie. He had bright buttons on his coat and pants.

"You shall have a tiny gold ring for your finger, when we go down town," said his mamma.

And Marguerite said to him:

"Oh, brother, how lovely you *do* look!"

Then she danced up and down, as she always did when she was pleased.

CHAPTER 4
A TALK

"Oh, how lovely we will look, won't we, mamma?" Marguerite said.

"You will look very nice, my darlings; but you mustn't

be vain and proud. Did you know that God wouldn't love you if you were proud?"

"Yes, mamma, Mrs. Brown told us that; she told us a good many things about God, and she was talking about Him the last thing before she died."

"Who was Mrs. Brown, my dear?"

"She was a nice woman, who took care of us, and when she died, we didn't have anybody to care a bit about us any more."

"I used to have a washer-woman by the name of Mrs. Brown, that I thought a good deal of."

"Oh, mamma, I do believe, maybe you are the very one she told us about, that she used to work for; she said she wished we could find her; but that it would be no use to try, for she went to Europe to stay two or three years. She gave us a card, with her name on, so that if we should ever come across her, we should know it was she; but I can't read the card."

"Run and get it, darling, and let mamma see it."

So Marguerite went to her room, and returned in a moment with a card, which read as follows:

Mrs. Edward Frank Esselstyne.

"That is the very card I gave her," said Mrs. Esselstyne, "and that is my name. So you see, my darling, God has heard Mrs. Brown's wish, and brought you to me. Now get dressed dear, as soon as you can, we are going to ride, you know."

CHAPTER 5
A MORNING RIDE

THE carriage rolled to the door, and Mrs. Esselstyne, and her son, and daughter, came out, and were handed in; Alphonso had on a seal-skin overcoat and cap, and brown kid gloves; Marguerite's furs were of ermine, and her kid gloves were a lovely shade of lavendar.

"Oh! Oh!" she said, as they rolled down the broad, handsome street; "what a lovely, *lovely* place; I didn't know there was any such street as this in all this large city. Oh, mamma! are we going to stop at this store? Won't that be splendid!"

"This is a bookstore, dear," said Mrs. Esselstyne. "I am going in to see about a book; you may both come with me, if you like; it is a very interesting place to go; you will see more books there, than perhaps you thought there were in all the world."

So they were helped out, and all went into the great handsome building, and the brother and sister wandered up and down the wide aisles, looking around in wonder and delight, while their mamma made her purchases.

The next place they stopped at, was a very large dry-goods store.

"Would you like to get out, and pick out some dresses, or would you like to sit in the carriage and watch the people pass by?"

"I think we would like to get out; wouldn't you, Marguerite," said Alphonso.

"Well, perhaps you had better," said Mrs. Esselstyne. "There comes papa now, and he will take you with him to see about your new clothes, then Marguerite can come with me; help them out, James."

"Yes ma'am," said the coachman, touching his hat.

"Margie," said her mamma, "how would you like this suit of navy blue, trimmed with silk?"

"O, mamma, it is perfectly lovely."

"Well, then we will take it; I have bought a bottle green, and a dark brown; now you want a cardinal red, and then I think you will have plenty of cashmeres. Now we must look at these white embroidered suits, and at sashes and hair ribbons to match your dresses, then from here we must go to the milliners to see about your new hats; you will need one to match every suit; I saw a white felt, trimmed with blue silk, and plumes, that will match the blue suit nicely."

"Oh, mamma!" said Marguerite, "how perfectly splendid you are!"

CHAPTER 6
THE BIRTHDAY PARTY

A WHOLE year rolled by; it was the children's birthday; they were to have a party. They were dressed and waiting in the parlor for their company.

"Ting-aling-aling-aling" went the doorbell.

"Oh, there are Fanny and Cornie Monroe!" said Marguerite; and almost in the same breath, Alphonso said:

"There comes Fred Burton."

And after that, the bell rang every minute until the company were gathered. At seven o'clock they went out to the elegant dining-room to tea. *What* a table it was! Oh, I couldn't *begin* to tell you of all the elegant things that were on it; it looked just *lovely!* Then they had more games, and pretty soon, when all were gone home except two or three particular friends, whose mammas were coming for them, they went into mamma's room and sat around the fire in the grate, and mamma came and leaned over Alfie's chair and told them a splendid story; it was about a little boy and girl who were out in the cold, and the snow; it made Margie think of the many days that she had wandered up and down in the cold, with hardly anything on her feet to keep them from freezing; and she pushed up her hand softly, and took hold of her mamma's, and put loving little bits of kisses on it; but Alphonso couldn't realize that he had ever been a poor little boy; it seemed to him that he had always lived in this elegant home, and worn just such fine clothes.

CHAPTER 7
TROUBLE

NOW you have heard all about the young lives of this brother and sister; I have only told you this, so that you would know about them. They are several years older now. Alphonso has not improved in every respect. He had a friend, Fred Burton, who did him no good. One day he met him down by the wharf, where he was talking with the mate of one of the boats. His going to the wharf worried Mrs. Esselstyne.

"He is getting reckless, I fear," she said, with a sigh; "Oh, dear me, I *did* try to bring him up right!"

Well, to go back to Alphonso. He was talking with Fred. "I don't know Fred," he said, "whether I can go, or not."

"Oh, pshaw! of course you can go; we don't start till nine o'clock; will you go?"

"Well, y-e-s, I guess maybe I will."

"I want you to *promise.*"

"Oh, I can't do that."

"Yes you can; promise now, and then it will be done with."

"Pshaw! well, I'll go if something doesn't happen to hinder me, and that's all I w-i-l-l say."

"All right—that's enough; I can trust you. Good-bye."

"Oh, dear!" said Alphonso, the minute he turned away; "I wish I hadn't promised him; I don't want to go; at least mamma would rather I wouldn't; but after all, I don't see what harm there is in it; they needn't be so dreadfully afraid of a fellow."

CHAPTER 8
PLANS

MARGUERITE had improved very much; for one thing she was a Christian; nobody knew it yet but mamma and papa, and Jesus. That same afternoon that Alphonso was at the wharf, she was out walking; she saw her brother with Fred Burton, and it troubled her.

"Mamma," she said, when she came in, "don't you think Alphonso goes too much with Fred Burton?"

"Yes, my dear," said Mrs. Esselstyne with a sigh; "I know he does."

"Mamma, some of the boys are going riding to-night, down to the willows, and are going to have supper; and I think they are going to have wines, and—a-n-d—"

"Yes, daughter, I know what you mean; and you are afraid our Alfie will drink wine; so am I. My daughter, you must pray for him."

"I do, mamma; but I can't bear to have him go to-night. There he is; I would rather not see him just now."

So she left the room and ran up stairs.

"Mamma, where is Sis?" said Alphonso, looking in.

"She just went to her room, my son."

Her brother wanted to see her about something, so pretty soon he followed her. As he was about to knock at the door, he heard her voice, and stopping to ascertain if any one was with her, this is what he heard:

"Dear Lord Jesus! please make my dear brother a Christian; *do* help me to keep him away from that supper to-night; I don't want him to go; I want him to go to the prayer-meeting with me; please make him want to. Please keep him away from places were they drink wine, and don't let him want to smoke any more. Hear me for thine own sake. Amen."

Her brother was dumbfounded! He did not know what to do. Just then, the bell rang, and off he went to his room to dress for dinner. After dinner he went back up stairs and stayed in his room until his sister came to ask him if he would not go to the young peoples' meeting with her; he said "Yes," very pleasantly. After meeting, several of their young friends came home with them, as Margie had invited them to do. She knew that Fred Burton was coming at nine o'clock to call for her brother; she had a plan for that; she told the coachman to be on the watch for Fred Burton, and let her know when he drove up; at nine o'clock, James, the coachman, knocked at the parlor door, and said in a low voice:

"Miss Margie, he is driving down the avenue."

Then Margie went to the door.

CHAPTER 9
AN IMPORTANT DECISION

"WON'T you come in, Fred?" said Margie, as she stood in the hall with Fred Burton; Alfie and I have a little company; I should have invited you; but you were not at meeting; we brought the boys and girls home with us from the meeting. Please come in.

"Well, I don't know," said Fred, very much embarrased. "Alf promised to go out with me this evening, and I called for him; I didn't know that you were to have company."

"*He* didn't, either; it is mamma's and my surprise; please come in, Fred, your sister Annie is here."

"Oh, I don't think I can, thank you; I have my horse with me, and must attend to him."

"Why, James will attend to him; there he is now. James, take Master Fred's horse and take care of him, please; now Fred, come in. You see, I took your affairs into my own hands," she added, laughing, as she waited in the hall for him to lay aside his wrappings. So, very much to his surprise, Fred Burton found himself attending a delightful little party in the Esselstyne mansion, with a supper very much nicer than any that could have been had in the Hotel at the Willows.

Alphonso did a good deal of thinking during the next few days; he could not forget that prayer that he had heard from Margie's lips. He was half vexed at himself for thinking so much about it; he said to himself, that he hadn't been good for anything since "that night," as he phrased it. Finally, one afternoon he shut himself into his room, and said:

"I will *decide* this thing, one way or the other, and I will decide *now*."

On the table lay the handsome big Bible that his papa had given him for his last birthday present; he hardly ever opened it, but this afternoon he did; and the first words he saw were: "My son, give me thine heart."

"I will," said Alfie; "I *will* do it."

And he *did*. After that you do not need to have me tell you that he became a splendid boy.

THE END

7

Safety First

MARCELLA KEMPER stood by the front window, looking out on a stormy sunset. Battlements of sullen gray loomed in the west like grim towers and gables, with flames of angry crimson bursting between, and here and there a thread of silver light like a bayonet on the ramparts. Overhead stretched an endless, steely sky, relentlessly shutting one in to the inevitable.

There was war in the sky and war in the air! One talked of nothing else; one lived but to get the next edition of the paper to see what had happened. Flags flapped desolately in the chill evening air, showing where patriotism had got the better of the appalling thought of war.

There were seven flags on the block. Marcella had not counted them before—two at the Baileys', small and rain-streaked; a fine, large bunting of magnificent proportions floating from a tall white pole in front of the Porters'; two crossed over the front door where the old Bingham sisters lived; a real old patched revolutionary, faded and blurred, hanging from Mrs. Coates's third-story window. Mrs. Coates was a Daughter of the Revolution and wore her jeweled badge proudly on her rusty black alpaca. The seventh flag floated over the door of the doctor's office just across the road. It was medium-sized cotton, faded and dimmed. Marcella could remember the Fourth of July, some ten years or more ago, when the doctor had brought it home and put it up all bright and new, while she and his young brother, Dudley Ward, had shot off firecrackers on the steps. It seemed but the other day!

Marcella marveled, looking drearily up and down the street. It was incredible that war was really upon the land again in this enlightened age of the world! War! The thing their grandmothers had told them about with quivering voices and dim, reminiscent eyes! Scraping lint and stripping bandages! High prices and lack of food! Farewells and death messages! War! There had been found no other way to righteousness and peace but to fight it through. All the agitation and protest had failed!

She began to wonder who on the street would go. The Bailey boys were scarcely old enough, yet they were just the kind—big, courageous fellows who would jump at the first call. Would the Porter money somehow provide a way to keep their one pampered son in a place of safety till the horror was passed, or did the size of their flag really represent the quality of their patriotism? Dudley Ward had just been graduated early from medical college to enlist. He would be coming home soon. The doctor had offered his services to the ambulance corps, and was conducting a class in Red Cross work. Marcella was planning to join.

And there was Frederick! Would Frederick enlist?

Frederick Morton was big and healthy, and just twenty-six. He would easily fall among the called if conscription should come. If he should go away to war, would he commit himself to her before he went?

It was four years, now, that he had been coming to see her two or three times a week, bringing her flowers and chocolates, taking her to entertainments, and generally monopolizing her, to the exclusion of all her other young men friends. His extreme intimacy had begun about the time that Dudley Ward had gone away to college, and he had been gradually appropriating her more and more until all her girl friends considered her engaged and laughingly asked when the wedding was to be; and yet he had never spoken a word of love or marriage!

For a long time she had been content, but of late there had been a growing uneasiness. Her mother had fallen into the habit of asking probing questions. She was beginning to be nervous and sensitive. Vague doubts stirred within her heart. Did he mean nothing but friendship? Was he, perhaps, waiting till her invalid mother should die? She always put this thought by as unworthy of her, and as far as possible forbore to analyze the situation lest the filmy meshes of her romance be broken.

Mrs. Kemper put her head in at the door.

"Marcella, did you remember to get the yeast?" Her voice was like a plaintive purr.

Yeast! In the midst of great events one must eat! How strange and mixed life was!

"No, mother. I'll get it now. They'll let me in at the side door. I won't be a minute!"

"But it's real dark! I hate for you to go alone! Since those munition places have brought so many strange people here to work, it really isn't safe!"

Safe! Marcella caught up her sweater and fled into the dusk. How strange that her mother could think of a little fear like that when so many larger horrors loomed on the immediate horizon! If war came, women would have to forget such little shelterings and be strong!

Frederick was sitting in the big chair when she returned. Mrs. Kemper's voice was mildly reproachful, as if it were Frederick's right to have Marcella always on the spot when he arrived.

There was a suppressed air of excitement about Frederick.

Marcella wondered if he were going to tell her that he had enlisted. She gave one glance out of the window as she pulled down the shade. Only a faint copper lingered in the inky clouds, like smoldering embers in a deserted camp. She did not call Frederick's attention to it. She had tried to make him see things like that before. He did not understand. It irritated him. Frederick was practical.

But Frederick did not talk about the war when they were alone. Instead, he asked her, quite as if he had often spoken of it before, if she did not think it was time they were married.

Marcella looked at him, astonished. It had come at last, that question for which she had waited so long, and it fell on her heart dully like lead that had missed its mark. She felt strangely apathetic about it—idly curious as to why he had asked her now and not before. Her eyes searched his face calmly, impersonally, in vain quest for an answer to her thoughts. Was he, perhaps, feeling that in these perilous times she, and possibly her mother, needed his protection? A soft color rose in her cheeks at the thought and a glow flamed in her eyes, but faded slowly as it met no answering glow in his. His cool, pleasant eyes regarded her steadily, practically, sensibly, contentedly, evidently sure of his answer.

He was, then, going to enlist? She saw herself bidding him good-by. His wife! Staying at home to wait for news of him. It was strange, but her heart did not stir at thought of his danger more than it had stirred for the Bailey boys or Twinkenham Porter or Dudley Ward. She was regarding him only as a part of the great army of those who must go. Where was the joy she would have felt a few days ago if this question had been asked her?

She studied his face tensely, silently for a moment, and her voice sounded harsh to her own ears when she spoke:

"Why do you ask me that *now?*"

A dull color stole into his handsome face. He seemed almost confused for a moment.

"Well, I hadn't intended to plan for this just yet, Marcella." His voice was almost condescending. "I wanted to wait till I was fixed a little better financially, and then I thought perhaps your mother needed you. But it begins to look very much as if the president were going to have his way about conscription, and—*unmarried* men will be called first."

He paused, puzzled over the expression on Marcella's face. Something he had never seen there before had flared in her eyes.

"And you do not *wish* to be called?"

"Of course not!" His voice rang sharply, accusingly. "Why, Marcella, you wouldn't want me to go to *war*, would you?" There were indignation and astonishment in his face.

Marcella looked at him with eyes from which all illusions had suddenly fallen.

"Do you think I want you to hide behind *me?*" she asked scornfully. "I've been reading about those awful soldiers over there who made screens of women and little children to shelter them as they marched into battle. How would you be better than they if you married me for that?"

Frederick sprang to his feet, white to the lips with anger.

"Marcella, I didn't take you for either a fool or a fanatic!"

"Perhaps I am both," said Marcella steadily, though her knees trembled beneath her as she rose. "Whatever I am, I know I never should have any more respect for myself— much less for you—if I allowed you to do such a thing!"

For a space, they regarded each other in silent consternation. The very room seemed hushed in panic. A dull roll of spring thunder rumbled above the house. The shade blew out with a sudden gust of wind, revealing an inky sky from which the copper had long ago died. It was as if war waited outside the door for the outcome. It was not what Marcella had dreamed it would be when he should ask her to be his wife!

A white anger burned over Frederick's face and left it dark and lowering like a coming tempest. His stubborn lips and well-chiseled chin with the cleft took on determined lines; his brows drew down enigmatically over eyes that had turned to steel points.

"You are not yourself, Marcella," he said coldly. "I'll leave you to think over what you've said to me and give me a fitting apology. I am sure no self-respecting man would care to remain and discuss the matter after his fair proposal of marriage had been met by a comparison so odious. You know how to find me when you've come to your senses."

He made his way with dignity from the house. The door shut with a dull thud. It seemed to be slamming in the girl's heart; and on its threshold lay her tattered romance, its filmy threads hopelessly rent.

Outside, the thunder rumbled exultantly, but Marcella stood where he had left her, unable to move, her hands clasping each other painfully, and all around on the horizon of the dark world, war hovered in legions of warriors coming on at the call of God and country.

Mrs. Kemper opened the dining-room door cautiously, alarm in her eyes.

"Why, what's become of Frederick?" she ventured timorously.

Marcella answered in a dry, dead voice:

"He's gone!"

"Gone! Why, isn't he coming back?"

"No, mother, he's gone for good! He's *never* coming back!" Marcella said it as if she were trying to get used to the fact herself.

Mrs. Kemper sat down as if the power that held her had suddenly been withdrawn.

"Why, Marcella! What's happened? You haven't quarreled, have you? Marcella, he *isn't* engaged to somebody else, is he?"

The girl in her agony turned on her mother desperately.

"Oh, *don't,* mother!" She dropped her head an instant and then lifted it again in a movement of strong despair. "He's a *coward,* mother! He wanted me to marry him to save him from going to war!"

Her mother looked at her bewilderedly.

"Well, why not, Marcella? You can't blame a man for not wanting to go to war. War's awful! He's been coming to see you a long while now. I don't think you ought to call him a coward."

"Yes, he's been coming to see me for four years, mother, and he might have married me long ago. He knew that. He didn't want me till he got good and ready. He didn't ask me till he needed me to protect him! It's no use, mother. I couldn't ever respect him, and you can't love where you can't respect."

Mrs. Kemper looked helplessly at her.

"It would be so nice to have a man around to protect us in these war times!" she quavered.

Marcella cast a pitying glance at her.

"Protect us!" she said with a bitter curl of her lip. "If he were a real man, he'd find a bigger job in war time than protecting us! No, mother! If war comes, it's up to you and me to protect ourselves or be too busy helping others to need protecting! Don't you fret, mother, I'll protect you!" and she gave her mother a fierce, impulsive kiss and rushed upstairs.

Far into the night she sat by her open window. The shower had passed. The moon had risen fair and clear above the street. Over to the left, in the valley, the great munitions factory twinkled its myriad lights, showing where thousands of men and women worked day and night to get ready for war. A sudden new appreciation of their part in the great conflict swept over the girl as the midnight whistle sounded from factory to factory. Up and down the street the dim flags waved in the soft moonlight and took on a new significance. They stood for liberty, justice, for love and home and heroism that was willing to lay down its life that a land of freedom and righteousness might be possible.

Marcella came downstairs early the next morning and announced that she was going to buy a flag.

"Do you think we ought to afford one?" asked her mother dubiously. "You need a new spring suit, and we have so little to spend. Prices are so high!"

"What are new suits when our country is in trouble? We're the only people on the block without a flag, and we're going to have one!"

"Do you think it's quite safe, two women alone?" Mrs. Kemper voiced her fear anxiously. "There might be a spy around, Marcella. You can't tell what they might do. You know they flew over London and dropped *bombs* right down. You don't read the papers much. A flag might attract them."

"Safe! Oh, mother!" gasped Marcella hysterically.

"Well, I'd get a small one that can't be seen very high up."

"Mother! Isn't your country anything to you? Don't you put any trust in the protection of your flag? Don't you believe in God and righteousness? You always brought me up as if you did!"

The mother cowered at the accusation of her beautiful, indignant daughter, and watched her go down the street with a deep sigh. She never had understood Marcella.

Marcella found that the flags she wanted were too expensive for her purse, so she bought material and came home to make one. For two days she sat and stitched, eagerly, tensely, scarcely stopping to eat, her mother watching gloomily and hoping that Frederick would repent his hasty action and return before the flag was finished. It seemed like calling him names after what Marcella had said to him. If they didn't make it up, Marcella would likely never have another chance to marry now. She was twenty-four!

As Marcella stitched her big stars into the blue field, all the history she had ever learned came back in review, and she began to realize how many struggles and heartaches and tears it took to make the flag what it really stands for to-day. She was beginning to get a world grasp on life.

It was just dusk when the last star was set, and she flung the bright folds of the flag from her upper window. The mother, hovering timorously behind the parlor curtain, looked up, half proud, half fearful. It seemed presumptuous for quiet, simple people with little means to flaunt a handsome banner like that.

It was the night for Frederick to return if he were coming. Marcella, in her heart, had given him this one hour of grace, and presently he came walking down the street—but *on the other side and with another girl!*

The girl was Cornelia Porter, fluttering along in her usual affected way. So this was his revenge! Well, he had his answer in her ultimatum, flung forth in red and white and blue. Marcella thought she saw him start as he looked furtively over toward the house and saw the flag. He did not pause, but walked up the street and did not return. She knew now what she had to expect from him. He knew what he had to expect from her!

Marcella flung herself on her knees beside the bed with a great gasp and buried her face in the pillow, her whole body shaking with soundless sobs. She knew now that there was no turning to this road down which she had started. The moment was made no easier by the thought of her mother, cowering at the window below. To her this would spell but one word—calamity!

It seemed incredible that the sun should rise bright the

next morning and the air take on that elixir of spring that stirs all the latent joy in the soul. Spring was going on in spite of war and lost love! The trees were putting on soft fringes of green. The munitions plant would presently be shut from sight by a wall of living green. Marcella, at her window, looked over hungrily toward the great acre of buildings which sheltered a host of workers who were akin to her in soul. She thirsted to be at work at something worth while.

Suddenly, as she looked, a great column of flame shot up into the air, with smoke and a soft, dull plung! *plung!* PLUNG!—three separate explosions shaking the foundations of the earth, rattling the window by which she stood, rumbling away into the depths of the earth. Instantly a medley of confused cries arose, a din of whistles and fire alarms.

Marcella stood stunned, stupefied, at the sight. She put her hands to her ears and shuddered. It was the opening of war! She understood as well as if it had been written across the morning sky in letters of fire, "An enemy hath done this!"

There were great flakes of cinders in the air. One could not see the munitions plant now for the smoke. The very sun seemed darkened. The fire engine went thundering down the street, and people ran out from their houses in every direction.

Mrs. Kemper opened the bedroom door fearfully.

"You don't suppose that's a submarine come up the river, do you, Marcie?"

The sight of her mother's distraught face brought the girl to her senses.

"No, mother. There's been a big explosion at the munitions plant. Some of the buildings are on fire. Look! You can see it from the window! I'm going to run down and find out if anybody was hurt!"

"Oh, don't, Marcella! You can't be sure but what it was

a bomb dropped from an aëroplane! There might be more! There was a woman killed over in London——"

But Marcella was gone, running bareheaded down the street.

Some one called to her from a car that slowed up beside the pavement. It was Dudley Ward.

"Get in, Marcella," he said gravely, as if he had seen her but yesterday. "You'll be needed. There were three or four hundred girls in that building and more than half of them are horribly burned—many are dead. There'll be need of all who can help!"

Marcella climbed in with relief. It was good to hear Dudley's voice again, to be going with him on a service of mercy.

War! If she had been suddenly conscripted and flung into the trenches, she could not have seen more horrible sights than she saw that morning as she toiled with the army of volunteers to save lives and alleviate suffering. Shoulder to shoulder with the young doctor she worked, obeying his orders to the letter; doing things she had never dreamed it would be possible for her to do; seeing and hearing enough to make the stoutest heart quail, the strongest nerves give way. White to the lips, yet strong and clearheaded, she moved among the dead and dying; tearing bandages; holding a disfigured head while the doctor prepared some soothing lotion for the lacerated flesh; hiding away dismembered bodies under decent coverings; receiving last words from the tortured lips of the dying.

It was long past noon when she returned in the doctor's car, and then it was to announce to her mother that they were bringing three of the victims there to the house to be cared for. The hospitals were crowded and private houses were being pressed into requistion.

Mrs. Kemper stood dazed, with silent protest in her eyes, as her daughter flew about putting the parlor in order to receive a cot.

"What will we do without the parlor?" she whimpered. "What if Frederick comes?"

"Frederick!" Marcella echoed the name as of one she had known long ago and almost forgotten. "Oh, *Frederick!*" and she laughed as if he were a child who was not to be taken into account. "Mother, will you see if that is Dudley with the ambulance? I must have this bed made up before he gets here."

The mother turned to look out of the window. She felt as if she had just picked up what used to be her child's most cherished possession and the child had suddenly scorned it. She was dazed and burdened. It all depended upon her to keep up Marcella's loyalty to Frederick, yet what could she do? Dudley Ward's face, streaked with soot and perspiration, as he helped to bring in his patient, was strangely unpleasant to her. She had never thought him a handsome child. He had not improved in her eyes now that he was a man. She had meant to protest against this invasion of her home as she had used to protest when he and Marcella had tracked mud on her clean kitchen floor. But when he came forward at the head of the stretcher, there was so much strength and power and gravity in his face that she only stood aside with a shudder from the poor creature on the cot. She could only wonder what they would do with such a state of things if Frederick should come back.

When Frederick did come back, several days later, it was Marcella who met him at the front door, coming with anxious, hurried step. One of the patients had had a bad turn and seemed to be dying. Marcella had not thought of Frederick for several days. Even now, she stepped back startled, with an anxious glance beyond him.

"Oh, it's you!" she said, disappointed. "I thought it was Dudley! Excuse me, but there's a woman in there dying, and I must get the doctor!"

Frederick stood in offended astonishment and watched her speeding across the street. Dudley! Why should she have thought he was Dudley? He turned with dignity and pushed open the parlor door, but an odor of disinfectants swept out in his amazed face and he caught a glimpse of a mummy-like figure swathed in bandages with Mrs. Kemper bending anxiously above it, and drew back bewildered as if he had somehow suddenly found himself in the wrong house. He beat a hasty retreat to the dining room, as he saw Marcella returning with the doctor. Oh, yes, Dudley was a doctor. He had forgotten.

It was an hour before Marcella came to him, an hour during which he had passed through several different stages of emotion—annoyance, bewilderment, chagrin, indignation. Many people he knew were nursing victims of the munitions disaster, but why should Marcella have cumbered herself with such burdens?

Marcella's manner was absorbed, anxious, withdrawn. She did not apologize for her long delay. She said she had but a moment to stay.

Frederick arose with an impatient movement.

"I called to see if you had changed your mind and were ready to be married next week, but as you seem to be so occupied, I would better go away again."

Marcella looked at him pitifully from the height upon which the experiences of the past week had placed her, and answered him gently, as one does a little child whom one must hurt:

"No, Frederick, I haven't changed my mind. I couldn't marry you next week—or *ever!*"

"Then you never loved me!" There was startled astonishment in his tone.

"I loved what I thought was you," she said thoughtfully.

"And you don't any more?"

"I couldn't," she said earnestly. "Things have all changed. I've seen life from a different angle. I've discovered that you and I are not the only people in the universe. There's something bigger than just pleasing ourselves."

"Something bigger than love?" demanded Frederick loftily.

"Yes," said Marcella steadily, "to be able to give up that love, if need be, that the world may have more of it!"

"Bosh!" declared Frederick angrily. "Sentimental twaddle! Bosh!" and he took his hat and strode angrily from the room.

Mrs. Kemper stood by the front window looking drearily out into the darkening street after the tall, angry form of the departing Frederick. Dudley Ward came across the street and passed her like a shadow, slipping silently into the room, but she did not see him. She was watching Marcella's last chance in life pass slowly out of sight.

The young doctor came to the cot and stood beside Marcella, bending to listen to the patient's breathing, touching the pulse with practiced finger. Then he looked up at the girl with a light of triumph in his eyes.

"She's going to get well," he said in a low, joyous voice, "and it is all due to your nursing, Marcella! She'll go back to her three little children, and she won't be scarred, either, thanks to you!"

Dudley Ward's voice was like a sweet, deep-toned bell whose music lingered in Marcella's heart. She was uplifted by a great ecstasy. She had entirely forgotten Frederick. It was enough that she could live, and save life, and receive Dudley Ward's commendation.

The happy days of service passed. The patients, one by one, recovered till all were gone at last and the little parlor restored to its old order. Marcella, suddenly bereft of her duties, stood again at the window looking out on the sunset battlements of cloud against a blazing sky, and faced her future. War was still in the air. Men in khaki or marine blue walked everywhere. There was talk of sending a regiment to France. Dudley Ward was expecting his call to duty any day. His comradeship had been a wonderful thing as they had worked together. It had been almost like being a soldier in service to work with him. What was life going to be now that the work was over and he was gone? Who was to take his place in her life? Frederick? She almost laughed at the thought. No, never Frederick any more. How had she ever thought it could be? But life was going to be very dull and empty without Dudley. This was the first night he had not come over at the evening hour, but of course there was no reason, now the patients were gone——

"Marcella!"

He was there, standing beside her in the shadow. His arm was about her, drawing her into the shelter of the curtain.

"I've got my commission, Marcella! I go to-morrow night! But I can't go without telling you I love you. I've tried, for it didn't seem fair to cumber your life with a man who might get shot any day. But I can't go without speaking. I've loved you, Marcella, since we were kids in school, and these last weeks together have been the greatest in my life! I was afraid, from what folks said, that some other fellow might have got ahead of me, and I can't go off to war without finding out. Marcella, am I too late? Do you belong to some one else?"

Marcella put out her hands with a beautiful motion of surrender and her voice caught in a quick sob.

"Oh, no! You're not too late!" she said joyously. "I was almost a fool, but the war brought me to my senses! How could I ever have thought that I cared for any one else when there was you in the world!" and her head went home to his shoulder like a bird to its nest.

An hour later, Mrs. Kemper opened the door a nervous crack and peered into the shadowy room to see what her strange child was doing all alone in the darkness. Marcella's voice vibrated to greet her:

"Mother, Dudley and I are going to be married in the

morning just as soon as he can get the license. Mother, won't you be glad with me? I'm very happy!"

Mrs. Kemper stood in the doorway, nervously gripping her hands together.

"Why, Marcella!" she protested tearfully. "Why, *Marcella!* What if Frederick should come back!"

Marcella laughed out joyously.

"Oh, mother dear! It won't make any difference if Frederick comes back. I've found somebody bigger and better than Frederick. I've found a real man!"

"You see—mother," said Dudley Ward, laying a shy hand on the mother's arm, "I'm going to war to-morrow, and I want to make sure you and Marcella are perfectly safe. I want the right to take care of you both in case of war coming to this country, or in case of anything happening to me. My uncle left me a little money, and I want it in Marcella's hands, so she can use it in case of trouble. It will save complications if we are married before I go. I shall feel happier to go that way, you know."

Mrs. Kemper sat down suddenly in the nearest chair and tears of relief slipped slowly down her cheeks. Then Marcella hadn't lost all her chances, after all! And he wanted to take care of her mother, too! How wonderful! Poor little mother! So long the burdens of life for herself and her child had rested upon her inadequate shoulders!

She laid her frail little frightened hands on their two heads as they knelt beside her and gave each a trembling kiss. Then she slipped away in the dusk and left them to each other.

Upstairs in Marcella's window, she stood and looked down on the big, bright flag waving below. For the first time since Marcella had put it there, she felt a sense of protection and shelter in its presence.

Quiet Hands

MARTHA came out of the back door with a basket of clothes and set the basket down hard on the neat turf under the clothesline. She was wearing her working clothes and a large gray cloth pinned firmly about her hair. She carried a basket of clothespins on her arm. The grass was green and well trimmed under her feet. The sky was blue and very clear overhead. A bird off in the distance piped a thin high note. Martha's lips were set in a hard line, and her chin showed determination.

She took a clean cloth from the clothespin basket and walked briskly along under the line, wiping it clean, then she reached into the basket and took out one of the tight rolls of wet cloth and shook it out till it filmed into a soft thin white curtain which she pinned briskly to the line. Then she reached into the basket for another.

"For pity's sake, Martha!" called her neighbor from the back door of the next house. "You're not washing again! Not twice in one week?"

Martha turned an annoyed glance toward Admah. "Just washing some curtains," she explained a trifle haughtily.

"But I thought you just got done cleaning house a few days ago!" said Admah curiously. "I thought you washed all the curtains in the house!"

"Certainly, I washed them all when I cleaned, but it's several weeks since these were put up and they really were beginning to look soiled again. I like to have them fresh. We're expecting company."

"Company?" said Admah eagerly. "That's nice. Who's coming? I wish I could afford to have company as often as you do."

"My brother likes to be hospitable," said Martha with a toss of her head. "I like to have things nice when people come."

"You certainly are particular!" said Admah. "Company wouldn't know just how many days since you had washed the curtains, I'm sure. I was looking over to your house just this morning and thinking how crisp and nice your curtains look. You certainly do take a lot of pains. I couldn't be bothered. Who did you say was coming?"

"The Master!" said Martha proudly.

"The Master?" cried Admah incredulously. "Why, He was only there a little while ago! He comes to your house often, doesn't He?"

"Yes," admitted Martha. "My brother is very fond of Him. And He seems to enjoy coming. We are very dear friends!"

"Well, when He comes so often I shouldn't think you'd have to be so particular about your curtains," said Admah jealously.

"I like to have everything as nice as it can be. I tell my sister that you can't have things too nice. Besides I don't grudge it when it's for the Master!"

Admah looked at her speculatively.

"They say the Master is a wonderful preacher," she said thoughtfully. "I suppose you get to hear a lot of talk when He stays at your house. Is He interesting?"

"Oh, yes," said Martha, "wonderfully interesting. He tells us about God and Heaven and Death and Life. It's very interesting, but of course I don't have much time to sit down and listen. I have to be waiting on Him."

"Why, doesn't Mary help? I shouldn't think there would be so much to do with two of you working together."

Martha's lips set thinly as she shook her head.

"No," she said with a sigh, "Mary doesn't do much to help. She's got an idea we must just sit down and listen every minute. She seems to think meals will cook themselves and the dishes will just hop on the table and set themselves. She simply loses her head when the Master comes, and camps on His footsteps listening. And the look in her face, why it's just enraptured! Of course what He says *is* wonderful, and very interesting, but she seems to lose all sense of the fitness of things. She doesn't seem to realize that He is our guest and everything must be perfect about the meal and the table and the house. She's just perfectly lost in what He is saying. It may be all very well to give Him attention like that, but she doesn't seem to stop to think that I have it all to do."

"But it does seem too bad, Martha, that you shouldn't enjoy His company too. Why don't you have a simpler supper, and make time to be with Him more yourself?"

Martha cast her a scornful look and tossed her handsome head. "I know my duty!" she said loftily, "and I try to do it. I feel that we should honor Him with our very best, and I certainly don't want it said that we didn't treat Him as well as anybody else who invites him. I want to serve Him just as well as I can when He comes!"

Admah studied her face. "You believe in Him, don't you?"

"Why of course," said Martha.

"You think those miracles are all genuine? You think He opened that blind man's eyes, and cured old Anna? You think He really made those few loaves of bread and the little fishes feed all those people? You think He raised the ruler's daughter from the dead?"

Martha looked a little startled. "Do they say He raised her from the dead? I hadn't heard that!"

"Yes, they say He did. Do you believe it?"

"Well, I believe He can do anything He says He can," admitted Martha, "and yes, certainly I believe in His miracles. A friend of ours was on the mountain that day and saw the loaves and fishes as they were given out. And we've known old Anna and how she has suffered for years. You can't doubt that! Look at her today!"

"Yes," admitted Admah, "it does seem wonderful! But if you believe it I should think you'd be at His feet, too, along with Mary. I shouldn't think you could bear to miss a word He says. My! There's a lot of things I'd like to ask Him if I had the chance. I can't understand how you can bear to miss a word He says if you think so much of Him."

"I figure that I am serving Him just as truly by cooking His dinner and serving things carefully and beautifully as if I just came and hung around Him all the time," said Martha proudly. "I know my duty and I feel that we should serve Him as befitting a King. I feel that we owe it to our family to have everything just right when He comes!" Martha snapped the last curtain out of the basket and pinned it firmly on the line. Then she turned back to her neighbor.

"I've got to get back and wash those windows now before it's time to iron these curtains and put them up again. Come in sometime while He's here and meet Him if you're so anxious to question Him," she added graciously, and then hurried into the house to be sure the savory soup she was brewing on the stove was simmering just enough and not too much, and to look into the oven at the rounded loaves of bread that were baking. There was satisfaction mingled with severity in her handsome face as she turned from closing the oven door and faced her beautiful sister who was entering from the street.

"Where in the world have you been, Mary?" she asked querulously. "I've been hunting the house over for you."

"Why, I've been down to the apothecary shop, Martha. I heard they had some wonderful new perfume in and I wanted to ask about it! It is marvellous, Martha! They had a tiny flask open and I caught a whiff of it. And it is done up in the most precious alabaster boxes!" Mary's eyes were shining with eagerness, and the sunlight touched her golden hair and brought out the beauty of her delicate features.

Martha looked at her in indignation and contempt. "And you went traipsing off after perfumery on this day of all days! You left me to do all the work, when you knew the Master is coming! You, who profess to honor Him so greatly!"

A troubled look came into the beautiful blue eyes. "Oh, I'm sorry, Martha! I didn't realize you would need me! I had fixed the guest room and thought everything was in order. I knew the soup was on and the bread in the oven. I didn't think you would want anything more just now! Oh, Martha!" in sudden dismay, "you have taken the curtains down! Why did you need to do that? They were just washed such a little time ago! I was looking at them only yesterday thinking how nice they looked!"

"Oh, you were, were you?" said Martha bitterly. "You thought they looked all right? You wonder why I took them down? Well, I wonder why you wanted to go and look at perfume? What possible use could alabaster boxes of precious ointment do in getting ready for our guest?"

The color stole slowly up into Mary's face. "I thought—" she began, and then closed her lips and turned away, a cloud over the brightness of her face.

"You thought?" said Martha contemptuously. "Well, what did you think?"

"Never mind," said Mary evasively. "Where are the curtains? I'll wash them."

"They're all washed!" snapped Martha. "I washed them and they're out on the line now."

"I'll iron them," said Mary quietly.

"No, you won't!" said Martha. "I'll iron them myself. You are so up in the clouds you'd be sure to scorch them! You with your costly perfume and your precious alabaster boxes! I do wish you'd get down to earth a little while and do something practical! Not moon around all the time. For pity's sake hunt out the best tablecloth and see if any of the silver needs polishing. I declare it does seem that I have to think of everything, and then do it myself in the bargain!"

"But you know, He said He wished you wouldn't go to any trouble for Him, Martha. He said He would so much rather have just what we have."

"That's all well enough for Him to say," said Martha, "but I know what is due our family traditions when we have honored guests. Suppose somebody from next door should come in while we are at supper and see us eating a simple meal with an honored guest like that? Why, it would be all over town before next morning that Lazarus had lost his money, or else was getting stingy!"

"Would it matter so much what the world thought if He was pleased?"

"Matter? What do you mean? Would it matter if the world thought our brother had lost his wealth? Of course it would. Oh, you are simply impossible! You seem to have lost what little sense you used to have! Well, get to work at that silver and linen and don't let's talk. You make me so angry I can't work!"

Mary's lips quivered sensitively and her eyes were misty but she drooped her head meekly and went to work getting out the best tablecloth and napkins, while Martha vigorously washed windows and then slammed off to the kitchen to put on the irons and peel the vegetables for dinner.

When the vegetables were ready in clean bowls of fresh water Martha tried the irons with a wet finger to see if they would sizzle, and then went out to feel of the curtains. Yes, they were dry enough to iron nicely now, and she began to unpin them.

Admah opened her kitchen door and came out to lean over the fence.

"What does He tell you to do, this Master?" she asked wistfully. "Is His creed hard to follow?"

"Do?" said Martha whirling about and looking startled at her neighbor. "Do? Oh, why—*do?* You believe on Him you know."

"Yes, but what do you have to do besides that?"

"Well, really—I don't know that I can answer that definitely." Martha looked confused. "You see I've been so busy doing that I haven't had much time to listen to His sayings. But of course the main thing is to believe on Him, and—and—*serve* Him. You better ask Mary about that. Of course you do good, or something like that! I'm trying hard to do the best I can."

"I'd be willing to *work*—" said Admah, "but I don't know much about believing. I think I'd have to see a miracle myself first. I wouldn't be sure unless I did."

"Well, you can ask Mary," said Martha. "I really haven't any time to talk about it now, I've got to get these curtains up. It would be simply dreadful if He were to arrive and the curtains all down in the living room."

Martha slammed into the house and Admah stood looking wistfully after her.

"Oh, well," she said to herself with a toss of her head, "I don't suppose it would be worth while. She has to work awful hard. I don't see that it would be much fun. You might have to give up a lot of things too, and I wouldn't be willing to do that. But it would be nice to have a friend who could feed you when you were hungry, and cure you if you were sick! I wonder if He really does, or they only just think so? I guess I'll ask Mary some time."

The bread was out of the oven, standing in crisp brown loaves on the table, filling the house with its appetizing fragrance, and the curtains were all ironed and hanging in crisp snowy folds at the windows by the time the Master arrived. Mary had set the table with a few flowers, lilies of the field, in the centre. There was meat broiling over the coals and the kettle was boiling. Dinner was almost ready.

Martha went hurriedly from table to stove, and into the dining room to put the butter on the table, and a pitcher of water. Through the open doorway into the living room she could see her sister sitting at the Master's feet on a low stool, a wrapt expression on her face.

A quick sharp pang of jealousy went through Martha's heart. She looked at the Master's face, so strong and sweet and tender, so different from the face of any other man they knew and suddenly her anger rose.

She stepped forward to the doorway and paused, looking at her sister. She spoke her name in a low summoning voice, but Mary was asking the Lord a question and did not hear. She did not even seem to be aware that her sister stood waiting there, expecting her to come away and help.

With a hardening of the lines of her face, she turned sharply toward her Lord, her eyes flashing indignation, her hasty temper giving point to her words.

"Lord, don't you care that my sister has left me to serve alone? Won't you tell her to come and help me?"

The Master lifted His eyes and seemed to look straight into Martha's soul, His gaze giving her an unexpected revelation of her own self as He answered: "Oh, Martha, Martha!" and His voice was almost sorrowful in its tenderness. "You are full of anxiety and trouble about so many

things. Don't you know that you are leaving out the most
important one? Don't you realize that I am only to be with
you a little while longer, and there is so much to tell you
both? Why will you not put aside your cares for a little while
and come and listen? Mary has chosen the things that are the
most important. Don't blame her. All these little matters
about the house and the meals don't matter. They will pass
away. But what I have to tell you is something that will not
pass away. It will stay with you even after I am gone. Come,
Martha, let us have very simple fare, and you come and talk
with us instead of worrying about the supper."

Martha drew a quick sharp breath that was almost like a
smothered sob, and turning quickly walked back into her
kitchen, and closed the door, choking back the hurt sobs
that kept threatening to master her.

Then Martha heard her brother Lazarus coming into the
house. She would not let him see her weeping. She set her
lips firmly and went swiftly to work. She would show them
that she could get the dinner on the table alone. Simple
dinner indeed! How His look and His words had rebuked
her! How they cut deep into her soul!

She called them to supper almost at once, and at the
table she was silent, with downcast eyes, busying herself
with the cups and viands, not once lifting her eyes to meet
that full strong wonderful gaze in which she so delighted.
She felt somehow apart from the rest in the conversation,
left out of the spiritual converse that had always been so
pleasant. Yet it was her own fault. They had tried to draw
her into the conversation, but she made some excuse to
hurry into the kitchen to get more bread, or to set the
kettle on again. And when Mary offered to go in her place
she shook her head summarily.

"No!" she said sharply in a low tone that was like a blow
to Mary's sensitive nature, "No, you stay and talk!"

When the evening was over and Lazarus was about to
lead Him to the room that had been set apart for His use,

Mary was there to say good night, but Martha was out in the kitchen attending to something for the morning meal.

In her own room at last Martha wept by herself, and slept but little, and in the morning her expression was hard, her eyes averted, her lips silent.

Mary hoped that perhaps the Lord intended having a little quiet talk with her sister after Lazarus was gone to his business, but there came a messenger in search of Him before He had scarcely finished His breakfast. There was urgent need, and need of haste. So He went with only a handclasp for Martha, and a deep look into her eyes, a look that searched again, and revealed, and hurt her soul, her soulish soul.

Martha went on with the days that followed. He did not come again as she had hoped. There were rumors that He had gone to another vicinity where He was needed. But His look stayed behind and searched her heart daily, especially nightly when she was alone, with no work to take her thoughts away from herself. She began to suspect that there were things in herself that made it impossible for her to get the vision that Mary had.

Daily she watched Mary with that tender gentleness upon her, saw how meek she was, how she strove to please, how careful she was to help in the housework now, how much more thoughtful than she had ever been before, and all these things acted like a mirror to show Martha more and more clearly herself. She saw the impatience and worldly ambition and selfishness that she had been cherishing as a virtue, and how she had made a fetish of her work, holding it above communion with her Lord. She had no time for just sitting and talking with Him!

Day by day she strove to defend herself. The work had to be done, didn't it? Hadn't she been serving her Lord even better than Mary, by preparing delicate dishes and inviting people to the house to meet Him? And yet, in her heart there was a troubled silence, in which was that searching look of her Lord, and nothing more.

One day Lazarus came home from his business at an early hour, and his face was ghastly. He stalked into the house, flung his coat on a chair and hurried to his room.

Martha followed him with fear clutching at her heart.

"I'm sick!" he said, flinging himself down upon his bed, and Martha gave one look at the pallor of his face, the anguish of terrible pain that swept over his countenance, and hurried for the usual household remedies. She called aloud to Mary who was out in the yard working among her flowers, and Mary came quickly, frightened at her tone.

The neighbors came in to help and brought their remedies, the old family physician came, and called a consultation. Lazarus was gravely ill. The doctors came and went and shook their heads. But Mary and Martha by common consent could think of but one physician.

"Have you sent for the Master?" asked Admah in a scared voice the second morning coming in to offer a remedy that her mother had always used in such sickness.

"Oh, yes!" said Mary quickly, a light of hope shining in her eyes. "We sent at once. It was the first thing we thought of."

"Then you really believe He can help?" said Admah wonderingly. "But why doesn't He come?"

"He will come as soon as He knows," said Mary quite positively.

"Where is He?" asked Admah. "I should have thought He would have been here by this time if He was coming."

"Why, He had gone out of the city on a little preaching trip, but we have sent a messenger after Him. I'm sure it will not be long now."

"Well, I'm sure I hope it won't be too late!" said Admah looking doubtfully toward the bed where the sick man lay.

"Martha and I are quite sure He will soon be here. He loves us all you know," said Mary quickly.

"But suppose He shouldn't get here? Suppose your brother should die. Would you keep on trusting Him just the same?"

"Why, of course," said Mary, that strange light shining in her eyes. "Don't you know *Who* He is? He might have some better reason than we knew."

Admah looked at her almost enviously, and lowering her head went out in a kind of awe before Mary's faith.

The days went on and Lazarus grew steadily worse, and still the Master had not come.

Martha nursed her brother fiercely, untiringly, day and night. She would scarcely let her sister touch him. It seemed as if she begrudged her even the privilege of bringing a glass of water to him. And her grim lips spoke few words save necessary orders. Her face was lined with sorrow, worn with watching, yet she kept on.

Friends brought in specialists and insisted that they examine the sick man, but they shook their heads. He was beyond their help they said; and Mary and Martha who had suffered their presence but had not wanted them, kept waiting, and watching out the window up the long winding road down which He had so often come to them, but still He did not come.

Martha, as she knelt beside the bed the night that Lazarus died, too weary to stand longer upon her feet, too desperate even to rest on the couch near by, for she felt Lazarus was slipping fast away from them, began to search her own heart, and to see how desperately she had been trying to have her own way, how fully she had been engrossed in her own ideas of serving her Lord. And now here was Death coming so unexpectedly down her way, and she had nothing to help her meet him.

Oh, if she had but listened to the Master as He talked of the things of the other life, there would be something now for her to lean upon! There was Mary whom she had blamed for listening too much, going quietly about doing the few little things that were left to be done for the beloved brother, with a beautiful peace upon her face, while she, Martha, was utterly prostrated. Mary had something which she did not have. Mary was being carried through this awfulness of approaching death with a serenity that she, Martha, could not feel. Oh, did she have to go through *death* to understand that the things of this life did not matter?

She got up and went to the window and strained her eyes up the road, but there was no sign of anyone coming, and she went back and knelt again beside Lazarus' deathbed.

Mary was praying. She could see her dimly in the room beyond, kneeling beside the open lattice where she could watch as well as pray. But Mary was not frantic as she was. Mary had sat at the feet of the Master and learned faith. Oh, that she had been less careful and troubled about the outward serving, and more careful about the service of the heart, the spiritual service.

And then he was gone! Lazarus, their brother was dead! And Jesus, who loved him, did not even know it yet! For it was unthinkable that knowing, He should not have come.

Martha thought about it as she lay upon the couch wide awake and suffering. Could it be possible that His power had failed, and He knew He could not keep Lazarus alive? Was there then some trick in those other seeming deaths, as people hinted?

Her heart wrenched away from the thought. It could not be. That face could not deceive! Those lips could never lie! Little as she knew about things spiritual, she knew that. Her faith clung to that. He was the Son of God. Whatever He might do or not do, He was still the Son of God. Of so much she was sure.

All through those awful days of preparation for the funeral, those days when the house swarmed with friendly tormentors asking questions, trying to help in their decisions, pitying them because the Lord had not appeared, suggesting trivial reasons, and looking more than they quite dared to suggest! How did they live through them? How the voices of mourners pierced them through and through!

Mary let the blessed tears flow down and ease her sorrow, but Martha went about with wan set features, pent up tears, and terrible despair. She could not believe that their friend had deserted them in their great sorrow. Yet the messenger had returned and told them that he had seen the Lord personally, and yet He did not come or send them any message! What could it mean?

And while the ritual for the dead went on Martha was judging herself. Martha was meeting death. Martha was seeing what she herself had been. Martha was living in bitterness and despair, as Mary sat and grieved with yet that peace upon her brow! For Martha was beginning to see more and more into her own heart and finding sin there. Beginning to understand the difference between mere outward service and the true service of the heart which Mary was rendering.

Walking back from the tomb where they had laid their brother, bowed with grief, Martha wondered about their Friend. What could have happened that He had not come? Not even to the funeral. Some of the disciples had repeated rumors of hatred among the Jews, a plot to kill Him, but the Master was not afraid of anything. Surely He would have come to the funeral! Martha refused to believe that He was afraid to come because of the Jews. She shut her lips in a thin hard line when Admah suggested the idea and shook her head.

"There is some other reason," she said, and remembered the look He had given her when He said good-by, that look that searched her very being. It seemed to her now almost as if He were trying to make her understand that she was grieving Him, and faintly she perceived now the difference between material service and spiritual devotion. It had taken Death to make her understand! Oh, that she might have learned without that! Her heart leaped sickly at the thought. Did He foresee when He went away that she was having to pass through Death to make her understand how superficial was her love for Him, her service? And could it be that He was staying away to teach her something? Was that what that strangely tender pitying look He gave her had meant?

Four long days had Lazarus lain in the grave when some of their Jewish friends came out from Jerusalem to Bethany to call on the bereaved sisters. They sat and talked about Lazarus. They told anecdotes of his childhood that they remembered. They said what a fine man he had been, what a canny business man, and how they were going to miss him. Casually they enquired if he had left his affairs in good shape and whether the sisters would be well off. It was hard to sit and answer their kindly, curious questions. It took strength and grace to stand it. Mary took it all sweetly and Martha brought out pleasant refreshment and wished for their leaving, that she might be alone again with her heavy heart. She was beginning almost to feel as if her brother's death had been her fault, as if the Lord had had to send this sorrow because she could not otherwise find out her own sinfulness.

She was out in the kitchen cutting more cake, and preparing more coffee when the messenger came. Just a little boy with silent bare feet, and bright eyes looking out from under a thicket of hair. She wondered if he could be the little boy who had brought the barley loaves and little fishes the day the Master fed the five thousand?

He came and stood in the doorway looking about furtively, glimpsing the guests in the living room through the open doorway. Then he slid over to her side and murmured in her ear: "The Lord is on His way. He thought you would like to know. He is resting now beneath some palm trees just outside the village at the crossways."

The boy slid back and out of the door like a shadow and was gone, and Martha dropped the knife with which she was cutting the cake and hurried after him.

Down the village street, without her formal garments for the street, scarcely noticing the neighbors whom she passed, out of breath she hurried on to the outskirts of the village. She knew the group of palm trees where He had often rested by the way. They could see it from the housetop. They had often gone up there to see if He were coming.

The last few furlongs she ran. It seemed that her wildly beating heart could not endure it to go slowly! The Master had come at last! She could see Him sitting there quietly as if nothing were the matter. And yet He must know that Lazarus was dead! Well, at any rate He had not been afraid to come, for He must know that the feeling against Him was stronger now than ever. Her indignation rose as she remembered how some of their guests had sneered when they asked if the Nazarene had not come to see Lazarus before he died. They laughed a little as they suggested that some of His strange power might have been used for His friend, if it was genuine power!

She reached the palm trees at last and fell low at His feet. "Lord, if You had been here my brother would not have died!" she sobbed, and the look He gave her broke her heart.

"But I know—" she added, lifting her tearstained face, "I know that whatever You will ask of God, God will do it for You!"

Ah! She had confessed her faith! She had not learned intimately of Him as she might have done, but she had found her faith, and acknowledged it. A wild hope clutched at her heart! Something, something, might be coming to pass! He had come, and anything might happen! She looked at Him with her heart in her eyes and His answering look understood her faith. He was speaking! His voice was exquisitely tender!

"Your brother shall rise again!"

Oh! It was nothing to Him, this awful separation from her beloved brother during the rest of her earthly life! He viewed life from eternity. But poor human ordinary flesh could not comprehend eternity. It was now and here that the heart ached.

"I know," she said sadly, "I know he will rise at the resurrection day. I believe that! But it was so hard to have him die. To live out our earthly life without him!"

"Listen, Martha!" He looked deep into her eyes. "*I* am the resurrection, and the life! He that believeth in me, though he were dead, yet shall he live! And whoever lives and believes in me shall never die. Do you believe this, Martha?"

Martha lifted her head and looked at Him, that wild hope clutching at her heart again. What did He mean?

"Yes, Lord," she said eagerly, hesitantly, "I believe that you are the Christ, the Son of God, the Messiah whom we've all been expecting!"

She searched His face for an instant more and then she arose, a strange hope growing in her heart. What was He going to do? What might not happen when the Saviour of the world was present? The Son of God!

"I'll go and call Mary!" she said breathlessly, and hastened away back to the house. She glanced back and saw that He was not following her. It was as well. She had sensed that He was waiting to see Mary, and He would want to see her without those guests present. She would slip in and call Mary out, staying there herself. Mary would know how to find out what the Lord meant. She, Martha, had made her confession of faith. It was all that she could do. Mary had ever been closer to Him. Mary was the one to be told if there was other comfort than the distant resurrection day. Mary could understand things that she, Martha, could not hope to understand, because she had not sat at the Master's feet to learn.

So Martha went back to her guests with more cake to pass,

and stepping near to her sister's side murmured low, so that nobody else heard: "The Master has come. He wants you! Yes, out by the palm trees." She went on passing the cake.

Mary arose quickly and slipped out of the room.

"What's become of Mary?" asked Admah who never missed seeing anything.

"She's probably going to the grave to weep," said one of the Jewish women who had come to comfort the sisters. "She oughtn't to do it. It won't make things any easier. We'd better go with her!"

"Yes," said one of the men whose word was law among them, "we'll follow her. It isn't good for her to give way to her grief. Somebody should be with her all the time. She might be overcome with grief. She might faint and nobody there to revive her!"

Martha tried to protest that her sister would rather be alone, but they did not hear her. They hurried on after Mary. So Martha dropped her serving and went with them.

"Yes," they said as they followed, "she is going toward the cemetery. If we had known it before she left we might have dissuaded her."

But Mary was already kneeling at the feet of her Lord, her tears falling down, and repeating the same words that had rung over and over again in the minds of the two sisters: "Lord, if You had been here my brother would not have died."

The visitors had got out their handkerchiefs and were wiping their eyes, looking belligerently at the Master. Here He was at last after it was too late. This Master who had professed to cure people yet had failed His dearest friends when they were in dire extremity! They wept copiously and properly with Mary. They had come out from Jerusalem to do this.

And Jesus, the Master Himself was weeping! Martha marvelled as she watched Him, vaguely sensing that He wept because of their lack of faith, vaguely questioning within herself about the power of Death. Was Death greater than the Master? Was that why He wept, because He could do nothing?

Some of the people took satisfaction in the fact that He wept. They felt it showed His weakness, His lack of power after all that was boasted about Him. But others whispered among themselves, "See! How He loved Lazarus! Couldn't He perhaps have saved Lazarus' life if He had been here. He *did* open the eyes of the blind, you know. I was there. I saw it myself!"

But Jesus was speaking. Martha held her breath to listen.

"Where have you laid him?"

And now some of those that hung around and were eager to have a part in telling the news answered eagerly: "Come and see!"

Oh, they ought not to have said that. Now Mary would go too, Martha caught her breath and hurried around near the Master, but He had already started out on the road that led to the cemetery and the others had fallen in behind Mary. There would be no stopping them. Martha writhed in spirit. If she only could have got Mary out without those visitors coming too!

It was not far to the cave where they had laid Lazarus, and the little procession halted and looked toward the Master, as much as to say, "See what a beautiful spot this is where we have laid our friend. See with what royal burial we have laid him away!"

There was a strange look upon the Master's face. They could not quite read it.

"Take ye away the stone!" he said in a tone of authority, and a shocked look came on all faces.

Martha was quite near to the Master now and she put out a protesting hand.

"Oh, no, Lord! He has been in there four days! It—will not be—pleasant!"

Then the Master turned His wonderful searching eyes upon her, with that look of mingled tenderness and sorrow.

"Martha, didn't I tell you that if you would believe, you should see the glory of God?"

The little crowd stood back startled and eyed them suspiciously. What was this? Some private conference that was being referred to?

But some of the men who had been with the Master stepped forward and removed the stone that sealed the mouth of the cave, and Admah who had crowded close stooped down and peered curiously into the tomb.

The Master, however, had lifted up His eyes toward Heaven, and they all looked toward Him. Was this to be some new and curious manifestation of this strange man who did so many unusual things?

He was praying!

"Father, I thank Thee that Thou hast heard me. I know that Thou hearest me always, but because of these people that are listening, I am saying it, that they may believe that Thou hast sent me."

What a strange prayer! He hadn't asked for anything, had He? They looked at one another with question in their eyes.

But suddenly the voice of the Master was raised and it startled them all. He was calling: *"Lazarus, come forth!"*

With suddenly blanched faces they watched the door of the tomb. What did He think He could do? Was He crazy? They had seen Lazarus dead themselves! They knew he was dead! There couldn't be any trick about it. They themselves had been at the funeral, had touched his cold hand, had seen the look of death upon his bloodless lips. They could not be deceived.

But—could they believe their senses? There was something white moving within that dim tomb. The dead man was coming forth. Swathed in grave clothes, bound hand and foot, and a napkin bound about his face, he slowly edged his way toward them, and they stood frightened and speechless watching, trying to think this thing out, trying to explain this phenomenon in some natural way. Probably Lazarus was still back there in the tomb and this was a man dressed up to represent him, to make them all believe that the Master could raise the dead!

But the sneer died on their lips. The Lord was speaking again, and still in that voice of authority: "Loose him and let him go!"

Ah! So! He was willing to have him loosed. They could look on his face! It wasn't to be blind deception then!

They pressed close while the men who had rolled away the stone unfastened the napkin and revealed Lazarus' face. Lazarus, well and looking like himself! Lazarus, who had been dead, was alive and standing in their midst with a strange startled look upon his face as if he had been brought away suddenly from a place that was full of brightness.

Afterwards Martha could not quite remember how they all got back home again, with their beloved dead walking hand in hand with them alive and well.

Some of their friends came back too. Martha wished they would go away. There was no need for words of comfort now, and they wanted their brother and their Lord to themselves.

But when she saw the light of joy in the Master's face as He heard their confessions of faith, she found herself rejoicing with Mary and Lazarus that those doubting sneering men who had seen what the Lord had done for Lazarus, had come to believe on Him. Martha began to understand at least in part how the Lord loved these also, and therefore for His sake she must bear with them, love them, be glad about them too.

But some of those men did not come back to the house. They hastened instead to Jerusalem, professing much pressing business, and went at once to report to the chief priests.

That night there was a meeting in Jerusalem as those high in authority consulted how they might not only put

Jesus to death, but Lazarus also, because since this miracle many people now believed on Jesus.

But that night in Lazarus' home there was rejoicing, and not only Mary, but Martha also sat at the feet of Jesus and listened, learning the great lesson of how Life can come only out of Death; seeing also vaguely the shadow of the cross in the distance as the Master spoke of Death in the offing, and the Resurrection Life that should come out of it; learning how those who were willing to share His death should also be raised to share His life, and bear His own image, even while they were living on this earth. And Martha gratefully accepted the life that her Lord was bringing to her own heart.

Oh, she would serve joyfully in the kitchen when it was necessary, but hereafter she would plan to make that secondary, and not do it for show or form or ceremony, and there should be plenty of time to sit at the Master's feet.

Six days before the Passover they gave a supper to the Master at Bethany and many of His closest followers were invited. Some friends came, not only for Jesus' sake, but because they were curious to see Lazarus who had been dead and was alive again.

"Please let me do the serving tonight, Martha," Mary had said lovingly. "You have done so much, and you will want now to stay with the Master, I know."

Gently Martha shook her head.

"No, I'd like to do it this one time at least, Mary, not because it's the first time since Lazarus came back, but because everything is so different now. You know, Mary, when I used to think I was serving the Master I was really serving *myself,* out of *pride!* Now I truly want to serve *Him!* I think He will know the difference."

So Martha's face was filled with a new joy and light as she went about her duties, quietly lest any word of her Lord should be lost.

And Lazarus was there, alive and well, sitting at the table with his friends. There was a faraway look in his eyes that seemed to say that he saw more than they did, but his smile was as warm, his welcome as earnest and his words as merry as they ever had been. Oh, it was a wonderful occasion and Martha's heart was full to overflowing.

Mary, though she had been helping Martha all along in the preparations for supper, was now among the guests, here and there, giving a smile and a loving greeting, and Martha watched her lovingly between her comings and goings to the kitchen and back to the dining room.

But suddenly Mary disappeared. Martha could not find her anywhere. She searched the room with wondering eyes. Why should she have left her place?

Her eyes roved about the room again and met the eyes of her Master, met such a loving gaze, as if He was well pleased with her, that it made her heart throb with a great joy. It was almost as if He had put her on a level with Mary, Mary whom she now loved and honored the more for her consecration to the Master. She no longer felt angry and jealous of her. She had come to know the Lord better herself, and to understand why Mary sat at His feet whenever she could. But where was Mary? Why had she left the room? She wasn't sick, was she? Perhaps she ought to go to her room and look for her!

But no, there she came in at the side door, a little breathless, her eyes quite starry, her long lovely hair falling about her like a garment, her soft white clinging dress in beautiful folds about her sandaled feet. Ah, Mary was lovely indeed! Her sister paused to admire her. The guests were all well served and there was time now to glance about and enjoy the scene.

Mary was coming to the feet of her Lord. She was kneeling there where He reclined at the table, and she carried something in her hand! An alabaster box! Ah!

Martha suddenly remembered and a soft color came into her cheeks. Was this what Mary had wanted? She had been to the apothecary's?

Mary was stooping now over the alabaster box, breaking it, and a heavenly fragrance filled the house! She was pouring it upon the Master's feet! And everybody was looking up. Such costly perfume to be poured out so lavishly upon mere feet! There was startled attention upon every face, wonder, even disapproval. Down at the foot of the table was Judas scowling. Martha wished she had not invited him. It had only been because he professed to love the Master so that he had been bidden. He spoke in a loud snarling tone that clashed into the perfumed air with a false note:

"Why was not this ointment sold for three hundred dollars and given to the poor?" His sanctimonious air suddenly reminded Martha of her own self before Lazarus' death. That was just what she would have said if Mary had told her why she wanted an alabaster box of precious ointment that morning when she wanted her help!

She, Martha, must have looked like this Judas when she came scowling into the Master's presence and demanded that he send her sister to help her! Oh, was she like that, and did her Lord see her so? Was that why Death had to come to teach her?

> My hands were filled with many things,*
>   Which I did precious hold
> As any treasure of the king's,
>   Silver, or gems, or gold.
> The Master came, and touched my hands,
>   The scars were in His own.
> And at His feet my treasures sweet,
>   Fell shattered one by one;
> "I must have empty hands," said He,
> "Wherewith to work my works through thee."

My hands were stained with marks of toil,
　　Defiled with dust of earth,
And I my work did ofttimes soil,
　　And render little worth—
The Master came, and touched my hands,
　　And crimson were His own.
And when amazed, on mine I gazed,
　　Lo, every stain was gone!
"I must have cleansed hands," said He,
"Wherewith to work my works through thee."

My hands were growing feverish,
　　And cumbered with much care,
Trembling with haste and eagerness,
　　Not folded oft in prayer.
The Master came and touched my hands,
　　With healing in His own,
And calm and still to do His will,
　　They grew, the fever gone.
"I must have quiet hands," said He,
"Wherewith to work my works through thee."

My hands were strong in fancied strength,
　　But not in power divine.
And bold to take up tasks at length,
　　That were not His, but mine.
The Master came, and touched my hands,
　　And might was in His own.
But mine, since then, have powerless been,
　　Save His were laid thereon.
"And it is only thus," said He,
"That I can work my works through thee."

*Reprinted by permission of Fred Kelker Tract Society.

9

A Journey of Discovery

LOUISE HASBROUCK stepped out of the suburban train at Norwood and stood on the platform looking haughtily about for a cab. A strange sense of peace and quietness struck her city-accustomed senses startlingly, as if she had been suddenly dropped into an alien world. She was a trifle frightened now that she was here. After all, how foolish of her not to have come in her own car! There was no cab in sight!

The station was an absurd affair of gray cement, with latticed windows and fluted coral tiles, like a doll's house. The country spread leisurely, invitingly about her, dotted with houses set down as if economy of space were of no moment whatever. A pleasant hill sloped gradually in the distance, also dotted at intervals with houses. A mild-eyed cow with a long golden straw dangling from her amiable mouth surveyed the stranger thoughtfully over the rails of her pasture fence across the street. The country did not seem at all to realize that she had arrived.

Inquiry from the genial, gold-spectacled agent elicited the fact that the only cab had just taken Mrs. Samuel Hawkins

Reprinted by permission of *Christian Herald Magazine*.

up the hill and would not be back for fifteen or twenty minutes, as they had to go around by the Plush Mills to get a passenger for the down train. If she was in a hurry she was advised to walk to Mrs. Van Rensselaer Blake's. It was only four blocks straight ahead, and then turn to the right, and three blocks. Stone porch with arches and green shingles. She couldn't miss it.

She stepped into the quiet street curiously, half bewildered at its emptiness and space; only milk-carts and a grocery wagon in view.

Louise Hasbrouck had been restless and unhappy ever since her friend Cecilia Radcliffe suddenly gave up her brilliant social career to marry Van Rensselaer Blake and live in an eight-room bungalow in the suburbs.

The marriage had been a distinct shock to their entire social set, and Louise had felt it so keenly that she had never as yet been to visit her friend in her new home, although it was now almost two years since the wedding. It seemed to her like going to the graveyard to trace a beloved name on a tombstone, and yet she had known all along that some day she would go. She must see for herself just what had come to her friend. If Cecil and Vannie could give up purple and fine linen and be content in the country without even a car of their own, why, there must be something in love in a cottage after all. Louise did not believe much in love. There had never been any manifestation of it in her own home. Her father dwelt abroad most of the time, and her mother was worldly wise.

It was Jimmie Jordan who had stirred up the unrest in her heart and caused her to go forth at last to discover for herself once for all if there were such a thing as love that satisfies. Jimmie did not belong to their set.

Louise had met him two summers ago on a yachting trip when he was just out of college and she a débutante. He was the roommate and college chum of their host's younger brother. He had been good fun and they had been splendid comrades during the trip, but it had been quite understood from the first that Jimmie was not one of them. He was a worker—whatever that might mean—something in engineering. He had worked his way through college and was now "doing things" in the world. Louise had only a vague idea of what they might be—something about bridges and tunnels. He was perfectly respectable and all that, but not at all in her scheme of living, merely a pleasant incident by the way, to be thought about at intervals occasionally.

And yet, when she thought about it definitely, it was really the memory of Jimmie Jordan's gray eyes and the unspoken things in them that sent her desperately out to Norwood to hunt up Cecilia in her exile and prove to herself once for all that the suggestions that kept knocking at the door of her restless soul were ridiculous and impossible. It seemed that nothing short of stark, disagreeable reality would drive them from her mind.

For Jimmie Jordan had spoken of how happy Cecil and Van were in their charming home and asked if she had seen them lately. He had told quite briefly how Blake had given up his man and his apartments in town, bought this bungalow, taken a bank position, and they were living on his salary, twenty-five hundred dollars! It seemed incredible! Why, twenty-five hundred wouldn't begin to pay for and keep the car that she and her mother went out in every day. How could Cecilia have done it? How could they get on at all and be decent on that poor pittance? And Cecil might have had her choice of men who were worth their millions!

"You ought to see how well they live on his salary!" Jimmie Jordan had declared, a ring of triumph in his pleasant voice. It was then his gray eyes had taken on that wistful look that haunted her. It haunted her the more because there was a longing for something in her own soul which she could not understand.

And so this sweet spring morning she had run away at last to see for herself and satisfy those doubts that would not let her do what everybody was expecting her to do. For she had promised to give, that very afternoon, a definite answer to Halsey Carstairs, the man whom everybody expected her to marry and she felt she could not give it until she had seen for herself.

Halsey Carstairs was good-looking, agreeable, comfortably attentive, and had plenty of money. He was dull and tiresome at times, perhaps, but still one could not have everything. Once she had dreamed that life would have something different for her, something more interesting and romantic than Halsey Carstairs; but she had waited, and nothing better seemed coming her way. Perhaps there was nothing better. Perhaps she was wrong to look for more. And yet she had to come. That haunting, unspoken question in Jimmie Jordan's eyes would not let go of the yearning in her soul until she had seen for herself. She could easily get back by five o'clock for the interview with Carstairs.

Perhaps it had been with the desire to let things seem as bad as they could that she decided not to come in her car but to take the common train, and to walk from the station. She wanted to let her sensible self see what people who did foolish, romantic things had to put up with. Yet as she walked down the pleasant little street of Norwood she searched in vain for signs of discomfort and barrenness. There was nothing to suggest unpleasantness or poverty. A little girl with shining brown curls danced out of a gate and down the street, humming a merry tune, gazing curiously at the richly dressed lady as she passed, admiring the beautiful furs she wore and the roses on her hat. The little girl went into a small grocery half a block ahead, where a jangling bell made known her entrance, and emerged with a big loaf of bread in a paper under her arm just as Louise passed her. Was that the thing they had to do in the suburbs? Fancy, having to carry one's own bread home!

When Louise turned to the right as the agent had directed she could not help feeling the beauty and picturesqueness of the street. The houses were all different, yet very pretty. Many of them of stone or stucco, with tiled roofs and quaint windows. There were porches everywhere, and the lawns were neat and trim, with hedges about them, and borders of tulips and hyacinths. There were children playing in some of the yards, with their kittens and their dolls, watched over by big shaggy dogs.

She passed the third block and came to the house which she knew must be the Blakes'. There were crocuses, purple, white, yellow and blue, stiffly dotting the grass, and there were soft creamy curtains veiling the windows. It was in beautiful taste and harmony, the very prettiest of all the homes she had passed. It was like Cecilia, and it brought a sense of brief relief, as if she had looked fearful into a coffin and found the face more lifelike than she had expected. Then suddenly she stopped short on the walk and gave a startled exclamation. A willow baby coach stood on the porch quite near the door, with soft wooly drapery falling over the side, as if it had recently been cast aside by the occupant. That too! She hadn't heard! How strange!

And yet, perhaps it was a mistake. Of course! She had come to the wrong house! She couldn't imagine Cecil with a child! But she would go up to the door and inquire.

She stepped up and sounded the brass knocker half timidly, and then stood looking curiously down into the little empty nest, at the soft embroidered pillow, lace-frilled and puffy; at the pretty afghan of white and blue knit wool, with wide blue satin ribbons run in. How pretty they were! It reminded her of her doll days, and the expensive toys wherewith her childhood had been crowded. It gave her a sense of relief to notice that the ribbons were of good quality and everything fine and dainty. And then the door opened and a trim little colored maid in white cap and apron with a silver tray in her hand opened the door.

"Yas'm. Mis' Blake lives here," she assented, smiling. "Step right in, please." And Louise was ushered into what seemed a spacious room for so tiny a house, and at once surrounded with an atmosphere of loveliness. The sense of peace and quietness that she had noticed on the street seemed almost to have its source from this spot, so sweet and happy did the room seem.

She sat down and gazed about her, almost dazed. This then was Cecil's home! This was what Jimmie Jordan had meant when he told her she should see? She might have known! How could Cecil be anything but harmony and beauty and quietness?

It was as if she had suddenly discovered that one whom she thought dead forever was radiantly alive. She looked about and tried to take note of things, but her mind could not grasp details. There was a rug of costly pattern, a few pieces of Chippendale and Sheraton, some rare pictures on the walls, and vases and bric-a-brac that all belonged to the great world from which she had come; but these were wedding presents, of course, and they were so arranged amid a sweet simplicity that there was nothing incongruous in all their surroundings. There was a piano, a case of rare books, a wide-open fireplace, and through the open doorway between heavy curtains she caught a glimpse of glittering glass and silver—more wedding presents! But yet none of these things seemed to be essential to the place. There was an impression all over the room that the house would have been the same lovely abode even if the rare things had been omitted from it. What was it that gave the room this charm? What a contrast to Cecilia's mother's reception-room in the city, so stumbling full of rugs, bric-a-brac and gold-encrusted cushions! What was it that made the charm here?

Then, before she could answer the question, a door

opened somewhere and there came a soft little coo; a queer little human sound of a baby voice, saying, "Ahh-hh-ah! Ooooooo!" and she was recalled with a start to the thought that had come as she entered. There *was* a baby in the house then! Cecilia had a child! How strange! How startling!

But before she could get used to the idea Cecilia herself came rushing down the stairs with a cry of great joy and flung her arms about her guest.

"Oh, Louie, you dear! How good to hear your voice again! And to think you've really come! I've just longed to have you here. I thought you had forgotten me! And now you're hear, I'm going to keep you at least for overnight. Take off your hat and gloves at once. You'll just have to telephone and call off all engagements. I've got a duck of a spare room, and I'm bound to have an old-time visit. Take off your coat and hat this minute and come right upstairs! You've just come in time. I'm going to give baby her bath and you can see her. You haven't seen the baby, have you? She's the darlingest thing. She usually has her bath earlier than this, but I took her in the coach to the station with Van this morning, and she went to sleep on the way home and just woke up, so all the day's régime is upset. But I'm glad now, for you can see her. She is so cunning in the bathtub!"

And was this the forlorn exile whom she had dreaded coming to see? This radiant creature with blooming cheeks and starry eyes arrayed in——? What was this she wore? A cotton shirtwaist with the sleeves rolled high, showing the girlish dimples in her elbows, and a large flannel apron covering the rest of her garb completely! This vivid, happy girl, who talked so joyously and continuously that her visitor could not get a word in edgewise even if she had been able to think of a word to say! Was this Cecilia Radcliffe, the slim, pale, dignified, almost severely sad girl she had known of late years? Was this the woman she had come to pity and be warned by? This happy, jubilant, carefree creature, more like the girl with whom she had gone to boarding-school!

Thus in wondering silence she suffered herself to be led upstairs past the landing, deep bay windowed, where cushions, ferns, and a magazine invited one to linger, and a yellow canary in a brass cage fairly split his throat to sing a welcome to the crocuses in the garden below.

The top landing gave a charming vista of three pretty rooms and a white tiled bathroom all flooded with the spring sunshine, as if a dozen suns were shining in as many different directions. They were airy rooms, with muslin-curtained windows, simple wall paper, neutral-tinted rugs and white furniture, with a touch of color in the borders of the wall and curtains, the cushion on a rocker, a knot of ribbon on the dressing-table. One room was rosy-tinted, one was white and gray, and the third a dainty blue, the wall bursting into a shower of cherry bloom over a deep sky background. Something pink and roseleaf-like was stirring softly in the blue and white draped basket-crib in this third room, and again the soft little voice sounded: "Goo-ah-gooo-oooo!"

Straight to that blue and white crib went the visitor and stood looking down at the little mortal lying in its dainty depths, moving fluted roseleaf fingers, kicking little pink worsted shoelets, gurgling softly to herself.

Louise had never cared for babies. "Ugly little squalling red things!" she had been wont to think of them. But this baby was different. She had a personality. She was the tangible presence of the bond that bound her father and her mother to a new world, and placed them irrevocably out of the world which they had renounced. She gazed at the baby half in awe, and resented the strange tenderness that stirred her; till suddenly the baby smiled most ravishingly, showing unsuspected dimples, and bursting into a delicious remark accompanied by the most delightful darting gestures of fluted hands and tasseled toes: "Ahhh-ooo-ah-oooo!" and ending in a chuckle and another smile.

"Isn't she a darling, Lou? She knows you are somebody extra nice. Just see her smile! She doesn't deign to smile at everybody. Miss Darnell was over here last week, and she would do nothing but pucker up her lips and cry whenever she looked at her. Now take off your hat and coat and sit over here in that chair while I get the bath out of the way. This young lady won't have any day left if we don't hurry."

Still in silence Louise sat and watched and wondered, letting her hostess do the talking for the most part, too surprised at everything to answer except in monosyllables.

She looked in amazement at the strong capable way in which Cecil prepared the bath, undressed the baby and held her so easily upon her flannel-aproned lap, touching the exquisite pink skin with loving, caressing movements, as if it were intensest pleasure. She studied the array of little blue toilet articles set out at hand like a dolly's outfit; she watched the soft wash-rag foamy with sweet soap as it moved over the little fluffy golden head and down over the happy gurgling face, making the baby gasp and gurgle and laugh and splutter. She wondered how Cecil dared, for fear she might choke the child. She stood expectant when the little pink-soaped Cupid, still gurgling unsubdued and smiling undaunted, was lowered into the big white tub and sat crowing and splashing in ecstasy like some young fountain of delight, and then was lifted, slippery and protesting, back into the flannel lap and enveloped in a great soft towel, from which she presently emerged with shining countenance haloed by soft rings of gold, and roseleaf body warm and dry.

"But haven't you any nurse at all, Cecil? Do you always have to do this?"

"No, indeed, I haven't any nurse," declared the young mother firmly. "But I wouldn't let any nurse do this for my child if I had ten servants. It's the happiest part of the day, and I wouldn't miss it for anything! People who let servants attend to their children never know all they miss."

"But doesn't it tie you down dreadfully? How can you ever go out?"

"It doesn't tie me down half so much as society life used to do. You don't understand, Lou. I don't want to go out much, because it's so much nicer here at home, and we'd be missing so much. Van feels that way too. He just loves his home, and we have such good times together! Sundays he always stays around and helps me with the baby. He thinks there's nothing like her, and she just worships him. Wait till he comes home this afternoon and you'll see how she laughs and crows to go to him."

The bath was over and the baby was being fed now. Louise sat in wonder and watched the sweet-faced mother with the little golden head nestled against her breast; the great blue baby-eyes looking trustingly, dreamily into the heaven of the mother's face; the long lashes drooping more and more until they lay still upon the soft cheeks. It seemed like the painting of some great madonna suddenly come to life. She had never dreamed of anything so sweet as this intimate relation between mother and child. It seemed a mystery incomprehensible. She had come to have her illusions swept away, and lo, more illusions were being thrust upon her! Suddenly she felt her eyes fill with strange, wistful tears. Was marriage and mother-hood a lovely thing like this? Then she thought of Halsey Carstairs and her heart said: "Not with him!"

A little later Louise went with the young housekeeper through the immaculate house; surveyed the wax-like kitchen with its mysterious gas range, its white enamel sink and rows of shining cooking utensils, the little maid standing at the sink peeling potatoes. Everything seemed so perfect, like well-oiled machinery.

"How do you manage it, Cecil?" she asked when they

were back in the living-room again. "She must be a wonderful servant to do all this. How did you know what to tell her to do? Or does she tell you?"

"Bless your heart! She didn't know a thing when I got her."

"You! But how did *you* know?"

"I went to cooking school and learned," laughed the young wife.

It was a wonderful day. It absorbed her so intensely that she almost forgot to telephone Halsey Carstairs in time to stop his meeting the appointment at her home.

When they got back to the house they found that Blake had telephoned he was going to bring a friend out to dinner, and Louise entered into the arrangements eagerly, herself arranging crocus buds in a glass bowl for the center of the table, and feeling as if she were in a play.

And who should the guest turn out to be but Jimmy Jordan, with his strong handsome face and his wistful gray eyes all alight with anticipation of the evening! The gray eyes fairly blazed with joy when they saw Louise.

"Why, I didn't know that *you* were going to be here!" he said with a thrill in his voice; and held her hand so long in both of his big hearty ones that her cheeks grew pink and her eyes drooped in panic lest Cecilia or Blake should see the gladness she knew was in them. But she need not have worried. Cecilia and Blake were altogether too much taken up with one another after the long day of separation to notice mere visitors.

Jimmy and Louise attended the good-night ceremonies in the nursery, standing on the outer edge of things as it were, and gazing with half averted faces at the pretty rite. They slipped away half embarrassed down to the little porch, with the evening breath of the crocus, and the clear near call of the thrushes' good-night in the trees of the neighborhood. In a moment more Blake joined them and suggested that they go through the new bungalow that was almost finished in the next block. Cecilia came and they went down the pleasant little street, with Blake and his wife nodding good evening and passing a pleasant word with the neighbors who were out on their porches and lawns. Jimmy and Louise walked together, and were silent under the spell of the evening and the pleasant home atmosphere of everything.

Oh, that lovely little bungalow! That charming fireplace with its cosy seats and bookcases and tiny lattice-faced china closet! How they followed their hosts about as Cecilia dilated on this advantage and that exactly as if she were an agent for the house! How Jimmy's eyes shone with that eager light again as he asked the price of rent and coal and things! And how Louise's throat suddenly filled up with a desire to cry, and her heart ached with a big something that kept swelling and swelling there! She had forgotten Halsey Carstairs entirely.

The evening sped on swift wings. Jimmy stayed till the midnight train and they sang around the piano together. He held Louise's fingers in a long warm grasp, and stood by the front door till the last minute, and then had to run for his train. In a few minutes she was upstairs in the pink and white guest-room; alone with her strange new thoughts and feelings. Through her closed door she could hear a gentle murmur of content in the subdued voices across the hall. They were happy! They were glad to be alone together again! What a mystery! What a beautiful wonder!

After breakfast the next morning, when Blake was gone and while Cecilia was giving the orders for the day and attending to the baby, Louise Hasbrouck, who was supposed to be reading the morning paper in the living room, slipped out the door and down the street. Something was drawing her to that little new house. She wanted to be there alone and think; try to imagine herself there keeping house with somebody; try to see if it would be possible! For now that the day was come Halsey Carstairs had become a reality again, and must be reckoned with. She had promised to come back to the city and give him his answer today.

Louise slipped softly in at the door and drew it gently behind her. She was alone in the little house with her thoughts!

Her cheeks glowed and she looked around with shining eyes. Suppose she had come here to live. Suppose Halsey Carstairs and she were married and were going to begin housekeeping here!

Something gripped her heart like a cold vise, but she went steadily through the little house and tried to imagine it. A strange tumult was in her heart, and a strange illusion was with her. Whenever she tried to think of the comfortable stupid face of Halsey Carstairs it took on the vivid strength of Jimmy Jordan; and try as she would she could not get away from the vision of Jimmy, with that eager light in his eyes, and that happy smile, asking how much coal and sugar and flour were. It completely swept the thought of Halsey Carstairs from her mind, and melted the ice in her heart. She went through all the tiny cheery rooms, and looked in every closet and cupboard like a child, pausing at last in the tiny kitchen beside the little shining gas range as if it were an altar.

She did not hear an automobile come purring down the street and stop before the door. She did not hear firm steps coming up the cement path, nor the front door pushed open. She was thinking, and there were wonderful lights in her eyes and a soft rose color on her cheeks; when suddenly her thoughts became a reality, and looking up she saw that Jimmy was there in truth! Something leaped from their eyes and told the story even before he spoke:

"Louise! *You* here!"

He was holding a small handkerchief in his hand. He did not stop to explain that he was on his way to a business appointment and had been drawn to stop and look at the little house once more; and that this scrap of a handkerchief with its initial had led him to search for the one who had dropped it. He did not even tell her that he had meant to call at the Blakes' and see if he might take her back to the city with him on his return from his appointment. He stopped for nothing. He merely gathered her into his arms as if he had a right to do so, and put his face down to her glowing face! And she did not resist!

And after a long sweet silence, during which the sink and the range tried to look decorously oblivious and not to smile in anticipation, Jimmy lifted up Louise's beautiful face and looked in her eyes: "Could you be happy in a home like this, Louise, until I was able to give you a better one?"

And Louise, with swift final vision of Halsey Carstairs' smug vanishing back, lifted up her joyous eyes and answered:

"Yes, with you, Jimmy!"

A King to Rule

ATTERBURY found his wife's note lying on the desk in his inner office three weeks before Christmas when he unexpectedly came back from Boston before going on to Chicago. At first he did not notice the handwriting, thinking the note too unimportant for his attention in his haste. But as he glanced at it again it seemed to flash a sudden recognition to him as he was about to sweep it aside to make room for his checkbook. He started, and stared at it. That was Alice's handwriting!

An unexpected thrill went through his heart like an old habit almost forgotten. How long was it since he had seen her handwriting on an envelope addressed to him? It must be three years at least. His checkbook dropped with a thud to the Persian rug at his feet. His fountain pen slipped from his fingers and rolled across the desk as he clutched at the envelope and tore it open. He had a sudden smarting recollection of the little loving notes she used to write him when they were first married. She used to send them down to the office by messenger while they were eating breakfast. How wonderful it had been to find them on his desk when he came downtown later.

But what nonsense. This would be nothing of that sort. They had gone their separate ways now for almost two years. He could not remember just when the notes stopped. They were not as much to each other now as two men would be who came back to the same apartment house at night. Days passed without their ever seeing one another. Even their engagements and friends were scarcely ever the same.

He tried to rub the sudden mist out of his eyes. He ought not to stop to read this letter now of course. His car was waiting downstairs. There was barely time to sign the checks, get the papers for which he had returned from his safe, and catch the Chicago Limited. It was most important that he get to Chicago in time for a certain business appointment.

Yet he stopped to read the letter! It was brief and abrupt. It beat its way into his unprepared consciousness like hail out of a June sky.

> I have gone to St. Luke's Hospital to be operated on tomorrow at two. If anything happens to me everything is in the little safe in my room. Hastily, Alice.

He was still holding it in his shaking hand, staring at it, when Hoskins came in for the checks.

"When did this come?" asked Atterbury, looking wildly around at his secretary, and holding out the letter as if he were responsible for its contents.

"That? Oh, Mrs. Atterbury's chauffeur brought it in about four o'clock yesterday."

"Yesterday!" He clutched desperately for his telephone. "Get me the number of St. Luke's Hospital! Quick!"

"You can be signing these letters while I look it up," said the efficient secretary calmly, laying a sheaf of letters before the lawyer and placing his fountain pen in his hand. "You haven't any too much time, you know," he reminded his employer as he took down the receiver and called a number.

"I can't go!" snapped Atterbury. "Tell Brinsmaid he'll have to go in my place. Open the safe and get the papers in the Barton case. Call up the garage and get him a taxi. Tell him to drop everything and go at once!"

"But he couldn't. He's not prepared," said the secretary with finality.

"Doesn't matter. He'll have to go. He knows just what has to be done in the case, and as for the rest he can take my suitcase. My things will fit him. Go! Quick!"

Hoskins cast a startled look at his usually self-contained employer, handed him the receiver, and beat a hasty retreat. When he and the amazed Brinsmaid returned, Atterbury was conducting a violent conversation over the telephone in a voice something between a sob and a shout.

"What time did you say? *NOW!? You say she's under ether now?* O, my God! Who's doing it? Who's the doctor? How soon can I see her? What? Not till— But I'm coming right now! Well, I'm *coming!* Yes, I'm her *husband!* I'm *coming!*"

He turned a haggard face on the two astonished men. "They're operating on Alice," he gasped dazedly. "They're operating *now!* You'll have to go to Chicago, Brinsmaid—" His voice caught in a great sound like a sob as he reached wildly for his hat.

The other two men exchanged significant, wondering glances. "All right," said Brinsmaid, and hurried out to close and lock his desk, and get his things together.

"You'll have to sign these checks before you go, Mr. Atterbury," reminded Hoskins in the tone of respect one uses toward a man in sudden trouble.

Atterbury wrote his name seven times without knowing what he was signing, pulled out a wallet containing tickets and money for Brinsmaid, and then without waiting to give further directions he bolted out the door, and down the stairs, not even waiting for the elevator.

"I never imagined he'd feel like that!" said Hoskins, looking wonderingly after him as Brinsmaid came back with the papers and put on his overcoat.

"You never can tell," answered Brinsmaid with a sneer. "I thought he was solid as the Rock of Gibraltar, but here he goes off his head like any nut. As if his wife was the only woman who ever went under an operation. My wife's had three, and I never missed a day at the office. Now what in thunder am I to do about this? The boob never told me a word about his investigations in Boston, and a lot depends on that. I'm all in the dark. The very idea of *his* going out of his head like that. I never saw him pay any attention to her before. I've been here nearly three years and I wouldn't have known he was married for all he ever seemed to think about her."

Down in the street Atterbury was dashing along in his car. The streets were thronged with Christmas shoppers. Resinous breath of Christmas trees was in the air; hawkers offered holly wreaths and mistletoe. A man up a pole was stringing Christmas lights across the way. *Christmas!* Just a farce! A lot of fuss about nothing!

Yet there had been Christmases not so long ago, when Alice— There! They were holding him up again! Fool women with their arms full of bundles and ridiculous smirks of satisfaction on their tired faces, insisting on going on across a crowded street when the lights had changed! How could the sun continue to shine, and the breath of the cedars be sweet, when Death was stalking him? His shoulders suddenly sagged and his head drooped.

"Alice! My little Alice! They're cutting my little Alice, and I'm not there!"

All the three years they had been growing apart were suddenly obliterated. Alice was a slim girl he had seen first in white with a bit of blue ribbon tucked in her dress, and blue beads around her neck, her gold hair in curls; the girl he had fallen in love with and married. And she had been so very young, little more than a schoolgirl. He ought to have remembered that. She was young, so young to be a wife. He had felt it so wonderful that she was his!

The capable, distant Alice, who had ordered his house, ruled his servants, gone her distant ways and looked at him out of alien eyes, was no more. It was blue-eyed Alice who lay alone on the operating table, just a little slip of a thing with dimples, and sometimes a rose in her hair—*his* rose.

It was not that they were unsympathetic at the hospital when this wild-eyed, rumpled husband appeared, his lips parted and dry with anxiety. But they had so many cases. They could not see that his particular Alice was the only woman on earth to him. They left him standing an unconscionable time in the hall, and then conducted him to a dreary desert of a reception room, where the single picture on the wall was a ghastly photograph of a skeleton in nerves, every lacy white nerve filament picked out against a black background. Some great specialist had skillfully, patiently worked it all out. Millions of tiny filaments of feeling, exquisite, beautiful—horrible! Intertwined, intermingled so intricately that it would not be possible to sever the human form anywhere without torturing the whole threadlike system!

And some thoughtless human brute had thought it appropriate to place that picture here for the edification of suffering visitors whose loved ones were under the knife! He turned and strode madly about the room like a caged thing.

The scent of ether pervaded everything keenly, and brought a vision of Alice lying still under its numbing breath. Somewhere in the distant halls a door opened hastily and a far, heart-rending scream rang and echoed, then was muffled by the closing of the door. Oh, why did they not come and tell him the worst? What hell could be more tortuous than where he was standing now?

A nurse came pattering rubberly down the hall with a starchy swish. She looked in at him curiously and moved away. He became aware that his face was wet with tears. When had he ever cried?

Desperately he sought in his pocket for Alice's note and read it again through the blur in his eyes, holding to it as if it were his only remaining hope.

How she had kept her nerve to the last, such a little, silent, courageous thing, fitting herself to the great city life in who knew what ways; always aloof in her plans. And now, at the last, she had taken this terrible risk alone!

There were no endearments in that note. Just plain facts, all that was needed from the point of view from which they had lived their lives lately. He shrank and quivered all over his big strong body as he realized this.

He knew now that it had been all his fault, this estrangement that had come between them. He knew that by his careless ways and hard words he had shut up and sealed the vaults of her tenderness. He began to know just when it had first happened, too. He had seen her delicate lips close tightly to hold back the hurt look. He had noticed her cheeks go white at his hard words, her lashes droop to cover the tears she was too proud to shed, and then her eyes flash wide in one great look of indignation. Just what was it he had said? He did not know, now. He remembered he had been ashamed of himself at the time, but he had been to bullheaded to say so. He thought she would forget. *He* had forgotten. But she had never forgotten. She had slowly turned to ice and had gone her way to the end alone.

There had been a time when he might have taken her in his arms and kissed her, said he was sorry—he knew the very moment now—and the breach would have been healed—but he did not—and now he was here alone—and she was upstairs asleep—alone. Oh, God in heaven, if she should slip out of life away from him forever, with only that cold little note between them always!

The house doctor paused in the doorway, curt, cool, hurried. There was power and knowledge in his pink, well-groomed face. Atterbury cringed before him. His voice trembled with anxiety as he tried to ask a question. The doctor's words were keen, incisive, like a knife.

"The operation is not over yet. You'd better come back, or call up, around six or seven. She'll be coming out of the ether then. There were complications, you know."

Complications! Not over yet! His head reeled. Six o'clock! It was eons away!

He tried to rally and ask a question. He could hear that the doctor was still talking, but the words meant nothing to him. They were obscured by his anguish. His soul was in torture. Couldn't he go to her? Now? The doctor shook his head and went away. Minutes dragged like hours. Hours passed like months. He tramped the room from end to end. He walked the long white ghostly halls, and then hurried back to the seclusion of the waiting room, stabbed by the curious eyes of any people who passed him. Dusk came and dreary lights sprang up high in the ceiling. The city twinkled through the darkened windows, threaded everywhere with Christmas lights. A city in which now his life seemed to have no farther part.

When he could no longer stand it in the hospital he went out and tramped the street a while, looking up at the many lighted windows of the building he had just left and thinking of all the Alices lying suffering there alone. His Alice, suffering, perhaps dying, all alone!

He had time to see all his sins, to accuse, suffer and repent. He even tried to pray as he marched the street, but he found he was groaning aloud so that people passing turned to look curiously at him.

Choir boys were practising in a chapel across the way. As he passed the window their voices broke forth clearly:

> *"Joy to the world, the Lord is come;*
> *Let earth receive her King;*
> *Let every heart prepare Him room—"*

Atterbury walked rapidly on out of sound of the old familiar words, a bitterness in his soul toward Christmas and all that had to do with it, yet the words kept ringing in his ears: "Let every heart prepare Him room!"

Well, there wasn't any room in his heart for a king, that was certain. If only Alice— Then he caught his breath in a moan and turned quickly about-face to go back to the hospital. No telling what had happened during his absence. He hastened his steps. Why had he come so far?

Back in range of the choir boys again the song burst forth as he passed:

> *"No more let sin and sorrow grow,*
> *Nor thorns infest the ground;*
> *He comes to make His blessings flow,*
> *Far as the curse is found—"*

Somehow the song seemed to come more from above than from the church. It was like a heavenly voice trying to show him what was the matter. Perhaps, after all, if he had had room for the King— Then it began to dawn upon him that it was sin that was in the world, and in him, that had made the trouble. Sin that must be blotted out before good could enter in. He suddenly began to pray as he hurried on to the hospital: "God, save her! Oh God I've sinned! Let me have another chance to show her! Oh God! Oh, God—!"

As he entered the building the operating surgeon was

coming down the hall. He had a look of quiet victory upon his face. His eyes were wise and kind. He regarded Atterbury almost tenderly.

"She has come through bravely so far," he said. "She is just coming out of the ether. There is every reason to hope that all will be well."

Atterbury reeled and put his hand to his head. It seemed almost like God's voice answering his heart's cry.

Someone across the road opened the choir room door for a moment and a line broke forth:

> *"The wonders of His love,*
> *The wonders of His love—"*

The doctor was speaking again: "You can go up to the door and take a look at her if you wish, and then I advise you to go home and go to bed. You've been under a heavy strain."

He wanted to weep on the surgeon's shoulder but he followed the white-garbed nurse through the marble halls with awe as if in the wake of a guardian angel. He stood with bowed head in the elevator, and his heart leaped up fearfully as he stepped into the upper hall and followed to Alice's door.

Two white-sheathed nurses were hovering about in there, doing something to the bed, patting and smoothing the white covers, taking away a pile of linen. They lifted their eyes once and dropped them again, going on with their work as if he were not there. No one noticed him. He stood within the shadow of the doorway. There lay Alice, his Alice, with her long dark lashes on her white thin cheeks, and her gold hair like a halo about her face. Strange he had not noticed how thin she was growing. But then he had seen so little of her lately. Alice! His Alice!

Her eyelids fluttered and she moaned and turned her head

from side to side. He could not bear it. The tears rained down his face silently and he turned away to hide them.

"She'll be out of the ether tomorrow," said the nurse gently. "You'd better go home now and get some rest. She'll be wanting you tomorrow."

His heart leaped up. *Would* she want him? Would she *ever* want him again?

The head nurse cheerfully manipulated him out of the room and closed the door. He felt as if the door were closing on his soul, and would have cried out but he dared not. He summoned his senses enough to enquire how soon he might see her in the morning and then he went home. He would have stayed all night in that dreadful reception room, but they seemed not to expect him to do so. It broke his heart to go away and leave her lying there in that great place so white and still alone with strangers. What if something happened in the night?

When he reached the house he sent the servants to bed. He forgot he had eaten nothing since his lunch on the train. He went up to his wife's room and stood a long time looking around. Everything reminded him of her, though he felt an interloper in her absence. He threw himself down upon her bed with his face in her cool pillow and cried out: "Oh, Alice, Alice, have I lost you forever?" And the soft cool fragrance of her pillow soothed him till he slept.

When Alice Atterbury had seen the door of her room open to the surgeon and his assistant, and known that her time was come, she lifted her clear gaze steadily. She knew what she might be facing. She was prepared. The doctor had spoken of the operation as not too serious but she was aware that there was always danger.

Then a whiff of something like a strong mountain breeze invigorating and spicy, swept across her face and she closed her eyes and took deep breaths. It was better than she had expected. She was glad to give herself up to it. The breath came stronger now and she found herself climbing a mountain made of ice, transparent, pure and clear, with blue lights through it. It towered above her out of sight into wonderful clouds, and so long as she took those deep breaths she moved upward rapidly; but if she stopped for a moment her lungs grew tired and there was a hitch somewhere. She could hear the nurse calling to her to keep on breathing deeply. She understood that she was being etherized and began to fear lest after all it would fail her, and perhaps they would operate on her while she was conscious, without knowing it. Then she was climbing the mountain again, the clear sunlit mountain, white like a diamond!

They were taking her rings from her hands. She could feel the tug of them. She wished they wouldn't. The thought came to her to wonder what her husband would think if he knew. But then he would not be home until the end of the week and it would be all over by that time, one way or the other. Just as well. Ah——! That was a sigh. She was almost to the top now! But just as she slipped over the border and went into restful nothingness, glad to be rid of it all, she seemed to see her little dead love slipped out of her heart and lying cold and still, encased in ice. She had thought it dead and buried long ago.

Sometime in the night she came creeping back. The mountain was gone and the cold; it was fiery hot and a light was burning above her, a tormenting thirst was upon her, but her body seemed a flame of pain. As if she were in a fiery pit down deep beneath them, the nurses and the doctor stood above her in cool air and spoke cheerful nothings to her. They soothed her as if she were a little child, bade her wait, gave her something that shut down upon her senses and made them dull so that she could not cry out her discomfort. She sank into a restless slumber.

When she awoke at last and found it was morning, the

sun was shining broadly across the room. There was good air and things were not so heavy; neither was there so much pain. They gave her a little water and she opened her eyes and smiled. There was a perfume in the air better than the mountain breeze that had sent her off to sleep. It seemed like flowers. She lifted her eyes and there they were, great sheaves of roses, Ward roses, the kind she used to love when she was a girl. Jim used to bring them to her when they were first married. That thought penetrated the vague walls of discomfort about her as something satisfyingly pleasant.

As she sank back into sleep again she was dimly conscious of something big and warm and strong clasping her hand tenderly. It was not the nurse's touch, nor yet like the feeling of the blanket. Her hand nestled in it contentedly. It made a rift in the cloud of pain that sometimes threatened to envelope her again. And when she rose again on the billow of consciousness it was still there, a big warm hand.

She lay a long time with closed eyes trying to think out what it could be, that old sweetly familiar enfolding of her hand. It was there when the pain gripped her like a vise in its ruthless clutch again. Her frail fingers clung to the hand and let all her thoughts centre there. She felt that if that hand had not been there she would have been forced to give up and let that awful biting, searing darkness envelope her once more. But the strong hand held and bore her upward, till there came a morning when her little life bark seemed suddenly to be floating to a peaceful quiet haven, and the pain was subsiding slowly but surely as she neared the shore. And when finally her boat came to a velvet stop upon the sand, she opened her eyes and looked up, knowing her ordeal was passed and she had come out fully conscious.

Her first great wonder was that she had not died. She had rather expected to die. Then her eyes rested on the roses! Who had sent them? Not any of the Clubs or women's organizations of which she was a member. She had taken great care they should not know where she was. Only her husband knew, and he would not be home yet from his business trip to Boston and Chicago.

Then the strong hand that held her own thrilled into gentle pressure, and she turned and saw him, like a great big awkward angel on clumsy guard beside her. He loomed strong and dear and protecting and her eyes met his in ecstasy, her lips trembling into a wondering smile.

"Jim!"

"Alice!"

He dropped on his knees beside her and covered her hands with kisses. There were tears of joy raining down his face.

All day he stayed there, and as far into the night as they would let him. They might not talk but it was enough just to be together, to bridge the years of soul-separation and know that it was past. They did not need words to say that it was so, they knew it. When she slept he was there, and when she awoke his broad shoulders loomed above her pillow. When he went away for the night she knew he would return and her heart lay still in a happy tumult.

She forgot to watch the slow receding of the pain, as it gave way hour by hour, now and then giving a spiteful bite back for farewell. She had something bigger than the pain. Joy had come to be her constant guest.

Atterbury went home nights to pace her lonely chamber, and recall over and over again the smile that came into her eyes when she had first seen him by her bed. Pausing before her portrait beside his own in a double silver frame that stood upon her dressing table he looked deep into her pictured eyes:

"Oh, Alice! Alice! Alice!" he would breathe softly, "you have come back, and I shall take care never to lose you again!"

Then he fell to planning about her return. What could he do to make things beautiful for her? What was it she used to wish for in those early days before he had money to gratify her tastes? A fireplace and a conservatory. Strange he had forgotten to give them to her as soon as he was able. Fool! Blind! To let a woman like that drift away from him over a mere difference of opinion. But he would make up for it now. She should have her fireplace and conservatory. That whole end of the room could be torn out and built in with glass, steam pipes could be run in, and glass doors. He would stock it with plants. It wouldn't take long. If he paid enough he likely could have it done before her return. He would get right at it the first thing in the morning.

And over there between the windows was where she had wanted the fireplace. That would work out very well, for the chimney from the furnace went up there somewhere. He would call a stone mason and carpenter tonight. Get them here at seven in the morning. Eagerly he strode to the telephone and arranged the matter.

When he came back he stared at the wall that separated Alice's room from his den. What did he want of a den? Dens were for bears and lions. Perhaps he had been something on that order in the past, but he didn't intend to be any longer. He would tear that entire partition down, enlarge the room, and refurnish the whole thing. Yes, he would do it before Alice got back. He would surprise her. And if there was anything about it she didn't like she could do it over. But she always used to like the things he bought her, liked them better because he had chosen them.

So he fell asleep dreaming of Alice in a white dress with a rose among the blue ribbons at her throat!

The next morning he was ready for the stone mason and the carpenter when they arrived, and they went to work at once, while Atterbury and the servants hustled the furniture into other rooms to make way for the workmen.

Down at the office Hoskins, coming in from the bank, hung up his overcoat and hat and turned toward the man who was taking Brinsmaid's place while he was in Chicago.

"Hasn't Mr. Atterbury come in yet?" he asked.

"Oh, yes, come and gone," sneered Mason. "He came in about a half hour ago and spent his time phoning to carpenters and stone masons and plumbers and florists. He didn't even look at his mail, and he told me to tell you to do as you darned please about the business. Said you could get him at the hospital if you needed him and then he went away. He was smiling from ear to ear when he left. He's daffier than ever. It gets my goat what's got into him! He's been married long enough to get over such fool nonsense. Just an operation! People have them every day and think nothing of it!"

"Well, his marriage must have been the real thing," mused Hoskins with a wistful sigh. He was young and still had ideals.

"Real thing!" snorted Mason who was divorced, "as if there was any!"

But Hoskins was standing by the great office window looking out over a vista of roofs and spires dreamily, and seeing the misty face of a girl he knew, and a vision of a little round table set for two.

And sometimes in the hospital when the nurses gathered, in little groups of two and three in an odd moment, they spoke about the Atterburys.

"My! Don't he think a lot of her though?" chattered the night nurse to the day nurse as they met in the upper hall. "He just sits and reads to her the whole livelong day, unless she's asleep, and then he just sits, and holds her hand, and looks at her as if he couldn't get enough. They talk a lot, too, in a tone as if they enjoyed it. He acts like a lover, yet she told me herself they'd been married almost five years. My! If I thought I'd get one like that I'd quit nursing today and go into society. I didn't think there was any real stuff like that in getting married. Flowers? I never knew there were so many in the world! He's real good looking too, and she's a peach! You never hear her complaining. She just lays there and watches him and smiles. And when he's away she just lays there and watches the door like she was afraid she might not see him first when he comes back. It's good to think there are such in the world today. They're plenty scarce, goodness knows!"

The days passed on and Alice Atterbury came slowly, steadily up from the brink of death into the great light of her husband's love, till all who saw her noticed the look of radiance in her face, and the doctor said: "Mrs. Atterbury, you're wonderful! You haven't the look of strain that so many have after an operation. You look as fresh and young as a girl!"

But Alice only looked at her husband and smiled.

As the days passed Atterbury was by her side almost constantly, snatching only an hour or so in the late morning to drop into his office and smilingly approve all that his partner had done. Or now and again he would slip downstairs to the hospital telephone booth and spend a few minutes in talking to the head workman who was making the alterations in his house.

Each day when he came he brought Alice a gift. Costly flowers or fruit when she was able to eat it, a jewel or a trinket of intrinsic worth. "It's almost Christmas, you know," he told her, and kissed her tenderly. And then the day she left the hospital he slipped a great blue diamond on her finger above her wedding ring, and looking into his eyes she understood it was the symbol of their new-old love come back to stay.

It was Christmas Eve when they let him bring her home,

carefully, in the great limousine, with skillful hands to tend her, and when they reached the house he carried her up the stairs in his own strong arms, and laid her upon the couch in her rejuvenated room.

For the impossible had been accomplished! The room was done, conservatory, chimney and all! By making appointments with decorators and florists for the late evenings, after he came home from the hospital, Atterbury had arranged for all the furnishing. Everything was in place even to a luxurious afghan flung across the foot of the chaise lounge. The fire was burning softly in the new fireplace, and the great stone chimney seemed entirely at home between the two windows, each of which was furnished with a deep seat with cushions. The sliding glass doors to the new conservatory were pushed back letting in the perfume of the tropics, and making it seem as if the whole south end of the room were aglow with blossoms. The walls were a delicate ivory tint, the hangings a soft rose, and the floor was covered with a rare old rug of heavenly Chinese blue.

The partition that had made the den was gone, giving breadth to the room, and in the alcove that gave two more windows stood a great wide-spreading Christmas tree aglow with lights, and heavy with treasure.

At last the nurse left them and they were alone together. Atterbury stood beside the couch and watched his Alice as she gazed about on the changed room, with almost that same daze and dawning wonder she had worn when she came to herself and saw him first in the hospital. She took in everything, letting her eyes travel slowly around the room, and then with her rare smile her glance came back to him with a mist of love in her eyes.

"Oh, Jim!" she said softly, putting out her arms to him. "It's all as I used to dream it might be. Everything I wanted, only a thousand times more gorgeous than I dreamed. But you are the best of all. I'd be satisfied just with you, if I hadn't anything else in the world!"

He dropped to his knees and put his arms about her, drawing her close in his arms. "Alice! My darling!" he said.

Then suddenly up from the street below came a sound of carolers, sweet and clear:

"Joy to the world, the Lord is come!
Let earth receive her King!"

Atterbury drew the afghan about Alice's shoulders, and stepping to the window flung it open, and the song came rushing in like a voice from heaven:

"Let every heart prepare Him room—"

They listened with their arms about one another, their faces close together, and as the last words died away, Atterbury whispered: "Alice, that song's been ringing in my heart ever since that night—that awful night—when you were in the hospital—I walked the streets and heard the boys in the Chapel practising it, 'Let every heart prepare Him room!' I knew I had no room in my heart for Him, nor for anything but you—and a great fear—and I resented all this Christmas fuss and talk and lights and everything. What was Christmas with so much pain in the world, and you and I as far apart as the poles, and maybe I'd never see you alive any more? And then, afterward, it stayed with me, and I thought a lot about it, and I began to realize that perhaps that was our whole trouble. Perhaps if we'd had room in our hearts and our house for God all these terrible things might not have happened! And I know now, Alice, that it was sin in my heart that made me so hateful with you—"

"But Jim—you weren't hateful—it was I who took

offense too quickly when you were tired—" Alice's fingers were softly in his hair, touching his head gently, lovingly.

"No, Alice, it was not your fault. It was sin in my heart. Sin of wanting my own way, and having the last word, and all that. Sin of wanting you to know I was boss. Just plain Sin! It was that that made it possible for me to treat you as I did, and to hate Christmas and all that it means. And Alice, now that I've found it out, I've been to God and asked Him to make me different, to take the sin out of my heart and make room for Him there, and I guess after this, Christmas is going to be in my heart."

Alice drew his lips down to hers and kissed him. "Yes, Jim," she whispered, "my heart too. Room in my heart for the King! Oh, it will be different, won't it, Jim? For it will be neither you nor I ruling— He'll be King!"

Then Jim suddenly bowed his head and closed his eyes; "Oh, God," he said earnestly, "You gave her back to me in answer to my prayer, and I didn't deserve it. I want You to come into my heart and live a life worthy of such a precious wife as you have given me. I thank You, Lord, for giving her back to me!"

Suddenly the carolers down in the street began to sing again, sweet and clear on the Christmas air:

> *"Silent night! Holy night!*
> *All is calm, all is bright!"*

They listened silently, hand clasping hand, till the melody died away, and the carolers moved on. Then Alice said softly: "'Christ, the Savior, is born!'"

"Yes," said Atterbury stooping to kiss her. "And now, dear, it's time for you to rest: 'Sleep in heavenly peace—!'"

And in a little while it was all quiet in the room, the lights had been turned out, even the lights from the Christmas tree were gone, and only the soft flicker of the firelight was left, with the light of a single star that Atterbury had put up in the far window of the conservatory, that hadn't been seen till now. Alice lay looking at it for a little, in the quiet dimness of her lovely room, her hand in her Jim's hand, and the star shining. Then she closed her eyes happily. Tomorrow would be Christmas, and tomorrow would begin the new life!

The Call

JOHN HOWARD had no intention whatever of going to a missionary meeting. He wouldn't get caught at a thing like that for a fortune.

Of course the speaker was to be entertained at his father's house, and he would be expected to drive him to the church and be there at ten o'clock to take him back to the house again, but that was a mere incident in the evening. What he intended to do in between his duties as chauffeur was to spend the evening at Dixie Manton's house.

Dixie was a new student at senior high school, and very popular. She certainly knew how to entertain. There was always something peppy going on at her house.

John wished his mother wasn't always entertaining missionaries. Why didn't the guy go to Africa, or wherever it was he was supposed to talk about, and shut up? He was sure he would give twice as much money—providing he were going to give any at all, which he *wasn't*—if the man would only stay away and let him alone. What was the use of preaching to the heathen anyway? They never amounted to anything after you did, and they must be a great deal better off not knowing something they couldn't possibly live up to. So reasoned John Howard.

However, that was before dinner, before he even went to the station to meet the missionary.

He had expected to see a little, dried-up, old-woman-ish man with fanatical eyes and an impertinent chin. Instead, Dr. Robertson proved to be a tall, distinguished looking man with white hair and eyes that had a light in them as if he could see things that other people didn't know about. He wore clothes that were well cut, and his baggage had a Paris label, though his tongue had a burr that made you think of scholarly halls in England, with a tang perhaps of Scotch heather.

John curled his lip when he heard this missionary's office was located in London. Great missionary that! Drawing a salary for converting heathen in Africa from an office in London! Long distance conversion!

Yet before he had landed the stranger at his father's house he had confessed to himself, "He's clever!" and he lingered at the door of the guest room after taking up the shiny suitcase to hear the end of a story Dr. Robertson was telling; and as he went downstairs he said to himself sagely, "He knows his onions!"

He went whistling out of the house and even took a special trip to the station to find out about trains the man had asked about for the morrow.

John Howard had planned to be absent from the evening meal, taking a solitary bite at the pie shop, and appearing only in time to take his mother and her guest to the church, but as the hour for dinner drew on he found himself thinking it would not be so bad to go back and hear that man talk. So he hurried home and tidied up a bit, and got down to the living room in time to hear a story about a tiger and a leopard the missionary had met with in a tour of mission stations. So he *had* been to Africa after all!

At the dinner table there were more stories. It appeared that Dr. Robertson and his wife spent several months of every year going about among the mission stations under their charge, and that they were personally acquainted with the heathen by name in their own district. Some field secretary! Knew what he was talking about!

They lingered so long at the dinner table hearing more stories that they had to hurry to get to the church in time, and then John's mother asked him to take the missionary up and introduce him to the minister while she went to hunt up some music for the soloist of the evening. John's mother hurried away lest he should refuse. John did not like to do things like that, but somehow he felt rather proud to be escorting this man up the aisle of the church, and when the introduction was over he lingered just a second. It didn't seem polite to leave him at once.

The minister and the missionary were talking about some literature to distribute at the close of the meeting.

"I have plenty of it in my bag," the missionary said. "I wonder if my young friend here would mind going back for it?" and he put a friendly hand on John's shoulder.

"Sure, I'll go," offered John smiling, and feeling a strange thrill to be a part of this man's work.

"You'll find them in the top of the bag, fastened with gum bands," said Dr. Robertson, and smiled.

John walked out of the church proudly, thinking about that smile, thinking of the missionary's eyes, eyes that searched you kindly and made you wish to be the best you could; thinking of the grace he had asked at the table that made you feel as if God had walked into the room. "Good guy, that!" John Howard owned as he threw in his clutch and struck out for home. He must get those circulars up to the platform before the meeting began.

But they were singing when John got back with the bundle, and there was no usher in sight. John Howard stood helplessly by the door looking around, till suddenly he was aware of the missionary standing on the steps of the platform motioning him to come forward, and of course there was nothing to do but go. John Howard, with his best blue serge on, and his hair a little rumpled from the wind, walked up the aisle like an elder, a trifle conscious of the three girls from senior high who sat in the back row whispering, but more conscious of the smile on the face of Dr. Robertson as he stood on the second step of the pulpit and watched him with friendly eyes. John Howard walked proudly, that all might see that he was doing an errand for this man.

Dr. Robertson came down the steps and took the bundle, one hand companionably on John's shoulder as he thanked him; and then pointing to a seat in the front row, he whispered:

"I had that seat saved for you, brother."

The people were all sitting down now, as the song was over, and there was nothing for John Howard to do but to sit down also. He had a sudden fleeting annoyance as he remembered his promise to Dixie for the evening, but of course he could not get out just now. A prayer was going on.

All through the opening exercises John Howard was planning to slip out pretty soon by the little side door at the right of the pulpit, but just as they were singing the last hymn before the address somebody from a side seat, feeling the air of the room oppressive perhaps, got up and tried to get out that door, and found it locked. John Howard was glad he had not tried that, and been left to face the audience afterward. He cast about in his mind for some other means of escape that would be unnoticeable from the platform— of course he could give the excuse of a previous engagement afterward, and the missionary likely would not have noticed when he left,—but by this time even the aisles were pretty well filled with people. It would really make a disturbance to try to get out. So John Howard sat still, feeling uncomfortable at the thought of what Dixie would say tomorrow if she found out he had gone to a missionary meeting instead of coming to her party.

But suddenly Dr. Robertson was introduced and began to speak, and from that time forth John Howard thought no more of Dixie Manton. For almost immediately the walls of the church in which they were sitting disappeared, and John Howard was gazing at strange scenes as Dr. Robertson began to describe graphically the country in which his mission stations were located in North Africa. Lush green tropical vegetation grew up on every side; great beasts and fierce loomed in the offing; he walked the streets of a village the houses of which had mud walls and a mud floor, where the lizards and other small vermin and reptiles made free, and where the only roof was a grass thatch. Army cots and no mattresses, that was the luxury of the missionary; coarse food and sometimes very little of it! A salary of thirty-five dollars a month for a missionary and his wife and child to live upon! Even a talk of cutting it lower because of lack of funds!

Dirty, ignorant people who didn't want the Gospel! Why did he bother?

Suddenly down the little thatched street walked a boy about John's own age, dark of skin, careless of garments, turbaned and dirty, and uninteresting.

The missionary was telling how this boy came into the mission and heard the Gospel of the Lord Jesus,—how He loved sinners, and had died to save them from their sins.

The speaker made it all so vivid that afterward John Howard thought he had watched the wonder grow in the dark eyes of that other boy, and the light spring up in his face. He seemed to watch him that first day after he had accepted Christ as his Saviour, and started out into the street to tell some of his friends.

John felt a tremor of anxiety for him, for Dr. Robertson

had explained that it was as much as one's life was worth
in that Mohammedan country to confess Christ, and throw
off Mohammedanism.

But this young convert went boldly out and cried out
to his friends openly on the street: "Come, hear what I
have found out! We have been deceived! Mohammed is
a big fake! Jesus Christ is a Saviour and has forgiven my
sins!"

John seemed to see the dark look on the face of the boy's
uncle who happened to be passing and heard his confession. He sat spellbound as the uncle protested to the boy,
warning him that his life would not be safe if he said such
things in the street; and then he thrilled anew at the
response of the young convert: "Well, they may do anything to my body they like, but they can't take my Saviour
away from me! And I *must* tell everybody about this
wonderful Saviour!"

John Howard felt a strange shamed color creeping into
his own cheeks. And he had said a few hours ago that the
heathen couldn't live up to what was taught them even if
they did know it! Why, this lad was braver than a whole
regiment of soldiers, braver than the greatest athlete that
ever made a touchdown or scored an inning; braver—yes,
braver than a white man and a Christian in America! John
Howard was supposed to be a Christian. At least he had
joined the church at the age of twelve, and always went to
Communion when he could not think of some good
excuse to get out of it. But he had never even thought of
such a thing as telling anybody about his Saviour. Indeed,
John Howard began to wonder if he even had a Saviour.
That is, if the Saviour would own him as a follower in
contrast with a convert like this one.

John Howard sat with his eyes riveted to the face of
the speaker while he told of the arrest of that
Mohammedan boy, later in the day, by a soldier who
rushed up and insisted that the lad lift his arm and declare

the oath of allegiance to Mohammed. How he held his breath waiting for that African boy's answer! How he thrilled to hear his refusal, and seemed to see him led off to prison!

Five days they gave him to retract, and each day led him forth to hector and torment him and try to get him to affirm his faith in Mohammed; and each day the lad's answer grew clearer, more definite, more ready to die for his faith in Christ.

John Howard's throat swelled, and something hot and wet came into his eyes, but he blinked it away and listened fiercely to the end: how they cut him in pieces, this brave lad of Algiers, and laying the pieces in the form of a cross, sent them around to other towns as a warning to other lads. And John Howard's heart thrilled as it had never thrilled before, not even for Lindbergh; at the thought of that brave true heathen boy, faithful even to death.

The story went on, dramatic in its details, of other lads who were not afraid even after the terrible warning, and of the story of Christ that was spreading, and reaching other hearts and lives, even under persecution.

Again the scene grew dark and pathetic as the speaker described the little unwanted girl babies who were given into the hands of the mission schools for a few short years, and then at eight or nine years and sometimes even so young as five years, were rudely snatched back by their parents to be sold as wives to cruel husbands, many years older than themselves. His jaw set in a stern new strength. For John Howard knew what he had to do.

He was very quiet all through the late part of the evening while the family sat up and talked with their guest, asking eager questions.

A little before the rest retired John Howard slipped up to his room and wrote a check for the entire amount in his savings account which he had been putting away for a new sports model of a racing car that he had wanted.

Dr. Robertson, just gone to his room, heard a tap, and here was John Howard holding out the check. Dr. Robertson looked at the check, and looked at the boy, and then putting his hand on the young fellow's shoulder, said:

"Come in, brother. Tell me, what is this?"

And John Howard told him, blunderingly, it was for his mission work.

"Ah!" said the servant of God with a great light in his face. "Ah! dear young brother! This is good. There is but one thing better! It is written of some folk in the Bible days who brought some money to the Lord that 'they first gave themselves.' How about it, brother, why don't you give yourself to the work?"

"Oh, I'd like to," jerked out John Howard, "but I'm not good enough. Why, I've never done anything at all at even just being a common Christian."

"Ah, but you have the Lord's righteousness to claim," said the missionary. "Come, let us see what the Book says about it, and let us kneel down and talk to the Lord about it."

John Howard's mother thrilled to think her boy was talking to the great man, but she reproved him at breakfast for it.

"John, you shouldn't have kept Dr. Robertson up so late," she said.

Said Dr. Robertson:

"Oh, it was quite a blessed time the young brother and I had talking together last night, and I'm thinking we'll neither of us forget it. How about letting the lad go with me for three months through Tunis and Tripoli this winter? I'm sure it would be a wonderful experience for him, and he thinks he could easily make up his schooling afterward by studying hard. We would take good care of him, Mrs. Robertson and I."

Later in the day, walking home from high school John Howard came face to face with Dixie Manton, who rallied him gayly for not being at her party the night before, and invited him to come that night to make up for it.

John Howard shook his head:

"Can't do it, Dix. I'm up to my eyes in work. Got to work like a one-armed paper hanger with fleas from now till Christmas. You see, I've decided to be a missionary, and Dr. Robertson is taking me to Africa the first of the year to see what I'll be up against so I can get ready quicker; and I've got to get ahead in studies or Dad won't let me go."

Said Dixie with a great laugh as if it were the best joke she had ever heard:

"What are you giving us, John Howard? *You* a missionary! Why, you're not the kind of person they make missionaries out of!"

"No, I know it," said John Howard good-naturedly, "but just watch me and see! I've been taken over by a great Trainer, and I'm certainly going to start in on a new line."

"Well," said Dixie with a toss of her pretty little head, "all I've got to say is, you better stay at home and missionarize the people here instead of going to dirty old Africa. There are plenty of heathen over here."

"Yes," said John Howard thoughtfully, "but they've heard the news and it doesn't do them any good. However, I may take your advice while I'm getting ready for Africa, and I'll probably begin on you, Dixie; for now I belong to the Lord, and I mean business, and there are a lot of things I'd like to tell you, no matter if you do laugh! A laugh can't hurt anyone!"

Dixie stared at him puzzled for a minute, and then tossed her head, and tried to laugh again as she went on her way; but her eyes grew strangely sober and thoughtful as she glanced back to see John Howard with his arms full of books and his head held high, going toward his home to get ready to go with the Good News to Africa.

Majority's Hearth

IT was a dull, cold day with a desolate leaden sky for a background and some dirty, slushy pavements for a foreground. Now and then a sharp little flake was flung spitefully from the sullen clouds, and where it fell it stung its life out. The city looked more wicked and heartless than ever this cold November day.

In front of a high board fence which screened a coal yard from the gaze of the passer-by, an old colored man was slowly and apathetically cleaning the sidewalk. He was cold and his movements were deliberate accordingly. Behind him the flaming posters on the fence only served to make his tall gaunt figure look more forlorn. He was old and his hair was almost white. His shoulders were much bent and his black face had a careworn expression as of one who in former years had hoped for much but had been disappointed in all. His clothes were whole, though thin and worn. He was working with an old coal shovel whose many years of usefulness had given it a gnawed appearance about the edges; this did not assist in the work of the morning. There had been a partial thaw the night before and now it had turned cold again and the slush had hardened itself over the sidewalk in such a way as to be extremely difficult of removal. The metal of the shovel twanged and scraped against the stone curbing of the pavement and kept up a mournful chant to the old man's thoughts.

Now and then he rolled his eyes toward the tattered posters on the fence, where bill after bill had been pasted, partially torn off and pasted over again, until now on the same board one might catch glimpses of several generations of gaudily attired women fainting in the arms of various styles of lovers, mingled with heads of elephants, people poised on one toe in mid-air, and touching scenes of all descriptions. But there was a comparatively new poster, in a reasonable state of preservation, which attracted the gaze of George Abraham Wiggins. It represented a cottage room, with a fire upon the hearth. Before the fire in a large chair sat a lady with a ghastly smile upon her face, while several children clung to her dress with troubled faces, gazing after a man's foot which was just disappearing through a door upon the other side of the room.

George Abraham had not looked at the lady in the chair, did not care what was the matter with the children, and did not even notice the man's foot, or the room at all, in fact. His eyes turned again and again to that open fire in the grate. One flame of it had been torn down in a zigzag triangular shape and was waving disconsolately in the air. When George Abraham had finished the first quarter of the sidewalk—he always divided his work into sections on cold mornings to encourage himself—he laid down his shovel on the slippery stone and ambled over to the fence, fumbled carefully about on the lapel of his old coat until he found a bent pin, and then laboriously and tenderly fastened the torn bit of paper back among its rightful environments. He stood a moment and gazed longingly into the tawdry coloring and then turned back to his work with a sigh. Somehow the picture was not satisfying when viewed from a nearer point. He could not imagine the warmth of the blaze quite so well as when standing at a little distance.

He shivered as he began his work again. Nobody noticed him. The passers-by, coat collars turned up to their ears, hands in their pockets, only went straight on, watching the sidewalk a few feet ahead of them. Even a little dog with a well-kept coat and a shiny collar did not glance at the old man, but picked up his small feet quickly to get them off the cold stones, and hastened on. But George Abraham did not notice, he was used to that; he expected nothing else. By and by, as was his custom at his work, he began to hum, and then to sing in a wavering old voice, which, thin and breaking as it was, showed that it must have been rich and full in its time. It was a song he had sung before many times at his work. He sang it now without much expression, rather chanting and groaning it out by force of habit:

> "I 's gwine back to Dixie,
>   N' moah I 's gwine t' wandah,
> My heart 's turned back to Dixie,
>   I can't stay heah no longah;
> I miss de ole plantation, my home, an' my r'lation,
> My heart 's turned back to Dixie
>   An' I mus' go.

> "I 's gwine back to Dixie, I 's gwine back to Dixie,
> I 's gwine whar de orange blossoms grow,
>   Foh I heah de chillun callin', I see de sad tears fallin',
> My heart 's turned back to Dixie,
>   An' I mus' go."

He stopped at the end of the verse and straightened up to look again at the paper fire, glowing and leaping so tantalizingly there on the fence. Then he began to croon once more:

> *"I 's hoed in fiel's o' cotton,*
> *I 's worked 'pon de ribber."*

He stopped suddenly and spoke aloud to himself with a surprised air as if a new thought had suddenly struck him, out of something old and familiar.

"Dat's all true, Jawge Ab'ham, all true! Strange I nebber t'ought o' dat a'foh! Yoh *has* hoed in fiel's o' cotton, an' yoh's done worked on de ribber!"

He began to sing again, curiously feeling his way through the words:

> *"I use to t'ink, ef I got off,*
> *I'd go back dah no nebber."*

"Zackly, Jawge Ab'ham!" he broke in upon himself, "dat's jes' what yoh did use to t'ink!"

He turned to his work again with a meditative air and went on singing:

> *"But time have change' de ole man,*
> *His head am bendin' low,*
> *His heart 's turned back to Dixie*
> *An' he mus' go!"*

He stopped with a sudden jerk and straightened up as these last words were quavered out, throwing down his shovel with a clang and looking straight at the lady in the chair by the fire.

"Yas," he said, addressing her, "dat am jes' what have been de mattah wid Jawge Ab'ham all dese yeahs. His heart 's done turn back to Dixie an' he mus' go. I 's gwine right off 's quick 's I kin git ready," and he picked up his shovel and worked away with a will, making the clanging notes of the iron and stone sound to quicker time than they had done for many a day, and while he worked he planned. There was a new joy in his face. Somehow the people that passed him were attracted to look again, and the shining of the old black face gave the first bit of brightness which had gleamed in that street that morning. The sidewalk was finished with more than his usual care and it was done with much more alacrity.

Now and again he turned his eyes to the fireplace on the fence, but with a less hopeless look than before. When he had finished his work he paused before it once more and looked a sort of parting, then started to go, half paused, and turned back again. New impulses were stirring in the old man's heart. He had not had so many new thoughts since he was a young man. With a hesitation and a stealthy glance about, which were new to him, he carefully removed the torn bit of paper blaze from the fence, then, as he folded it quickly and placed it his pocket, looked ruefully at the dismantled hearth with that yawning gap in the fire. However a face of a little red demon from the paper beneath glared through the opening at the woman in the chair, which she seemed to like fully as well as the red and yellow blaze, so he went on his way with a tolerably comfortable conscience. He chuckled to himself as he went along, giving occasional pats to the paper in his pocket. His shovel was over his shoulder and he shambled with a sprightlier gait than he had used for years.

"Jawge Ab'ham, yoh jes' bettah quit wuk ride now, 'cause yoh got a ride smart lot o' tings to tend to 'foh yoh go. Yoh jes' hab to stop in 'n tell de jedge he don' need git yoh all any moh wuk."

Suiting the action to the word he presently brought up in front of an office, and, after shuffling his feet about on a wornout hole in the center of a mat for a few seconds, entered the room, taking off his hat and bowing low to a benevolent-looking old gentleman.

"Mohnin', Jedge, mohnin'!" he said with much deference, "I 's jes' callin' to say I 's mightily 'bliged to yoh, but yoh need'n' take no moh trubble 'bout findin' wuk. I 's 'bout to leab dis year part ob de country."

The old gentleman looked over his glasses with a smile of surprise that pleased George Abraham immensely.

"Why, you don't say so, George! That's pretty sudden, isn't it?"

"Yas, sah; yas, sah," said the old man with a chuckle, "reckon 'tis, sah. Sudden, sah, but my min's made up. Got my 'rangements 'bout made, sah!"

"You don't say so!" reiterated the judge. "Well, I'm sorry to hear it but I hope you'll have a pleasant journey. When are you going?"

"Well, sah," began the old man cautiously, looking thoughtfully out of the window at the little flakes which were coming down thicker now and promising to be quite a storm, "I ca'c'late I 's gwine 'bout t'-morrah." The sentence was brought out with a triumphant flourish intended to astonish the judge, but he only took up the morning paper and said:

"So soon? Ah! Well, good-by to you. I wish you well, George."

When the interview was ended and the old man again started toward home he felt as though he were much nearer the desired Dixie than before he had entered that office, for had he not confided his purpose to some one, and had he not already begun to say good-by?

It was a forlorn little cottage which he called home. The tan-colored paint was worn and dirty and the green blinds were mostly off or had a broken, discouraged look. The floor of the small porch was warped in places and the snow was gathering there, getting ready to warp it more. One step was a little loose and shaky, and bent under the weight of George Abraham as he went up to the door. The key was left inside the broken blind for him. His son's wife had gone out to wash and had taken the baby and the youngest boy along. The rest of the children were in school. Eliza had cleared up the room pretty well before she left, though the door was half open into a dismal bedroom beyond, where an unmade bed yawned amid heaps of ragged garments, thrown just where they happened. On the table in the kitchen was a plate with two cold boiled potatoes, a very small bit of cold bacon, and a loaf of corn bread. These had been set out for George Abraham's dinner. The stove with its fire had gone to sleep. The ashes lay grim and cold upon the hearth, and the rusty iron top gave forth no pervading warmth. The old man walked to the stove and held his shivering body up straighter, spreading out his fingers to see if there was just a little heat left, then mournfully shook his head. The prudent woman had been much too careful to leave a spark of fire when she went away for the day.

"Dis yer kine of 'rangement ain't no kine of 'rangement fer gettin' wahm. De ain't gwine stan' no show 'tall 'side o' de fiahplaces down Souf. Jes' wait till I get to Dixie."

The old man shivered with delight and threw back his head, laughing, as though he already felt the warmth from some old cabin chimney place. He put his hand into his pocket and cautiously drew out his precious fire-picture, feasting his eyes upon it a moment or two. Then he made a fire, throwing in chips and shavings with a prodigality that would have horrified his frugal daughter-in-law.

"It take a mighty powahful lot o' stuff to make a fiah in dis yer black hole 'rangement," he muttered, as he knelt to blow a sickly flame into life.

After as good a fire as could be procured was roaring in the rusty cook stove, George Abraham looked about the room and his eyes rested upon his noonday repast. Although it wanted a good two hours and a half to the earliest possible dinner time, still he felt the pangs of hunger keenly, for the sidewalk had been hard work and the excitement of his thoughts had helped to erase from his mind the memories of a not over-bountiful breakfast.

After a moment's consultation with himself he decided to take his dinner immediately, for there were many things to be done in preparation for his journey, which he could better do if the cravings of his stomach were satisfied. With a stealthy look at the windows to make sure that no little black heads adorned with pigtails were peering in at him, he seated himself at the table and prepared to enjoy his meal. As he ate he mused:

"Dis yer house ain't no place for Jawge Ab'ham, now de cold wedder am comin' on; Liza, she ain't no ways pahshall to hevin' yoh stay; Joe 's off, an' he won't cah, I don't reckon; de chillun dees too little to cah, an' so I'll jes' slip off an' not say a wohd. It'll come mighty hahd to leave dem little pickaninnies, but I 's made up my min' an' I mus' go!"

He half chanted the last words waving his fork aloft with a piece of cold potato stuck on it on the way to his mouth.

"Reckon I might sen' fer dem pickaninnies some o' dese yer days, p'raps. Anyhow dat ole stove an' I can't stan' nudder wintah togedder nohow yoh put it. I 's gwine whar de fiah is in great monst'ous fiahplaces, an' de has chimblies to set in an' smoke, like my ole mammy's. *Wa'nt* dem hoecakes good when de come out de ashes? I 's gwine have some first ting I gits dah," and he laughed aloud, putting down both knife and fork and leaning back in his chair better to enjoy the thought. Then the business part of the affair came uppermost and he sobered down again.

"How 's yoh gwine git dah, Jawge Ab'ham? Yoh ain't got no money to buy yoh ticket, 'cept de money fer yoh buryin'. Yoh's a good 'spec'ble niggah, Jawge Ab'ham, an' I don't want to hev yoh goin' back on all yoh ole frien's princ'ples and preceps. Yoh's ben tole time an' 'gin dat it ain't no way to do not to lay by money to be buried good an' 'spec'ble. Yoh know Jedge Lawrence, he say so, an' dat odder white man yoh wuk foh, an' Joe 'n' Lize, *especially,* dey say so. Now, *how's* yoh gwine git back to Dixie when all de money yoh got am in dat ole rag on de top shelf ob yoh closet in buryin' money?"

The old man brought down the front legs of his chair which had been raised in the air during the main portion of the meal, and with a thump and a shuffle straightened out his legs under the table, his head drooping forward, his whole body taking the attitude of deep thought. The question evidently was a poser and stunned him for a moment.

"I jes' tell yoh wha' 'tis," he said, raising his head after a moment, "I don' see no use totin' buryin' money all roun' de country. I wouldn't want de 'sponsibility of dat ar rag o' money what ain't my own to use, cause ef it's buryin' money it's like it ain't my own. An' I don't wan' leab dat money 'hind me 'cause Lize might not like hevin' de bodder o' takin' care o't, I jes' make a 'ves'ment ob dat ar money in a railroad ticket, dat's what I 's gwine do! Ef it pays den I gits buried with two ho'ses 'stead o' one, an' ef de 'ves'ment don' pay, den tain't my fault. I 's done de bes' I knows how. Anyhow, I 's gwine souf, and I ain' gwine let a little mattah like gittin' buried stan' in my way, not so long's I 's Jawge Ab'ham Wiggins!"

With this sudden determination he finished the last mouthful of corn bread and arose from the table. Having settled the question of finances he felt easier. After a little more deliberation he found no reason in his mind why he should put off his journey until the next day. He had just eaten a full meal which was more than he could expect again for some hours to come. Indeed he could not be sure that there would be anything so good in the house again for several days as that bit of cold bacon had been. Eliza might object to his departure, or something might turn up, especially if any one should suspect that he meant to take his burying money to pay for his trip. It would be better to slip quietly off without any formal leave taking. So he tied up his few possessions in a bundle, and taking his small hoard of money from its place on the dusty shelf, he bade a hasty farewell to the dismal little house and took his departure.

Through the city he hastened once more, not minding the cold this time, or the snow which was driving thick and fast. Warmth was in his heart and he cared not how cold the winter grew if he was going out of it; going to a land where hoecakes came at every meal and where flapjacks were a plenty; where the fires always glowed on wide-open hearths and where he should grow young again.

The matter of a railroad ticket was a little difficult to settle, inasmuch as his destination was uncertain, but with the assistance of a kindly disposed railroad official he finally decided upon a through ticket to Jacksonville, having first questioned anxiously whether he would be allowed to get off from the train if he should wish to, before his ticket was used up. The clerk assured him that he could get off as soon as he pleased, provided he did not get back on again, and so the ticket was bought and paid for, and he found that from the burying money there was a little left, enough to justify him in laying in a small store of eatables. Some crackers and sausage were finally purchased with a few other little dainties, and he sat down with an air of pride to wait three hours for his train. He had often passed through that waiting room and looked with awe and wonder upon the people who lounged about with such an air of indifference to wait for their trains, as though a journey were an everyday affair. Now here he was himself—his clothes in the bundle at his side, his best tall hat that the judge had given him, upon his head, his ticket in his pocket—waiting for a train like any of them. He watched the comers and goers for an hour or so, until it suddenly occurred to him that some one who knew him might come in and see him, and even yet, with his ticket bought, he might be stopped from going. After that there was no more rest for him, though he changed his seat to the darkest corner of the room and sat behind a pillar. Every time the door opened he started up with a sudden jerk and cautiously peeped around the pillar to see if Eliza had come or sent any of the children. Perhaps the kitchen fire had not been out and the house would burn up and Eliza would say it was his fault. Oh, why had he not thought of the fire before he left the house? It would be dreadful to be called back now. But time went on and at last the great man who called out the trains appeared at the door and shouted, "Passengers for the south take the train to the right. Train leaves in fifteen minutes!"

There was a rush and a bustle and every one started for the door as if the train were already moving, and poor old George Abraham hastily picked up his bundle with fingers that were numb with cold and anxiety, and speedily got himself into the thickest of the crowd, for he felt sure that fifteen minutes would be up and the cars gone before he could get out of the door.

He was in the train at last and wondering why it did not move, dreading yet the apparition of the dauntless Eliza or some of her children, and drawing a long sigh of relief when the whistle blew, the train began to move, and they were at last whirling—actually *whirling*—out of the city. There was only exultation in his heart as he watched the familiar streets pass him swiftly by and realized that he was bidding adieu to them perhaps forever. His eye caught a facsimile of the poster he had studied so carefully that morning, as they rushed by a fence, and it made his heart leap with a feeling of joy that he was really started on his way to a great fireplace somewhere, where he was to get warm and enjoy himself.

He began to croon over a verse of his favorite song as the spires of the city grew dim and snow-covered fields came into view:

"I 's trabblin' back to Dixie;
  My step am slow an' feeble:
I pray de Lawd to he'p me,
  An' lead me from al ebil;
But should my strength fohsake me
Den kin' frien's come an' take me,
My heart's turned back to Dixie,
    An' I mus' go."

The rumble of the train covered the low quavering notes and so the old man remained entirely unnoticed, as the short cloudy day drew near its close and the night began to shut down.

He took a lively interest in all that went on about him. When the lamps were lighted and smoked away in dimness he leaned his head back against the cushions and stared up at them and marveled at this palace on wheels which was rushing along so fast, bearing him to his own dear land once more. There was no thought of past hardships, or whippings or harsh words, scanty fare and separations. Only the dear cabin home, the orange blossoms, the sunny skies, and the shining black face of his old mother came to cheer his heart. He was so lost in his reflections that the surly conductor had to give him a rough shake before he was sufficiently roused to present his precious ticket to be punched.

"It ain't gwine make no diff'unce to yoh all ef I 's gwine git off some place 'long de road, is it, Gin'ral?" he asked politely, touching his tall rusty hat with the air of a gentleman.

"I don't care where you get off. Pay your fare, it's all the same to me," was the rough reply as the conductor passed on.

But the old man was relieved and leaned back in his seat with the air of a king.

George Abraham slept peacefully that night with the

roar and rush of the train in his ears. The cries of the babies who from time to time sojourned in the car did not disturb him, but perhaps only brought to his remembrance the favorite lines:

> *"I heah de chillun callin'*
> *I see de sad tears fallin'."*

The first day on the train was passed in a sort of blissful dream. George Abraham watched every bit of landscape with an artist's eye. He looked upon his fellow pilgrims with a benevolent air. He ate sausage and crackers and cheese and drank cindered ice water from the rusty tin cup with as much relish as though they had been nectar and ambrosia, and he smiled and touched his hat to all the conductors and brakemen as though they had been angels conducting him to heaven. He grew somewhat weary however, with long sitting in cramped positions and began to wish for the end of his journey. During the second day he kept his eye out at all the little villages, towns, and cities they passed, but none quite suited him. He wanted the far south. He was not content with any halfway place. There were no open doors revealing wide fireplaces as yet. His ticket was growing shorter and shorter, and his heart began to fail him lest after all he would not find the place of his desire.

It was growing dusky among the pine and the air was quite cool and damp as they approached a large town in the South. For some hours the soil had been growing sandier and was dotted over with sharp, faded palmettos, with here and there a baby pine-tassel of a tree setting up housekeeping for itself. They had passed several cypress swamps with their tangle of wild vines and old gray moss, and the old man strained his eyes to watch for each indication of the beloved southland he used to call home. He had kept very much to himself for the most part for he still had a guilty feeling as of a boy who had run away from home, and therefore he had made few acquaintances during the journey. In fact his traveling companions had not been of the sort with whom he cared to make intimate friends. Therefore he was feeling somewhat lonely and forlorn as night drew on and there was yet no prospect of a home. The train began to move more slowly as they entered the town and the houses ceased their dizzy flight past the windows.

The old man with his worn face pressed against the car window was peering eagerly through the gloom. There was desolation everywhere. A misty, driving rain was setting in, spreading a haze over the landscape. Suddenly there flickered across the lacework of tiny drops on his window, a light, bright and warm. It caught in every drop and made the window shine like a sheet of crystal, and it shone on the tired black face and brought hope once more to the poor old heart. It was only a little cabin home across the road from the track, where the door stood ajar and the light from a great open fire came brightly out to gladden the dreariness of the surroundings. Nearer and slower the train moved, and George Abraham's breath came quick and fast as he watched the spot of brightness. The train halted just in front of this bit of a home so that the old man had a good view.

It was a tiny, square, shantylike dwelling, with a wide door above two small steps, and one window. Inside there was no light save that splendid fire, but the chimney, which was built on the outside of the house of mud and sticks, was an immense affair covering nearly the whole end of the little room, and the flames leaped up with a joyous freedom to meet the outside air. Moving about in that bright little room, standing occasionally in front of the fire, then disappearing again into the gloom, was a dark figure. Presently, just as the train halted, it came to the door and stood with hands on hips and elbows akimbo, looking out. A woman of ample proportions she was, dressed in something dark and exceedingly classic in its drapery, with a handkerchief crossed over her broad shoulders and another knotted into a picturesque turban. That was the way it appeared to the passengers in the train. A nearer view would have shown the dress to be calico, old and faded, and made by a pattern whose object seemed to have been the saving of labor rather than the fit of the garment. But viewed in this misty light with the glare of the fire behind and the little square cabin for a setting, it was an exceedingly pleasant picture. To the sad eyes of George Abraham it was a view into paradise. He looked and looked, and seemed unable to take his eyes away from the spot. Indeed he could hardly think, and he was only roused to consciousness by the sound of the whistle and the lurch of the train as it began to get into motion once more. Then he started to his feet, clutched his bundle with one hand, jammed his high hat on and held it with the other, and started for the door as fast as his cramped limbs would carry him.

Several men were in the aisle and obstructed his passage, so that by the time he had reached the door of the car the train was under pretty rapid motion.

"Hy'ar!" he called excitedly, shaking off the detaining hand of a brakeman which was laid upon his arm, "I 's gwine git off heah. Dis yer 's my place."

Then as his face was struck by the outer air rushing quickly past and he realized at what a rate of speed the train was moving, he became fairly frantic and turned beseeching eyes upon the man.

"Can't yoh stop dis yer train jes' a minute? I 's *got* to git off at dis yer place. De man in de depoe tol' me I could git off whah I like. I 's got to git off heah!" and with a determined look he made one more plunge toward the car steps.

"This ain't the staion, you old idiot you!" said the brakeman angrily, jerking him back with so much force that he sat plump down in the lap of the neighbor who occupied the seat by the stove, much to that individual's disgust. "You can get off at this place if you want to, but you've got to wait till we get to the station. It's about half a mile down." And with that the brakeman planted himself in front of the closed door with his back to the old man.

Hastily rising from the seat into which he had been so suddenly precipitated, George Abraham bent himself over to the window and watched as long as he could see, the faint glow from that cabin hearth, and wondered if the train would carry him so far away that he could never find that place again. It seemed hours to him before it once more halted. He made his way out eagerly, the first one from the car, and turned his steps back up the track without stopping a moment to look about him, fearful lest he should lose his way. His feet, and whole body indeed, were stiff and lame, and the sand along the track was not easy to walk in. The half mile back seemed long and it was growing quite dark when he again saw the glow of the fire flickering across his path. With slow, painful steps he dragged himself up to the door of the cabin. No thought had he save that this fire was meant for him. It was for this that he had come so long a distance, and to this he would go and get warm and dry. What would come after he did not know. The woman who owned this home and this hearth did not enter into his calculation at all, except as she made a pleasant home-like accompaniment to the fire, and was in a dreamy way connected with possible hoecakes. But George Abraham was tired, lame, cold, and hungry. He could not be said to have thought about anything since he had seen that fire. His one desire was to get to it.

The lady of the mansion had left the room for a few minutes apparently, for there was no one in sight as he reached the door. The fire was leaping and glowing in a most enticing manner, saying as plainly as a fire could say:

"Come, and I will warm you; come, and I will cheer you." And George Abraham, tired and worn and cold as he was, came.

He crept to the fireside and stood looking to his heart's content, at the great soft flames as they chased one another gleefully up the chimney, pushing upward and onward the lazy blue smoke that curved and curled gracefully, caring not much whether its course lay by the way of the chimney or by the room of the house. He held his old hands up to the pleasant warmth, and shuddered as he thought of the cold pavement those hands had worked so hard to clean but a few days before. He remembered the bit of paper blaze in his pocket, too, and almost with scorn. Ah! This fire was so much better than that. *This* was a *fire!*

He had not had time to get used to the fire nor to feel the aching void in the region of his stomach, and wonder why the hoecakes were not forthcoming along with the fire, when the mistress of all this luxury appeared.

She was a stout black woman of perhaps fifty years of age, though of that one could hardly judge. Her frame was large and she had a ponderous tread like an elephant, as she rolled from side to side carrying her head with a masterful poise and her ample chest in a self-respecting attitude. The loose folds of her short gown followed her majestically as she rolled along, and the sharp points of her red turban waved and trembled with the motion. Her face was as black as ebony and her eyes large, with enormous whites, which helped the great white teeth to light up the dusky face. She came in with a package in her hand which she carried as easily as if it had been a feather, and she was quite inside her own door before she noticed the intruder standing by the fire. She stopped and, placing her hands on her hips, package and all, stood still and rolled her great white eyes at him for almost a full minute. George Abraham turned to look at her and for the first time since he had entered the cabin he realized that it did not belong to him; that, in short, he was a wanderer upon the face of the earth, with no home, no friends, and scarcely any money.

"What yoh doin' hy'ar?" demanded the astonished mistress of the house; "jes' yoh git ride 'long out'n hy'ar, yoh good-for-nothin' niggah yoh!"

The old man stood still with a dazed expression. To have found paradise and enjoyed several minutes of it, and then to be ordered out in this sudden manner was too much for humanity. He made no motion, but looked at her with a piteous gaze. It must have had some softening effect for she demanded again in a less harsh voice,

"Who is yoh! Whah d' yoh from? What yoh doin' thah, anyway?"

George Abraham's tongue found words and he said in a conciliatory tone, "I 's jes' gwine git wahm, ma'am! I ain't gwine do no hahm!"

"Laws! I never did see nothin' jes' like dat!" exclaimed the lady of the house after an astonished pause, then, "Whah d' yoh come from, yoh say? You lib 'roun' hy'ar?"

"I comes f'om de No'f!" answered George Abraham with a low bow.

"O shoo now! You can't fool dis niggah, you nebber come f'om de No'f. You jes' bettah git ride outen dis yer house, foh I ain't gwine have no moh nonsense roun' hy'ar." And she took a heavy step toward him and stood in a belligerent attitude.

Over George Abraham's face there swept a look of indignation mingled with despair. He was faint and weary and knew not where to go, moreover it was too much to have one's respectability thus doubted. Straightening himself with a dignified mien, and bringing up with a mighty flourish the hand holding the tall silk hat which had been concealed behind his back, he bowed a grave important salute to the woman and said, in tones which might have fitted old Judge Lawrence himself, so full of haughty self-importance were they:

"I 's gwine go ride away ef yoh say so, ma'am, but I ain't gwine hab no niggah, No'f or Souf, tell me I lies. I 's as 'spec'able a pusson as dar is in de city ob Noo Yo'k. I 's jes' come to de Souf foh little jouhney, an' I 's lookin' round fer a place I likes to lib in. I 's ben in de city ob Noo Yo'k foh yeahs, eber since befoh de wah. I 's made up my min' dat de Souf am bettah for my healf, an' so I 's come down. I jes' see yoh fiah when de cyah pass de doh, an' I make up my min' dat dis yer place am de place foh me, an' findin' no one hy'ar I come in. Dis yer fiahplace am jes' prezackly like de one whah my ole mammy cooked de hoecakes foh me when I was leetle pickaninny, an' my heart been a achin' an' a longin' to see one an' git wahm by de light ob one all dese yeahs, an' dat's what brung dis niggah back to Dixie.

"'My heart 's turned back to Dixie an' I mus' go.'"

He finished the sentence in a slow quavering chant, waving his long body from side to side keeping time with the words, and raising his hand with the silk hat in it once more to make it impressive.

The black woman was evidently impressed though she was not quite ready to admit it. Some fear and resentment for the cool possession the stranger had taken of her house and fireside still remained, but they were mingled with feelings of pity and sympathy, and a love of romance which was fast getting the better of her.

"What's yoh name, yoh crazy niggah yoh?" she asked in a half-relenting tone.

"Jawge Ab'ham Wiggins," he replied with a low bow, showing all his teeth. Then as she still stood in the same attitude, saying nothing except the simple ejaculation, "Law!" he went on in an explanatory tone: "Jawge, after

Jawge Wash'n'ton, de greatest man who hab ebber libed in dis whole country; Ab'ham, after Ab'ham Link'um, de *great* Ab'ham Link'um, yoh know. I see him once, jes' foh de wah close. An' aftah dat some folks say I gettin' to look like Link'um, so I jes' up an took dat name, Ab'ham, an' eve'ybody say it was mighty good name. Foh dat I use t' be call Jawge Wash'n'ton, but now I 's Jawge Ab'ham. I 's called Wiggins aftah de ole massa whah I was foh I went up No'f."

George Abraham was growing quite voluble, but the pangs of hunger began to assert themselves and he suddenly collapsed from his dignified straightness and said in a rather weak voice: "Yoh all ain't got no cawn bread nor nothin' round de house has yoh? I 's powah'ful hungry, an' I don jes' know whah de rest'ram is."

The last scruple of the woman was overcome. Her code of etiquette was not quite so strict as her dusky northern sister's would have been. She considered herself to have had sufficient introduction to the stranger within her four walls. Indeed she was almost persuaded that he might be an angel unawares. She straightway drew a chair, the best she had, to the fireside, and with a majestic wave of her ponderous arm said: "Sid down, sah, I'll git yoh some suppah."

She put another great stick on the fire and rolled around on her heavy feet preparing the meal. George Abraham watched her as though she had been some fairy creature, while she hung a great black kettle on a curious arrangement over the blaze, and did some mysterious baking in the hot ashes. His old heart warmed with recollections.

"What's yoh name?" he asked suddenly as a marvelous brown cake appeared from the ashes, giving forth an odor delicious. "Pears like yoh mus' be a 'lation ob my ole mammy's. She used t' make cakes jes' like dat ar!"

"I 's M'jority Wash'n'ton," said the woman straightening up from her bent position and putting her hands on her ample hips to look at her guest.

"M'jority Wash'n'ton—Wash'n'ton!" he repeated in amazed delight. "I knowed it. I knowed we's 'lations. What d' I tell yoh? Wash'n'ton! Didn't I tell yoh my name war Wash'n'ton foh I took de name ob Ab'ham?"

The lady did not quite seem to understand the relationship, but she showed her white teeth and chuckled appreciatively. In due time the supper was ready and the two sat down to a more sumptuous repast than old George Abraham had tasted for many a year. They ate heartily, conversing meanwhile, and then the old man following Majority's directions, shambled out to find lodgings near by. He lingered at the gate first to say a voluble thanks for the welcome he had received, promising to let her know immediately what were his plans.

As soon as he was out of sight an emaciated old neighbor of Majority's hobbled in to find out all about it, having watched the parting at the gate from her own doorstep with a good deal of curiosity and not a little disapproval.

"Who dat man come way f'om heah, 'Jority?" she asked as she entered the door and viewed the table still uncleared.

She was a thin old woman, like Majority very black, but with an unhappy face, worn and bony. Her eyes had a sharp, disagreeable look in them, and her enormously thick lips were rolled well apart always with goodly display of toothless gums. There were a few crinkled threads of gray among the woolly tails of her head. Her nose had a dissatisfied turn to it and curiosity stuck out all over her face.

Majority was evidently prepared for an onslaught of this kind for she replied to the question without any hesitation, and with a majestic condescension in her voice: "Dat ar man am a frien' ob mine f'om Noo Yo'k. A kind ob 'lation ob mine. He's berry nice man, visitin' de Souf. He's tinkin' ob settlin' heah'bouts. He might like to buy yoh house,

Mis' Lovett, ef he tink it good 'nouf," and with this sharp speech she sailed over to the fire and gave it a tremendous poking, after which she attacked the table and cleared it off. Her guest meanwhile was too much overcome with these statements to make any reply at first, but after her astonishment had worn away she roused herself sufficiently to mutter angrily, "Dat ar house ob mine's plenty good 'nuf foh any niggah, f'om Noo Yo'k or anywhah else, 'f I want to sell it, but I ain't gwine to. Not to any stuck-up niggah f'om de No'f, I ain't!"

With that she hobbled back to her own door in indignation, leaving Majority alone in her glory, feeling twice as important over the fact that she had been entertaining company. There was going to be a certain *éclat* about it which would set her up amazingly among her neighbors. Majority liked it and resolved to invite the old man to dinner the next day, which she did. With many chuckles of delight he accepted the invitation, and it was not many days before he was more at home in the little cabin by the fireside than ever he had been in his son's kitchen in New York.

George Abraham found work little by little, odd jobs here and there, enough to keep him from day to day, not much besides. Occasionally he laid aside a five-cent piece in the old rag when his conscience troubled him about the burying money, but that was not often, for he found life too comfortable in this new land to be very sorry he had come, even for conscience' sake. To be sure he lived in a desolate little hole of a room, but then what did it matter where one lived so long as one could spend the evenings by a pleasant fire with an agreeable companion?

Truth to tell, this fireside was rapidly becoming a necessity to old George Abraham's happiness, and he shortly began to cast about in his mind how he might make it his own. Money would buy one like it if he worked hard, and for a few days he worked as hard as he was able, but then the thought of a desolate hearth with none to enjoy it but himself did not seem a bright prospect and he meditated upon another plan.

"Mis' Wash'n'ton," he said one evening as they sat beside the fire. There had been a long talk during which George Abraham had given a full account of his own history together with that of several of his friends and relations, and Mrs. Washington had told most minutely about her own life, the death of her husband and two children, the burning of her house, the subscription paper passed about by herself among the townspeople and many strangers who were there, and finishing with an account of her life in the present cabin up to the time George Abraham appeared upon the scene. This appearance, she admitted, was a pleasant relief to the monotony of life.

"Mis' Wash'n'ton," he began again clearing his throat and moving his hands up and down before the blaze, "I has a prop'sishun to p'opose to yoh. Yoh see," here he raised the forefinger of his right hand and touched it eloquently with the thumb of his left, "yoh hy'ar is lonesome an' so 's I. Yoh ain't got no man to take cah yoh, an' I ain't no woman to git my meals. Yoh see," he passed to the second finger of his right hand here, and turning his head a little more toward her went on without looking up, "when I was mahried de fust time,—dat is,—when I was *mah*ried, Sally was a gal without any sense 't all, and she didn't wan' t' stay t' home an' cook, an' she war mighty young an' on'sperienced. Co'se she knowed how to do tings, but den she didn't seem to take no kind ob signature ob de fac' dat I want tings jes' right. Aftah she die I look round a spell, but I cou'd'n' seem to see no one bettah 'n she'd ben, an' so I went to lib with my son Joseph Jeff'son. He's mighty smaht man, Joseph Jeff'son is, but his wife Lize's no count. She kin' wuk well 'nuf, but she ain't no kind ob comp'ny. But now, 'Jority, ef I could a foun' yoh, I'd a jes' up'n mahried right smart quick."

With a satisfied chuckle he passed to the third finger and began under another head.

"M'jority, now, see," and he leaned forward and looked at her closely as she sat with her large arms folded peacefully over her ample proportions, and her luminous eyes fixed full upon him, while a broad grin was on the eve of lighting up her face, "'spose we gits mahried, yoh an' me." He stopped and leaned further forward eagerly watching her face.

Majority considered the question a moment, then she said in a calm deliberate tone, "Is yoh Meth'dis' or Bap'tis', Mistah Wiggins? 'Cause ef yoh's Bap'tis' I ain't right suah 'bout it. Yoh see Mistah Wash'n'ton was Bap'tis' and we never git 'long jes' right 'bout goin' to chu'ch. Dem Bap'tis' down hy'ar is dredful on'ligious-minded folks, an' I don't tink I could stan' one ob dem roun'."

"Oh, I 's Meth'dis'," answered George Abraham hastily, edging his chair a little closer to hers, and then he fairly held his breath with expectation as Majority considered.

"Wal, Mistah Wiggins," said Majority and then, mindful of the curious neighbor, she arose and closed the cabin door before she finished her remark.

They settled it between themselves behind that closed door, and George Abraham went to his lodgings with joy in his heart. This was the last night he would spend in the little forlorn room that had been his resting place since he came to the South. He arose quite early the next morning and began to make inquiries for a minister from the North. At last he found one.

"Will yoh mahry me jes' like you mahry white folks?" he inquired anxiously of the good man, "cause I 's f'om de No'f an' I 's used to no'th'n ways, an' I wants tings all right. Dat's why I come to yoh, 'cause I tink yoh knows how bettah. I 's f'om Noo Yo'k, sah!"

The clergyman assured him that he should be married after the most approved method.

"Well, sah, now I has 'noder question to perpound, sah. How much is dis yer business gwine to cos' me? I got t' know b'fo han' so 's see 'f I kin 'ford it."

"Cost you, my friend? Why nothing unless you choose."

"No, sah!" said George Abraham emphatically shaking his head. "I ain't no objec' ob charity. I 's good 'spec'able niggah, an' I wants to git mahried like white folks, an' I 's willin' to pay de cos' pervided 't ain't moh 'n I kin 'ford."

"But, my dear sir, there is no charge for marrying people. You can give what you like."

"No, sah. I wants de price stated. I 's gwine know befo'han' how much dis yer business gwine cos'. What 's de price?"

The minister was unable to get rid of the proud old man until he had stated a sum to be paid down at the close of the wedding ceremony, and although it was exceedingly small, George Abraham's conscience again troubled him as he counted it out from the hoarded five-cent pieces in his "buryin' rag."

It would be hard work to support a wife and replace all that money, but it must be done, now all the more, for it would never do to leave Majority to bury him with her own money.

The happy pair took a wedding trip in the one street car the town afforded, going to the limit of the road and back for five cents, two more bits of burying money paying their fare; after which gayeties, they came home to eat an unusually fine corn cake baked in the ashes, and to sit beside their own fire and talk over their new-found bliss.

Three years of happy life passed over the little cabin home in the southland. The master of the house took great delight in his new possessions. The small dooryard was neatly kept and two oleander trees stood on either side of the gate. The few boards that formed a path from the gate to the steps were bordered with periwinkles nodding gaily.

The rickety fence became a mass of Cherokee roses. The house itself had changed its weatherbeaten hue for an honest coat of thick whitewash and made a good setting for Majority's dark smiling face as she sat on the doorstep at her work. She never went out washing as in former times, nor out to do a day's work. She had become more respectable. She had a husband to "s'poaht" her now, and she only took in washings from a few rich tourists. These washings George Abraham always went after, for his pride would not allow his wife to go, and he dressed for the occasion in the starchiest white shirt and collar he owned and brushed his rusty silk hat till it shone almost with pristine brightness. He bowed low to the ladies when he asked for "de washin', ma'am, ef yoh please," until the ladies declared that they felt as if he were conferring a great favor upon them to be willing to carry it, and wished he would be a little less magnificent; it seemed like giving their washing to a minister or college professor.

The burying money had all been collected by hard labor, and given into Majority's keeping, consequently George Abraham could once more hold up his head with "de 'spectables," as he said. But the old man was growing feebler. A day's work tired him and though he was always ready to chuckle over the least little thing when he came in, Majority could see that he sat more quietly of an evening in his corner of the chimney, than he had done the first few months after their marriage. He sang often, now, his favorite song about Dixie. Majority had not heard it much until recently.

As the days grew shorter and cooler and occasionally there came quite a cold snap for Florida, the old man was to be found more and more by the fireside, where Majority kept a good fire for him all day long. Here he would sit bent over toward the blaze, crooning to himself. Sometimes he varied the favorite song with other plantation melodies. One that he often sang was:

> *I 's gwine lay down my life f' my Lawd,*
>   *Foh my Lawd, foh my Lawd,*
> *I 's gwine lay down my life f' my Lawd,*
>   *One o' dees maw'nin's, bright an' fair,*
>   *Put on m' wings an' try de air.*
> *I 's gwine lay down my life f' my Lawd,*
>   *F' my Law-aw-awd, f' my Lawd,*
> *I 's gwine lay down my life f' my Lawd.*
>   *Way down yon'er 'bout twelve o'clock,*
>   *Place my foot on de solid rock,*
> *I 's gwine lay down my life f' my Lawd.*

He would chant this over by the hour till Majority was wrought to a high pitch of excitement and she would sometimes join in the singing.

But one morning George Abraham did not arise from his bed. He said he did not feel just right and he guessed he would lie still. Majority built up the fire so that the brightness would reach over to the bedside, and he lay all day watching her at her work. But when the next day came and he felt no more like getting up, his wife began to be troubled. Day after day went by and still the old man lay there; quiet, contented, happy, singing his songs, it is true, and talking a little to her. Every day the voice grew weaker and the talking less. More and more he dwelt on the verse,

> *One o' dees mawn'in's, bright an' fair,*
> *Put on m' wings an' try de air.*

One day he said to his wife, "M'jority, yoh reckon dey has fiahplaces in heaben?"

"What foh yoh ask dat?" asked his wife sharply, looking at him suspiciously, and then with her tone growing more gentle she added: "Yoh don't feel bad, does yoh, Jawge Ab'ham? 'Cause ef yoh does I 's gwine hab de doctah."

And the doctor came soon but shook his head, left a little medicine, and went away.

Majority hovered about her husband, doing this and that for his comfort, making unnumbered dishes to tempt him, but he seemed not to be able to touch them. Her black face wore a dull hopeless look as day after day he only grew weaker and his voice more faint.

"M'jority," he said one day, "yoh 's ben a good wife, yoh has. I don't jes' 'zac'ly know what I'd a done ef yoh hadn't a mahried me an' ef yoh hadn't took me in to yoh fiah dat fust night I come. I 's enjoyed yoh an' dat fiah mos' monst'ously, an' I reckon it'll be hahd to leab, but I sort o' seem to feel I 's got my call. My heart 's set on gwine to de heabenly home, an' I can't seem to git it 'way. I'm glad de buryin' money 's all right. Las' night I hear dat song a goin' ober an' ober in my head 'bout Dixie, jes' like it did foh I come down hy'ar, only t'war all diffunt. I seem to say:

> "I 's gwine home to heaben,
>   No moah I 's gwine to wandah,
> My heart's turned home to heaben,
>   I can't stay heah no longah,
> Foh time hab changed de ole man,
>   His head am bendin' low,
> His heart's turned home to heaben,
>   An' he mus' go.

> "I 's trabblin' home to heaben,
>   My step am slow an' feeble,
> I pray de Lawd to help me
>   An' lead me from all ebil;
> But should my strength fohsake me
> Den kine angels come an' take me,
> My heart's turned home to heaben,
>   An' I mus' go.

"I 's gwine home to heaben, I 's gwine home to heaben,
I 's gwine whah de orange blossoms grow,
   Foh I heah de angels callin'
   An' I heah King Jesus callin',
My heart's turned home to heaben,
   An' I mus' go."

And with the last words of the song lingering on his lips the old man died.

A Fair Foreclosure

THE thills dropped with a dull wooden reverberation on the hard earth, and the old horse stalked toward the barn with his head down. He was weary, and the thought of oats was good.

The sound of his heavy hoofs on the worn barn floor echoed alternately with the clanking of the harness-buckles that hung about him.

He waited patiently in the stall until the old man took the harness off and hung it on the wooden peg, then snuffed the empty floor of the manger suggestively, lifting the soft, hairy, upper lip from his teeth, feeling all over the familiar wood, and blowing his breath into the corners.

The old man threw some hay down from the loft; but the horse continued to snuff the bottom of the manger, and was not satisfied with the puny ear of corn that was thrown to him. He wanted his oats. But there were no oats.

The old man passed the stall with a sigh, not seeming to notice the horse; and the patient animal looked after him with a kind of sad surprise, and then turned slowly to his hay as the barn doors fell shut with a hollow sound and the

Reprinted by permission of *The Christian Endeavor World*.

padlock clicked into place for the night. The evening star peeped coldly at him between the cracks over the manger while he ate his supper, and he mused drearily over the days when oats were plenty.

The old man walked slowly toward the kitchen door. His heart was going over and over in dull, aching thuds the events of the past three hours, trying to find a place where he might have done differently and so have changed the result.

He could feel the shaking of his hand now as it had shaken when he opened Stephen Lawrence's office door in the sunshine of that afternoon. He could see the bare floor, the leather-seated chairs, and the cold look on the face of the clerk seated at one of the desks. He felt again the blankness that had come over him when he looked about and found that Stephen Lawrence was not in the room, and his bewilderment when he was told that he had gone to New York. At another time it would have made his heart leap just to know that some one of his own town and acquaintance was in New York, because that was where Elizabeth was; but now it had only brought dismay.

Gone! He was gone! Stephen Lawrence was not there, and the mortgage was due that day!

It took some time for him to comprehend that he must tell his business to the clerk sitting there with that cold, hard face and annoyed smile. His lofty manner and city-made clothes gave the old man an uncomfortable feeling. Stephen Lawrence never wore his clothes so ostentatiously, although he had been in the city a great deal, and was a rich man.

The old man, standing out there on the wide stone flagging in front of his kitchen door, shivered as he looked up at the stars, and remembered the words that the clerk had said. Somehow the clerk's voice reminded him of a chisel cutting a name on a gravestone, *his* gravestone, *his* name.

"If you can't pay, we'll have to foreclose. That's the only way to do business." Those were the words, and the speaker's eyes had been as hard as steel.

The old man did not know that the clerk was anxious to do a neat little stroke of business while his employer was away, in order to cover up some laxity in other directions; he only felt the unmercifulness of the voice that belonged to an unrelenting world of business, and his whole soul writhed within him.

To think it should have come to him! He, who dreaded a mortgage as a man might dread the plague. He, who had owned his own little home, free of debt, these many years, and had hoped to leave it so for Elizabeth after he and mother were done with it.

It ought never to have been mortgaged. He ought to have managed somehow. And yet, when Elizabeth was taken sick and needed so much, off in New York, and mother had to go to her, there seemed no other way. There had been trouble with their few little investments here and there, and the interest that usually dribbled along enough to make both ends meet failed just at the time of need. He did not want to tell mother and Elizabeth then, when they were in so much trouble; and so he went to Mr. Lawrence. Stephen Lawrence was a young man, and he did not know him very well; but Stephen's father had been a lifelong friend. It seemed the only thing to do. Elizabeth was worth it.

Elizabeth came through the illness all right, and was well again and back at her post in New York—had been for a year or more. She hoped she could earn enough for them all to live upon by and by, when her salary was raised, and he had kept on hoping that that would be soon. He had kept up the interest on the mortgage until now; but the last three months no money came in at all, and to-day the interest was due, but he could not pay it. He had watched every mail by day, and watched it over again on his bed by night, hoping for some money from somewhere before the day for paying the interest, but none came. Then, when he hoped to gain a little time by asking Stephen Lawrence to wait, lo, he was not at home, and the man whom he had left in his place made it very plain that Stephen was no such merciful man as his father had been. It seemed there would be no kind of use in appealing to him. He would exact the last penny due him, and precisely at the moment due.

The old man bowed his head, and groaned beneath the stars. In a moment he must go in. Mother would be wondering what kept him. He must not make her anxious. There would not be much cheer inside; for they had been economizing for some time on account of the absence of their usual income, which used to come so regularly, though mother did not dream there was any further reason than that to be anxious. Mother did not know, and Elizabeth did not know—and how could he tell them—that he had mortgaged their home, and lost it from them! That was the burden of his thought, Oh, if he might escape from telling them! He felt a sneaking wish that he might die tonight before he would have to say anything about it. Mother would blame him for losing their home that they had worked for and saved for—for Elizabeth! And Elizabeth would blame him for sending mother out from her home at her time of life. He could not tell which would be the worse blame.

And now he must go in.

He put out his trembling hand, and touched the cold iron of the latch softly. There would be only a little fire, and he was shivering. A little fire seemed worse than none. It was better to stay out here under the stars. And there would be but a dim light in the kitchen; for the oil was almost out, and mother had been expecting him to bring oil. She had given him the can the last thing before he left, and told him to be sure not to forget to have it filled. It was standing in the back of the old buggy in the barn now, empty! He would have to make some excuse. How could he say he had forgotten it? He, who prided himself on never forgetting anything, even though he was growing old! Mother would not understand.

With another smothered groan he lifted the latch, and stepped into the kitchen, knowing all so vividly in mental picture just how it would look. Then he stepped back, blinded, startled, at the contrast of the reality.

Two things forced themselves on his consciousness. It was bright, and it was warm.

The brightness dazed him. Where did mother get the oil? He blinked blindly at the best lamp glowing on the kitchen table in all its parlor splendor, remembered that it had been filled the last time the minister took tea with them, and had never been used since. Mother was extravagant. Poor mother! She did not know! Her gentle old steps were going about the pantry now. He could hear the loose boards creaking with the familiar sound.

Supper was ready. The kettle was singing, and there was the smell of coffee. Coffee! They had not had so much as a pinch in the house for weeks! And the meek old cat no longer sat patient with closed eyes and tucked-up tail beside the stove. She was bristling all over, licking her whiskers and sniffing the air with her pink, suspicious nose.

He took in all these details as if with an extra sense. His usual mental faculties seemed dulled. He felt every item keenly, and could have turned and fled. But mother appeared in the pantry door with a light in her eyes and a smile of joy on her face, and called girlishly,

"Father, Oh father, Lizabeth's come!"

Then from the entry-way opposite came a rushing sound of soft skirts, and Elizabeth was in his arms, even while she mildly rebuked her mother for spoiling the surprise.

His heart gave one wild leap of joy, and then seemed to him to fall down, down to illimitable depths. He could scarcely force his languid arms to press the precious daughter close. He kissed her softly upon the hair, but could not bear to let his eyes meet hers, lest she should read the secret of their loss and shame. He tried to speak a cheery greeting, but his voice refused to give utterance except in hoarse tones; and his features were drawn and pinched, like one suddenly grown very old.

"Father's tired," said the mother, her quick old heart at once divining that something was amiss, and seeking to hide it from the beloved daughter because she saw he wished it so.

"Are you father?" Elizabeth asked tenderly. "Here, let me help you off with your coat. Give me your hat. I'm home again, father dear. Do you realize it? Did I surprise you very much?"

The old man passed his tired hand tremblingly over his bare forehead, and swept the few wisps of white hair into place, trying to drag a forlorn smile into his face.

"Why, I'm all struck of a heap, 'Lizabeth!" he managed to say, and then sat down heavily in his chair by the table.

Mother eyed him furtively and anxiously while Elizabeth went to hang away his hat and coat in the entry, but she did not question him. Long experience had taught her when to hold her tongue. Some women never learn that, and so miss half their usefulness and reward.

Elizabeth filled the water-pitcher, cut the bread, and brought the butter. There were white grapes on the table, and some wonderful little cakes from New York, besides all the good things from mother's company store; but the old man could not eat. He took a grape between his rough fingers, and looked at its transparent green, and tried to say the things he would have said if his daughter had come home to a house upon which no mortgage was to be foreclosed. He did not succeed in hiding from his wife the fact that there was something seriously wrong with him.

Elizabeth had much to say and a bright way of saying it, and so they got through supper under her happy talk; but her father did not know the next day any of the nice things her employer had said to her, and could not have told if he had been asked why she had come home so unexpectedly. Perhaps he did not listen. His eyes were upon her, but his thoughts were in the office in the village, hearing the glib sentences of the hard young clerk.

At last mother could bear it no longer. She arose to put the bread away.

"Father, you've got that pain in your head again," she said in her unobtrusive way that made the matter not so noticeable. "'Tain't no use to try to hide it from me. I see it the minute you come in the room. Just you go in the bedroom, and lay down a spell till it passes by." Then she went on into the pantry with the bread, leaving only Elizabeth's gentle solicitations to be dealt with. She knew the shrinking nature of the man with whom she had lived for nearly forty years.

"Wall, I will just lay down a few minutes if you don't mind," said the old man eagerly. It seemed to him that he could bear the strain of the beloved presences of his wife and daughter no longer. He must cry out if he stayed.

He tottered across the kitchen floor to the bedroom, glad that the entry-way was between it and the kitchen, that he might not hear so plainly the happy voices of the two as they went about clearing away the supper dishes.

He made as if he were preparing for an elaborate rest by pulling off his heavy boots and throwing them hard upon the floor. He momently feared those two would come upon him with medicine, hot water, and flannels, as was their wont. Perhaps if he had not been so deeply absorbed he would have noticed that they did not, and would have been pained by the omission.

He had not even thought to ask how Elizabeth got up from the station alone and unmet. It did not occur to him now. He sank down on the edge of the bed with a groan, and let his discouraged old head drop into his bony hands. He had never in all the long years of his life come to a spot of such utter discouragement as this. His whole nature bowed and gave way before it. He could neither reason nor pray. He was fairly stupefied by what he felt he had done to his family.

Now Elizabeth was in the pantry with very red cheeks, the uncleared supper-table quite forgotten, while she poured her confidence into the eager ear of her mother.

The wise old cat, having waited decorously a suitable time for her supper, made up her mind to help herself. Cautiously she stole upon a chair, and put her velvet paw upon the forbidden cloth. Shy, watchful, but determined, she took her stealthy supper.

The mother and daughter stood in the candle-light of the cold pantry while the girl told her story. The mother watched the flicker of the candle-flame upon the girl's face, and it was a goodly sight to her, one that her soul had fainted for for many a day past. She noted with loving eyes the deep touch of pink in the firm cheek, the sweet curve of lip, and the lines of eyebrow and forehead and hair. Nothing seemed wonderful that happened to Elizabeth. The wonder was that it had not happened before.

The mother forgot the sticky spoon she held in one hand, wherewith she had been scraping out the dish of preserves she held in the other. She stood and held them breathless, and listened, her wrinkled face lit with the joy of the remembrance of her own youth. She looked on her daughter not merely as her daughter, but as the lovely, gracious young woman that others must see in her. She watched the color steal into the beloved cheeks, and the eyes take on a tenderer light as the story grew more personal, and the long lashes droop shyly lower as the lips halted and came to the final closing words. Then the face was lifted appealing for mother's benediction.

She stooped, sticky spoon and all, and gave the mother kiss, wrapping her arms around that daughter in an ecstasy of joy; but her heart had flown straight to the bedroom where her old lover sat in trouble of some kind. This was his joy, too, and he did not know about it. He would rejoice with Elizabeth, and be proud.

Just then came a knock on the kitchen door. Elizabeth turned pink, and started to answer it. The cat gulped her last mouthful, descending to the hearth with a sudden, velvet thud, and sat innocent, licking her whiskers and blinking at the lamp, thankful to be unnoticed.

Mother, half divining what the knock meant, had the presence of mind to remain hidden in the pantry for a suitable length of time, whence she presently emerged with hastily tidied hair, minus her gingham apron, as consciously unconscious as a mortal woman could be. She tried to greet the guest as if it were the most common thing in the world for him to run in of an evening before the supper things were cleared away, and as if she knew nothing of his errand.

She tried to get them away into the stiff front room, where there had been no fire all winter, and then in dismay at the possibility of their taking cold she tried to carry away all the supper things at once. It amazed her to see Elizabeth take things so coolly, and actually scrape and pile the dishes in full view of the guest.

The cat watched the remnants of the supper disappear with disappointment in her blinking, innocent eyes. She had hoped they would all go into the pantry again, and give her another chance. But they did not. Instead, Elizabeth and the guest drew their two chairs up to the table, and sat together talking in low tones, and mother disappeared down the little hallway into the bedroom.

She opened the door softly, and held the latch firm until she had closed it again lest she disturb father if he was really very bad. Her soul was in a tumult between the news she had to tell, and the thought of what it could have been that troubled him at supper.

She stood a minute, quiet, beside the door, her eyes blinded at the dark; then, groping her way toward the bed,

"Father," she said. "Father," more gently, "does it ache so bad?" She put out her hand, and touched his gray, bowed head; then, drawing back with an astonished start: "Why, father! You ain't in bed at all! Does your head ache so bad as that? Then why don't you lie down?"

She sat down beside him on the bed, and drew his grizzled head to her lean shoulder.

"Why, father, I'm 'fraid you're real sick," she said in a sudden anxiety. "Your throat ain't sore, is it?"

"No!" the old main fairly groaned. Oh if it were! How he wished he could say, "Yes!"

But the faithful hand of his wife was investigating. Yes, his head was hot, but not hot enough for a fever. Ever since Elizabeth's illness she knew the feel of fever. Down his face her hand passed, and paused. What made her hand feel wet? She felt again. His eyes? Could that be tears?

"Why, father, you're a-feelin' real bad about somethin'! Has anything happened? You don't seem to sense it that 'Lizabeth's come."

He stifled another groan, but his wife was absorbed in her important news. In a tone of suppressed excitement she added:

"And here's Mr. Lawrence come, and like's not he'll be wantin' to see you pretty soon. What is it, father? You didn't have a fall on the slippery streets, did you? Nor a runaway?"

She peered anxiously into his face by the dim darkness that the light from the crack under the door only made more visible, but the old man started up with a movement of despair as he took in her words.

"Heh? What, mother? Mr. Lawrence? You didn' say he

had come a'ready? And 'Lizabeth just home! Oh mother! To think it should 'a' come to this!"

"Why, father! What do you mean? I would 'a' thought you'd 'a' been glad, hard as 'Lizabeth's had to work, and he rich. Don't take it so hard, father! However in the world did you find it out? I never suspicioned, even from her letters, though I can see now—"

But the old man interrupted her. He had not heard a word.

"I wouldn't 'a' thought he'd be hard on his father's old friend like that," he murmured strickenly. "To come this first night. He might 'a' waited till to-morrow. Besides, they said he was in New York."

"He was," said his wife. "He come down in the same train with 'Lizabeth."

"He did! Then he must 'a' known she was home and come a-purpose. And he used to be a nice boy, I thought, used to carry her books home for her, don't you mind, mother? Oh, it must be riches hardens men's hearts. Give me my best pants, mother; I'll go out and have it over. But you call 'Lizabeth in here, and keep her till he's gone. Mind. Don't you let her come out and hear us talk. I can't have her know to-night."

"Father, have you gone clean, stark crazy?" questioned his bewildered wife. "Didn't I tell you he'd just come? They don't want you nor me neither out there now. They want the place to themselves a spell. Stay here, and get slicked up nice. There's no hurry. You don't seem to understand. Your head must be real bad. You ought to lie down awhile first. Here, you put your head on the pillow, and I'll get you a cup o' tea before you try to get up at all. There, now, father; it's too bad you have these poor turns, and 'specially to-night."

"No, mother, I can't lie down, and I don't want no tea. It would choke me. I must go out and get this business done. Hand me them pants. I'll go right away."

"But, father, you mustn't, you know. It ain't proper yet, till they've had a little chance together," said the woman, laying a detaining hand on the Sunday garments. "You might as well have the tea; it'll hearten you up. Just get ready slowly. The teapot's on the stove yet, and 'twon't disturb them a mite for me to just tip in there and get it, and go right out again. 'Lizabeth will understand it. She knows you've got a headache."

"Mother, you don't understand!" said the old man, taking firm hold of his trousers with determination. "Mr. Lawrence's come to see me on business, and I must go right out and have it done. Maybe I'd best wear my old ones, and let him see what we've come to; but I guess I'll be decent 'slong 's I can, ennyhow. Where's my collar? Is there a candle in here?"

"Dear heart! What's come over him? Now, father, don't you see it ain't the thing for you to go in there right away? 'Lizabeth wants to kind of get things up to the right point 'fore you get in. It seems 's if we was a bit too anxious if you resh things so!"

"Mother, what on airth do you mean? And what in the name o' common sense does 'Lizabeth have to do with it? I'd like to know. You don't understand."

There were two red spots on the mother's soft cheeks, and she gripped her toil-worn hands with exasperation as she tried to make it plain.

"It's you that don't understand, father," she said; "and of course you don't; how could you? and she so far away all the time, and never saying a word about it. I never suspicioned myself, I tell you. 'Lizabeth's got all to do with it. Ain't a woman got all to do with the man she's going to marry?"

"Marry!" ejaculated father. "Who's she going to marry?" Here was a new trouble to be dealt with on top of the old one.

"Why, Mr. Lawrence, of course," said the mother with satisfaction. She was not denied the joy of telling the good news, after all. "He went clear down to New York to get her, 'cause he couldn't wait any longer. She wanted to stay in her place till spring, but he wouldn't have it so. He said he needed her right away, and—" here her voice choked happily—"he said he thought you and I needed her, too. Ain't that nice of him? It wouldn't seem like losing 'Lizabeth to give her to a man like that."

The bewildered old man could scarcely take it in, and was unable in his perplexity to make out just what effect this would have on the matter of the mortgage. He rubbed his forehead while his wife chattered happily on, relieved that her husband did not insist on going out to the kitchen at once. He wondered whether he ought to tell mother, and ask her advice, and, wondering, still hesitated as he "slicked up" at her bidding, and at last stumbled blindly through the dark little hallway, and made out to shake hands with the guest.

By some mysterious process known only to woman-kind Elizabeth and her mother suddenly melted away from the kitchen, and left the old man stranded with his guest.

He had scarcely been able as yet to take in the news his wife had told him. Elizabeth's going out at this moment made it seem all the more unlikely and impossible. The mortgage loomed up in terrible proportions. He crossed his right knee over the left, and unclasped his hands, then clasped them again, and put the left foot over the right. He grasped the chair with his roughened hands, and shoved it creakingly across the painted floor till he rumpled the rag-carpet strip that lay on the floor by the stove. There was no denying that he was embarrassed. He felt that he ought to speak of the mortgage at once; but the voice froze in his throat, and his brain would not inform him what he had meant to say. He cleared his throat, and cleared it again, and was not aware that the whole horrible process of thought had occupied but the infinitesimal part of a second, and that he had no need to open the conversation; for the guest had matters well in hand, and meant to do all the talking.

"I have something very important to say to you to-night," began the pleasant voice, and the old man's heart almost stood still.

"I was at the office to-day," the old man began tremulously, his voice sounding strange even to himself. It seemed as if he were delaying the calamity that was about to descend upon him and his.

"Oh, were you? And you did not find me there. I am sorry. They told you I was in New York. But I suppose you understand. And now about this matter. I know it's a very great thing that I'm about to ask of you."

The old man drew himself up as if to meet a blow. Then it was the mortgage after all.

"Yes," he murmured sorrowfully. "We've never been able to live very great nor fine, but it's all we've got."

Stephen raised his eyebrows in amazed surprise. He had not expected to be met with dignified sorrow.

He frowned slightly, and began again more earnestly. Perhaps gentle reason would overcome the old man's scruples. For Elizabeth's sake he would try.

"Great enough and fine enough for me, Mr. Bushnell," he said quietly, "and precious enough for me to understand how hard it is to you to think of giving up——"

The poor old man dropped his head in his hands, and groaned softly. Stephen's face flushed, and his eyes grew misty.

"Why, Mr. Bushnell, I didn't think you'd take it so hard. I thought you and I were good friends, and perhaps you'd welcome——"

"It's all right, I s'pose. It's your right, and I ain't murmuring. I know the law'll bear you out. I only thought perhaps, being your father and I were old friends, you might 'a' waited a little, and give us a chance——"

"I'm sorry it has come so suddenly to you. I thought you would understand," said the young man, a note of real trouble beginning to dawn in his voice. "I supposed Elizabeth had told you more about it."

"'Lizabeth don't know a thing about it, poor child! It was for her I done it. I ain't blaming anybody. I didn't need to be told, for I s'pose I ought to 'a' known it was the right thing in business. They explained it all out to me at your office this afternoon. I ain't complaining. I only thought if I could have a little more time I might be able to get the money together somehow——".

"They explained it to you at the office!" said the puzzled young man. "What in the world did they tell you?"

"They told me you was going to foreclose!" The solemn words were out, and dull despair spread over the old face.

"Why, Mr. Bushnell!" Stephen fairly laughed as he sprang to his feet, a joyous light spreading over his face, the while he fumbled in his breast pocket for a paper. "Here you have been talking about that mortgage on the house all the time, and I have been talking about Elizabeth. I wish I had a mortgage on her, and I would foreclose quick enough. And I don't know but I have a slight one, after all," he added as he caught the light of the plain gold ring on his hand. "I've brought that old mortgage along in my pocket somewhere, and I meant to give it back to you; but it slipped my mind, I was so full of the other thing. Now suppose you and I just write the name of Elizabeth in here in place of the house and farm, and I'll quietly foreclose, and we'll have it all over with? Are you willing? Don't you understand, Mr. Bushnell? I love your daughter Elizabeth. I am asking permission to marry her. May I hope to have it? And here"—laying the paper in the trembling hands opposite him—"here is the mortgage. You see I have had it 'satisfied,'" and he pointed to the writing in red ink across the end. "As for that rascally clerk of mine, I'll attend to his case to-morrow. No, don't talk of interest. Elizabeth is interest enough for any man. She's been interesting me ever since we went to school together. You're quite sure you're willing to trust her to a man you thought a moment ago was cruel enough to foreclose a mortgage on you and take your home away? No, never mind; don't apologize. I'm too happy tonight to allow it. It's all right. Elizabeth!" He raised his happy voice in pleasant protest, and Elizabeth and her mother came smiling from the dark bedroom, their eyes suspiciously wet with happy tears.

The old man, hardly able to believe the good fortune that had come upon them, hovered around the group uncertainly, looking at first one and then the other with glad eyes. The legal paper was resting in his breast pocket over his heart. Now and then he laid his hand over it to feel if it was safe, and its crisp rattle sent little shivers of delight down his back, just as he used to feel when a boy going off for the first swim of the season.

He stole away from the kitchen when they were all talking, so that he would not be missed, and slipped out to the barn.

The old horse awoke from his first grieved nap, and pricked up his ears as he heard the rusty key turn in the padlock. His master had not forgotten him, after all. The old cat saw him as she paused in her stealthy round after mice under the barn. She held herself well poised, a shadow among shadows, one velvet paw outstretched for the next step, her eyes glinting green fire against the dark. She wondered what strange things these people of hers were doing to-night, so out of the ordinary routine.

The barn door fell back with its usual creak, and the moonlight flung itself in across the worn boards of the floor, lighting the way to the oat-bin.

The old man stooped down, and groped with his hands till he gathered up a stray handful or so from the empty corners, and carried them over to the horse, feeding them to him from his hollowed hand.

"There, Billy!" he said tenderly, stroking the soft nose. "Missed yer oats, didn't ye? But never mind; I'll get some more to-morrow. Billy, if you had a mortgage on a bushel of oats I reckon you'd foreclose, wouldn't you, old fellow? There, good night, Billy!"

He fastened the door again, and the horse whinnied softly, protesting that he had not had enough, but it was music to the old man's soul. He walked happily back to the kitchen door, whistling an old tune that he had sung in meeting when he and mother were keeping company. On the flaggings he paused, and looked up at the stars gratefully. It seemed as if God were up there, and he wanted to acknowledge His benefits. One moment he stood reverently, looking up, and then humbly walked in to the joy that was awaiting him.

14

The Forgotten Friend

THE night was inky black and growing colder. Occasional dashes of rain brought a chill as it touched the faces of the hurrying pedestrians. The pavements gleamed black where the electric lights struck them, like children's slates just washed.

Gordon Pierce drew down his hat, turned up his collar, and dropped his umbrella a little lower to breast the gale, but just as he turned the corner into Church Street the uncertain wind caught the frail structure and twisted it inside out as if it had been a child's toy, and the hail pounded down Church Street rebounding from the stone steps of the church on the corner with such vengeance that the young man was fain to take refuge for the moment in the inviting open doorway till he could right himself or the severity of the storm should pass.

Hail storms are so unexpected that one cannot calculate upon them. This one lasted longer than was usual and pelted most unmercifully in at the doorway so that the refugee stepped further into the lighted entrance way of the church, taking off his hat to shake the hail stones from

Reprinted by permission of The Board of Home Missions.

its brim. As he did so his ear caught the sweet strains of the pipe organ within, and a rich tenor voice floated out faintly through the closed leather swinging doors from the lighted room beyond.

Gordon Pierce was fond of music and knew a fine voice when he heard it. This one attracted him. He stepped nearer and listened a moment, then stealthily pushed open the noiseless door and stepped inside the audience room.

There were only a few people in the brightly lighted church and they were gathered up toward the front near the pulpit and the choir gallery. The stranger stepped softly in and stood with hat in hand listening to the sweet music, then drawn irresistibly he moved silently a little further down the aisle to a seat somewhat behind the audience and sat down.

A prayer followed. Until then he had thought this a small private rehearsal for a favored few. Of course he could not go out during a prayer, and he bowed his head in annoyance that he had cornered himself in a religious meeting by coming so far forward, when he was extremely anxious to hasten home.

He was meditating a quiet flight as soon as the prayer should be over, when the same sweet voice that had first lured him in, broke the stillness that followed the petition. And this time it was a hymn that was sung. Yet the voice was insistent, clear, demanding attention.

> "I gave my life for thee,
>   My precious blood I shed
> That thou might'st ransomed be
>   And quickened from the dead.
> I gave my life for thee,
>   What hast thou given for me?"

The words were so old, but to the young man they sounded new. It was as if the question had been asked of his own startled heart by an angel. He forgot about trying to slip out before the meeting went further on and listened.

The quiet faced man who stepped to the edge of the platform as the singer ceased and began to talk in a low but impressive voice was a missionary, but the unexpected listener did not know it. He would have been amazed beyond measure if he had known at that moment that he was to be enthralled with interest in a missionary meeting, but this was the case. It was not like any missionary meeting he had ever heard of before though, and he did not recognize it as such even after it was over and he had dropped the last fifty-cent piece his pockets contained into the collection basket with a feeling of annoyance that he had no more.

He had heard things that evening that stirred him deeply.

The storm had ceased when he picked his way out into the slippery streets now white with a fine sleet it had left as a parting salute. As he made his way thoughtfully to his boarding house his mind was still intent upon the new thoughts the speaker had left with him, but when he turned the lights on in his own room he saw a pile of paper parcels and boxes on the bed and floor which made him forget his evening experiences completely.

"Great Scott!" he ejaculated aloud, "did I buy all those things? There'll be a howling big bill to pay when my next month's salary comes, and no mistake."

Then with the pleasure of a child he gave himself up to the investigation of his purchases. Most of the things were Christmas presents he had that afternoon purchased for his friends and the various members of his family. He felt a deep sense of satisfaction in their fineness and beauty as he opened first one and then another. He had done the thing up fine this time as became a young man who was away from home in business for the first time in his life and getting what in the eyes of his family was an exceedingly large salary for one who had been a boy but the other day.

There was the silk dress for mother. He had always said he would buy his mother a silk dress when he got a chance, and he had saved for this for several months. He felt its rich shining folds with clumsy inexperienced fingers and shook it out in a lustrous heap over the bed to admire it. It was all right, for he had asked Frances to tell him just what was the suitable thing for his mother, and she had said black *peau de soie,* and he had carried samples for her inspection one evening when he called, and she had bent over them and studied and talked wisely of texture and wear while the soft light from the opal lamp shone on her pretty hair, and he had thought how sensible she was to advise for the medium price, even though her father was reported to be a millionaire. He smiled at the innocent silk on the bed as though it brought a vision of Frances.

For his sister Mildred he had bought Hoffman's boy head of Christ. He knew that she fancied this particular picture and wanted it. It wasn't exactly the picture he would have selected for her if she had not expressed a strong desire for it, but it was a pretty thing and he placed it on his mantel and surveyed it pleasantly and critically, and as he did so something in the frank, deep gaze of the boy in the picture reminded him of the strange meeting he had attended that evening and the new thoughts that had been stirred by it. Somehow a wave of compunction went through his conscience as he turned back to the new possessions on the bed and remembered the paltry fifty cents he had put in the collection plate.

Last of all of his purchases came the article which had cost him the most thought and care in selection. It was a delicate little bronze statue, fine of workmanship and yet not speaking too loudly of its price to be in keeping with the position and salary of the donor, and it was intended for Frances. After all, he acknowledged to himself, this was the gift in which he took the most pleasure, this was for the friend—the dearest—and he drew his breath quickly as he dared to say it to himself, and wondered what she would think if she knew he thought in this way about her. Then the eyes of the picture drew his irresistibly and, as he looked up, by some queer twist of memory, or hidden law of connection, there came to his mind the song that had been sung that evening:

> *I gave my life for thee,*
> *What hast thou given for me?*

and, closely following upon the thought it brought, came the verses he had learned from the Bible long ago:

> There is a Friend that sticketh closer than a brother.

It came with startling clearness, as if it would remind him that there was a Friend whom he had forgotten, left out of his Christmas list after all, the very one for whom the Christmas festival was made in the beginning.

He sat down bewildered, and all the pretty prideful gifts he had arrayed stared back reproachfully at him. He sat ashamed before the pictured Christ.

In the sudden sense of shame that had come upon Gordon he looked away from the things he had bought so proudly but a few hours before, annoyed and unhappy, only to see what he had not noticed before, a chair on the other side of the room also piled high with packages. There was a large suit box, two of them in fact, and a hat box, with several paper parcels. They bore the advertisement of a firm of clothiers and men's furnishing goods on their covers.

The blood flamed high in the young man's face. He felt as if suddenly brought before a court of justice and convicted. These things were all for himself.

That great pile! And fifty cents in the collection basket the only thing he had shown as a Christmas gift to the Saviour of the world—his Saviour, for so in his heart he counted Christ.

He had a generous nature. He liked to give—when he had plenty to give from. He had never considered it so necessary to give very much toward religious institutions until to-night. Why was it that these thoughts were crowding out all the pleasure he was having in his purchases and the anticipated delight in giving them?

He turned impatiently and drew the chairful toward him with a jerk. He cut the strings viciously and unwrapped the parcels. Neckties! Why did he want more neckties? His bureau was simply swarming with them now in all the hues of the rainbow. But these were so pretty and so unusual! And just the colors Frances liked—and Frances had said those shades were becoming to him. Well, they were small things to scowl over. He tossed them gloomily aside.

Gloves! Yes, he must have new gloves to wear to the oratorio with Frances the night after Christmas. But he didn't need to buy two pairs just now. He could have waited for the others until after Christmas, and they would have been cheaper then, too.

The raincoat he had perjured his conscience to buy because it was a sample bargain and the last one of the lot, cut in a most unusual way, imported from one of London's great tailors, so the salesman had told him; that raincoat was disappointing now he looked at it with dull, critical eyes. It lay in a limp heap in the box with none of the crisp style to it that had charmed him when he saw it in the store and fancied himself swinging in its embrace down the Avenue holding an umbrella over Frances. He slid the box along on the carpet with the toe of his shoe, and opened the other box. He half hoped that the suit that he had had sent up would not fit. His old one would have done well enough for the oratorio of course, only this one had attracted him, and in the store he had felt quite virtuous to be buying a ready-made suit instead of one made to order, as Frances' brothers always did. Now it seemed even his virtue was an error. He sighed deeply and turned to the hat box for comfort.

To take Frances to the oratorio with this crown of well-dressed manhood upon his head was the fulfillment of a dream he had long dreamed. But now he took the hat from its box with little of the elation he had expected to feel. Somehow he did not like to look at the picture on the mantel and think of the souls without knowledge of Christ that he had heard about that evening, while he held that costly top-piece in his hand. After all, was a high hat so very desirable as he had thought? Was it as necessary to his earthly happiness as it had seemed but that afternoon?

He wished he had never seen it. He put the hat on his head viciously and glared at himself in the mirror, but the reflection did not do justice to his anticipation. He took it off and settled it on again, and looked at it critically, wondering if it was not a little too small, or maybe a little too large, and then threw it back ungently into the box and sat himself down to think.

He was unhappy! He felt that the only thing that could take this unhappiness away was to make it right with his conscience in some way. The only way to do that would be to give a goodly sum as a Christmas gift to that missionary or some other religious cause, he didn't care what. He felt mean, and that was the truth of the matter. He did not stop to tell himself that he had passed many Christmases before without a thought of giving a gift to Christ and been none the worse for it. Over and over until it came to be a din in his ears did that tenor voice ring,

> "I gave my life for thee,
> What hast thou given for me?"

He felt that he could not bear that reproach. Well, then, he must reconstruct his list. Perhaps he would have to change some of his presents for cheaper ones and get a little money that way. He glanced up at the mantel instinctively. The little statue posed in its costly elegance. Not that! He could not change that. Frances headed his list. He could not make her present one whit less costly or beautiful, for she was dearest—here he paused. Was he setting Frances above his Lord? And could he hope to be blest in trying to win her love if he did so? This was not a thought of his own. He distinctly felt it was not. It was sent.

He looked hopelessly at the bright little things strewed about the bed. After all, was that giving a gift to take it out of his other friends? Had he any right to deprive them of their gifts? Ought it not to be a gift from himself rather than one cut off from what he had intended giving all his friends? And the gift to Christ should have come first in the planning. Christ should always stand first. Had he nothing he could give? Some sacrifice? Was there anything he had that he might sell, or—stay! There were the gold cuff buttons he bought last week. He had never worn them. They were three dollars and a half and were charged on father's bill. He could return them and have them credited, and that would be so much toward a gift to Christ. It would not seem as if the fifty cents stood so very much alone. But still, taken in contrast with the goodly gifts that lay about the room it was small and mean for the Christ of heaven—his Saviour.

Again the heap of clothing he had shoved aside called his attention. Those things were bought and paid for. He told them decidedly they could not be taken back. He was a stranger at that store. How would he look returning all those things? They would think he was crazy. But even as he thought this he remembered that the salesman had told him he could return the suit if it did not fit and the raincoat had been spoken of in the same way. The salesman had said that if he did not like it on looking it over he could bring it back.

Then began a fight that lasted far into the night. Once or twice as he turned in his restless pacing to and fro he caught a glimpse of the face in the picture he had bought for his sister, and a fierce wish came over him to take that back where it came from. It had been the cause of all his trouble after all. But his better self knew this was folly, and the fight went on between himself and his selfishness.

At first it seemed to him that he was only giving room to an idle thought that troubled him and was trying to explain it all right to himself, but it did not explain. The more he thought about it the more there seemed to be something morally wrong about a professed Christian giving goodly gifts to those who needed them not, and buying fine raiment for himself and giving *nothing* to the Lord. The more this thought became clear to his mind, the more irritated he became, until suddenly facing his mirror, he saw his troubled, angry face full of petulant, childish self-will. Then, and behind it, reflected from the picture on the mantel, was the clear-eyed, boyish face of the pictured Christ, serene in the contemplation of matters of the Kingdom and his Father's business.

Himself in contrast with the Christ was something Gordon Pierce had never thought of before. He was startled. Not so much in the difference of the outward expression of his face and that of the picture, but in the character that both revealed.

He went back to his chair and dropped his face in his hands, and to his startled understanding there came a vision of the man he ought to be beside the man he was. For a little while the first question that had troubled him was lost sight of in the deeper thoughts that stirred his soul to their very depths. Even Frances was forgotten for the time while his soul met God and learned wherein he was found wanting.

A little while later he arose and reverently knelt beside his chair. It was the first thoughtful and unhurried prayer he had uttered since he was a little child and had needed something very much from God.

"Oh, Christ!" he prayed. "I have not been worth much as a Christian. I've been thinking too much about my own pleasure. Forgive me, and help me to do better. I give myself to Thee as a Christmas gift to-night. It is a poor gift, but make it worth something for Thee."

When he got up from his knees he quietly and deliberately picked up the raincoat, the new suit, the neckties and the gloves and carefully folding them laid each in its individual box or paper as it had come. Over the hat he hesitated a moment, started to put it on again, and then abruptly put it in the box and tied the cover down. After that he went to bed.

In the brilliancy of the clear, cold morning that succeeded the night of storm, he started down-town an hour earlier than usual, his arms laden with many bundles. His fellow boarders eyed him curiously, for he did not usually burden himself with anything when he started out in the morning. He affected an elegant leisure in all his ways. This was not because of his upbringing, but because he had supposed it would beget him a dignity in keeping with one who aspired to friendship with one like Frances. But this morning he had forgotten all such thoughts; his set face showed determination and a will that would carry it out.

From counter to counter, from one department to another in the great store he went. He blessed the happy custom that made is possible for him to return these ill-advised purchases without wranglings and explanations.

When he reached the last place, however, and opened the box containing the beloved hat, the young salesman who had waited upon him happened to be sauntering near the exchange desk and recognized him. He raised his eyebrows slightly as he glanced significantly at the hat, and said enquiringly: "What's the matter? Didn't it fit?"

The blood flushed the customer's cheek and he felt as guilty as though he had stolen the hat. He answered unconcernedly: "I've decided to do without it." But he felt as though the whole miserable business was written in his face.

He was glad when his hands were empty and the money he had received in exchange for the various packages he had brought down-town was safely in his pocket. He counted it up mentally as he boarded the car that went toward his office, inwardly thankful that there was not much doing in his business this cold weather, and his presence at the office at an early hour was not so necessary as it would have been at another season of the year.

When he reached the office he found the general manager had been there and ordered some of the men off to another part of the city, and there would be nothing for him to do that morning. He sat at his desk for a little while doing some figuring and counting his money. At last with a happy face he counted out thirty dollars and rolled it together by itself. Then he took up the morning paper and turned to the notices of religious services held the night before. It took him some time to find the mention of the meeting he had attended, but at last he found it in an obscure corner. It gave him what he wanted, however, the name of the man who had spoken so eloquently about missions and the name of the pastor in whose church the meeting was held.

With a brighter face he donned his overcoat and hat once more and hailing an up-town car was soon on his way to find the pastor. He was not at home, but his wife came to see the caller and explained that he would be away for a couple of days.

This was disappointment. When Gordon Pierce did anything he wanted to do it at once. Somehow those heathen in India would weigh on his soul and remind him of his lost high hat until the money he had decided to send them was out of his keeping. He drew his brows in perplexity. It had seemed so easy to hunt up this minister and ask him to send the money to the man who had spoken the evening before. The minister's wife studied the handsome young face before her and her heart went out in sympathy. She was used to helping young people through all sorts of trying times, from getting married to getting out of jail, so she asked a simple question sympathetically, and he opened his heart to her at once glad of a way out. Her face brightened as she heard that it was money for the missionary.

"Oh, then, it will be all right!" she said eagerly. "Just take it to Mr. Adamson. He is the treasurer of our church and has charge of the money for Dr. Hanson's work. You will find him at his office on Chestnut Street. You know Adamson & Co. Just ask for Mr. Adamson, senior. I am so glad there is someone interested enough to take the trouble to bring some money. It was an interesting meeting last night, was it not? Too bad there were not more out, but, then, it was wretched weather and so near to Christmas, too. People are selfish at Christmas in spite of everything. They will not come out or give. It was not a good time for a missionary meeting anyway, but we could not get Dr. Hanson any other time. Good-morning. I am glad you have called. I will tell my husband."

She bowed and smiled him out. He went down and gave his thirty dollars to the surprised Mr. Adamson, who looked with his keen business eyes at the young man glowing in the fervor of his first sacrifice for Christ, and wondered, but took the money and made a record of it with the name of the giver.

It was the night of the oratorio, and Gordon Pierce, with many a sigh, for the glow of sacrifice does not always last through the real part of the sacrifice itself, had arrayed himself in his old clothes, which were not so old except in comparison with new ones, and had donned his hat with many a thought of the hat that might have been, and gone after Miss Frances. He had been invited to sit in their own private box with the family, and he knew it was a great honor. He always felt that when the sharp gaze of Frances' father rested upon him every defect of his life stood out in bold relief, and so he had been particularly anxious to appear as well as possible, for with Frances' father rested, after all, the final giving away of Frances herself to any young man, no matter how much he might love her or she love him.

And very nice indeed he looked as he sat beside her waving her unnecessary little fan just for sheer pleasure of doing something for her. Frances' father sat watching him critically and could not deny that he was handsome, but wished that he would not look so ardently into that beloved daughter's face. He had happened to pass through a store and had seen the young gentleman trying on a high hat, and Frances' father was a self-made man. He knew what high silk hats cost, and he happened to know the size of Gordon Pierce's salary. He could not forget that hat. He expected to have it in evidence very conspicuously this evening, but had been surprised to find that the young man did not wear it, and took pains to keep his hat out of sight. His observations at this point were interrupted by Mr. Adamson, his friend, who had seen him in the audience and at the intermission came over to the box to consult him about something important. The business finished, Mr. Adamson glanced up at the young man beside Frances.

"By the way," said he, "who is that young man?"

"That?" said the father, dejectedly brought back to the thorn that had been troubling him. "That is a young kid who thinks the universe centers around Frances. His name is Pierce. He is a civil engineer and doing well, but I'm afraid there isn't much in him."

"Well, he did not strike me as that kind," said Mr. Adamson decidedly.

"Where did you meet him? What do you know of him?" asked Frances' father.

"He came to see me two or three days ago to give me some money for Dr. Hanson's mission. What did you say his salary was? I asked him if he was giving it himself, and he said, 'Yes.'"

"You don't say!" ejaculated Frances' father turning and regarding the flushed young man with a new interest. It was characteristic of Frances' father that he requested young Mr. Pierce to call at his office the next day.

"Young man,"—the millionaire knew how to come directly to a point when he saw one, "where did you get that thirty dollars to give to missions?" he asked abruptly.

It seemed to Gordon that every folly and every tender feeling of his heart was to be stripped from him here and now, and he stood trembling as one condemned. He felt a sudden desire to cry as when a small boy he had seen the big boys run off with all the fun after he had helped work to get it. Then a rare quality of his came to the front, and he saw the funny side of the whole thing.

"From the fine clothes that I didn't buy," he answered with a choking laugh. "There was a high hat and an imported raincoat and a new suit and a lot of neckties."

"H'm!" said the old man regarding him severely, "and what did you want all those things for?"

"To appear well before your daughter, sir."

"Indeed! And why didn't you get them?" The face grew quizzical.

A glow came into Gordon's eyes. "I did buy them," he answered quietly.

"What! Then how did you get the money back?"

"I bought them and had them sent home. Then I went to that meeting; the storm sent me in. It was not my own doing. I thought perhaps God sent me."

There was something grim in the older man's face. He had heard sentimentalists talk of God's doings in their lives before, and blame their own weaknesses on a higher power.

"I heard that man talk about those people who do not know about the Gospel. I heard some singing, too. I know you will not understand how I was stirred by it. Perhaps it will seem weak to you, but when I got home I got to thinking about it all, and looking over the things I had bought for myself and what I got for Christmas for my friends, father and mother and my sister—and the best I could afford for your daughter, for Frances, and something reminded me that I had given nothing to Christ. I can't explain to you, sir. It was only just that I felt that I had not been doing right by the Lord. I've never been any great Christian, but I never felt so mean in my life as I did that night. So the next morning I took all the things back that I had bought for myself and I figured up and found just how much money I could spare and get through the month, and I hunted up the man who talked and gave him the money. I don't see how you found out about it, sir." There was quiet respect in Gordon Pierce's tones as he finished.

The old man wore a curious look of grim satisfaction. "H'm!" he said at last, after calmly surveying his visitor. "And might I presume to enquire why you wished to appear well before my daughter?"

"Because I love her."

The face of Frances' father softened about the grim mouth and keen eyes. He was remembering his own youth.

"And had you ceased to love her when you took back your fine clothes?"

"No," said he, "I loved her all the more, but I loved Christ best. I had bought your daughter's Christmas gift, but I had nothing for my Lord."

"Well," said the old man, turning toward his desk, "you did well. Perhaps you won't mind adding a little from me to that Christmas present you gave." He was writing in his check book now as if nothing had happened. The young man looked at him curiously and wondered how he should say what he must say before he left that office.

"There, I'll trouble you to hand that to Mr. Adamson from me to go with yours to missions. I don't mind encouraging a Christmas gift like that. I'll go without a high hat myself another year," and he chuckled dryly, and rubbed his hands together.

Gordon Pierce studied the check in his hands bewilderingly. It was filled out for three hundred dollars made payable to Mr. Adamson. His face brightened as he suddenly understood. He was glad beyond measure to have his gift recognized by one so much larger, and he felt the joy of the old man's approval. But there was something else he must ask before this interview ended.

He went over by the millionaire's desk and dared to grasp the hand that had held so many dollars. "Sir, I have told you that I love your daughter. I want to tell you that I am going to try to make her love me. Have I your permission to do so?"

The hands were clasped for a moment while the old eyes looked long into the young ones.

"Well, I guess you can do it, my boy. Go ahead."

Alone in his own room that night Gordon's first act was to kneel and thank his heavenly Father for the great gift of a woman's love that had been bestowed upon him. Then in glad resolve to make this new year a new life in every way he took down his neglected Bible and turning over the leaves, scarcely knowing how to begin a long broken habit, he lighted upon these words:

"Give and it shall be given to you—good measure, pressed down, shaken together and running over, shall men give into your bosom. For with the same measure you mete withal it shall be measured to you again."

Reverently he bowed his head as he realized that even then all gifts of his would never requite the great gift God had given to him that night.

About the Author

Grace Livingston Hill is well-known as one of the most prolific writers of romantic fiction. Her personal life was frought with joys and sorrows not unlike those experienced by many of her fictional heroines.

Born in Wellsville, New York, Grace nearly died during the first hours of life. But her loving parents and friends turned to God in prayer. She survived miraculously, thus her thankful father named her Grace.

Grace was always close to her father, a Presbyterian minister, and her mother, a published writer. It was from them that she learned the art of storytelling. When Grace was twelve, a close aunt surprised her with a hardbound, illustrated copy of one of Grace's stories. This was the beginning of Grace's journey into being a published author.

In 1892 Grace married Fred Hill, a young minister, and they soon had two lovely young daughters. Then came 1901, a difficult year for Grace—the year when, within months of each other, both her father and husband died.

Suddenly Grace had to find a new place to live (her home was owned by the church where her husband had been pastor). It was a struggle for Grace to raise her young daughters alone, but through everything she kept writing. It 1902 she produced *The Angel of His Presence, The Story of a Whim,* and *An Unwilling Guest.* In 1903 her two books *According to the Pattern* and *Because of Stephen* were published.

It wasn't long before Grace was a well-known author, but she wanted to go beyond just entertaining her readers. She soon included the message of God's salvation through Jesus Christ in each of her books. For Grace, the most important thing she did was not write books but share the message of salvation, a message she felt God wanted her to share through the abilities he had given her.

In all, Grace Livingston Hill wrote more than one hundred books, all of which have sold thousands of copies and have touched the lives of readers around the world with their message of "enduring love" and the true way to lasting happiness: a relationship with God through his Son, Jesus Christ.

In an interview shortly before her death, Grace's devotion to her Lord still shone clear. She commented that whatever she had accomplished had been God's doing. She was only his servant, one who had tried to follow his teaching in all her thoughts and writing.

Don't miss these Grace Livingston Hill
romance novels!

TITLE	PRICE
Where Two Ways Met, Vol. 1	3.95
Bright Arrows, Vol. 2	3.95
A Girl to Come Home To, Vol. 3	3.95
Amorelle, Vol. 4	3.95
Kerry, Vol. 5	4.95
All Through the Night, Vol. 6	4.95
The Best Man, Vol. 7	3.95
Ariel Custer, Vol. 8	3.95
The Girl of the Woods, Vol. 9	3.95
More Than Conqueror, Vol. 11	3.95
Head of the House, Vol. 12	4.95
Stranger within the Gates, Vol. 14	3.95
Marigold, Vol. 15	3.95
Rainbow Cottage, Vol. 16	4.95
Maris, Vol. 17	4.95
Brentwood, Vol. 18	4.95
Daphne Deane, Vol. 19	3.95
White Orchids, Vol. 28	4.95
Miss Lavinia's Call, Vol. 64	3.95
The Ransom, Vol. 77	3.95
Found Treasure, Vol. 78	3.95
The Big Blue Soldier, Vol. 79	3.50
The Challengers, Vol. 80	3.95
Duskin, Vol. 81	4.95
The White Flower, Vol. 82	4.95
Marcia Schuyler, Vol. 83	4.95
Cloudy Jewel, Vol. 84	4.95
Crimson Mountain, Vol. 85	4.95
The Mystery of Mary, Vol. 86	3.95
Out of the Storm, Vol. 87	3.95
Phoebe Deane, Vol. 88	4.95
Re-Creations, Vol. 89	4.95
The Sound of the Trumpet, Vol. 90	4.95
A Voice in the Wilderness, Vol. 91	4.95

The Grace Livingston Hill romance novels are available at your local bookstore, or you may order by mail (U.S. and territories only). Send your check or money order plus $2.00 for postage and handling to:

Tyndale Family Products
Box 448
Wheaton, Illinois 60189-0448

Prices subject to change. Allow 4-6 weeks for delivery.
Tyndale House Publishers, Inc.